M000013382

THE CAPTIVE

(GRIFFIN TASK FORCE #1)

OTHER SERIES BY JULIE COULTER BELLON

Canadian Spies Series

Through Love's Trials
On the Edge
Time Will Tell

Doctors and Danger Series

All's Fair
Dangerous Connections
Ribbon of Darkness

Hostage Negotiation Series

All Fall Down (Hostage Negotiation #1)
Falling Slowly (Hostage Negotiation #1.5)
Ashes Ashes (Hostage Negotiation #2)
From the Ashes (Hostage Negotiation #2.5)
Pocket Full of Posies (Hostage Negotiation #3)
Forget Me Not (Hostage Negotiation #3.5)
Ring Around the Rosie (Hostage Negotiation #4)

Griffin Force Series

The Captive (Griffin Force #1)
The Captain (Griffin Force #2)
The Capture (Griffin Force #3)
Second Look (Griffin Force #4)

Lincoln Love Stories

Love's Broken Road
Love's Journey Home

THE CAPTIVE

A NOVEL BY

JULIE COULTER
BELLON

This is a work of fiction. The names, characters, places, and incidents are either the product of the author's imagination or are used fictitiously, and are not to be construed as real. Any resemblance to actual person, living or dead, business establishments, locales, or events is purely coincidental. The opinions and views expressed herein are the responsibility of the author.

Copyright 2015 by Julie Coulter Bellon.

All rights reserved. No part of this book may be reproduced or transmitted in any manner or by any means, electronic or mechanical, including photocopying, recording, or by any information storage or retrieval system, without permission in writing from the author, except for the inclusion of brief quotation in critical reviews and articles.

The scanning, uploading and distribution of this book via the Internet or any other means without written permission of the author is illegal and punishable by law. Please purchase only authorized electronic editions, and do not participate in or encourage electronic piracy of copyrighted materials. Your support of the author's right is appreciated.

Cover Design by Steven Novak Illustrations
Copyright 2015

ISBN-10: 0692603220
ISBN-13 978-0692603222

Printed in the United States of America
First Printing December 2015

10 9 8 7 6 5 4 3 2 1

ACKNOWLEDGMENTS

Thanks to Jon Spell, GG Vandagriff, Robyn Wood, Jordan McCollum, Dawn Allen, Jan Holman, and Faelynn Butler who are the most amazing readers and friends an author could have. Thank you for the late nights, last minute additions, and for being there when I need you.

Thank you to my SWAT team who are an incredible support to me and add some fun to my author life.

And last, but never least, my unending thanks and love goes to my family who put up with deadlines and late dinners, who are always there to cheer me on, and pick me up when I need them most. I love you.

For Jared, who completed a mission of his own this year and returned with honor. I'm so proud of you!

CHAPTER ONE

Special Agent Jake Williams had plans for today. Plans that included going to Texas to track down a terrorist. But instead, he'd been pulled off a plane and was now cooling his heels at the U.N., waiting to be taken to Admiral Moore.

He couldn't be more annoyed.

He rolled his neck, wishing the security personnel would hurry up. The two men were clustered behind a monitor, clicking through screens and giving him that we'll-say-whether-you-get-through-or-not look every now and then. Jake stood there, trying to smile at them instead of grimace, swallowing words he'd probably regret later if he said them out loud. He worked for Homeland Security Investigations for crying out loud. Why was this taking so long?

With one last polite smile at the two slowest-security-people-in-history, he pulled his phone out. There was a chance he might be able to save what was left of the day if he could get through this meeting with Admiral Moore in record time and back on track with his case. If only he could have refused the meeting in the first place. But there were few people in this world that could say no to Admiral Moore. Trying to distract himself, he tapped on his messages and waited for them to download.

Still nothing.

Why hadn't anyone emailed him an update? Did Tyler have anything? Had they lost their lead on Nazer? His finger hovered over the phone icon. He'd already called Tyler twice on the way here and been told to wait for an update. He probably wouldn't appreciate a third call. As tempting as it was, Jake moved his finger away from the call icon and clicked off his phone instead. He blew out a frustrated breath. He shouldn't be waiting for updates, he should be the one in the field giving them.

He put his phone back in his pocket. Maybe no news was good news. Tyler Coughlin was the go-to guy on his Homeland Security Counter-Intelligence team and he could track a bee in a blizzard. But even with all Tyler's skills, Nazer al-Raimi had slipped away every time they'd gotten close and that stung. Today was supposed to have been the day to put that all in the past, the big reward for spending the last six months tracking this guy and his operations in the U.S. He needed Tyler to give him good news.

"Here's your pass. You're cleared." The security guard closest to him handed him a card to clip on his jacket like he was bestowing an Academy Award on Jake or something.

Finally. He took it and put it on. "Thanks."

The other security guy waved as Jake passed by. "Sorry for the wait. You know how it is."

Jake nodded and gave him a real smile, sorry he'd been frustrated with them before. They were only doing their jobs. If anyone should understand the importance of checking and double-checking when it came to security, it was Jake. And he'd learned that lesson the hard way, too.

He swiped a hand over his face, eyeing the couch in the first lobby he passed. He'd been up nearly thirty-six hours straight and he was starting to feel it. The thought of meeting up with Admiral Moore gave him a little shot of adrenaline, though. He'd served under him when he'd been with the SEALs and he was the toughest commanding officer Jake had ever been privileged to work with. After another glance down at his tie, he hoped his suit still looked pressed. Admiral Moore's opinion mattered and it was one more reason he couldn't have refused this meeting.

He walked down the beige-carpeted floors of the Secretariat building, door after door of conference rooms on either side of him. His job at Homeland required him to be inside a lot of the time, but he always had options of going into the field and that was what he loved. It was what he'd loved about the SEALs, too. But today he just wanted to find the right room, get it done, and get out. He resisted the urge to take his phone out again. He needed to be out there, squeezing every source he had about why Nazer was in the U.S., and hopefully capturing him before he got across the border.

Unfortunately, all the doors looked the same. Several people milled around an information desk of some kind. Jake waded through them to the very young and very serious man behind it. "Jake Williams. I have an appointment and I can't seem to find this room." He showed him the paper he'd been handed the moment he'd gotten off the plane this morning.

The guy behind the desk looked at it, then back at his computer. "You're almost there. Go down the hall and around the corner."

"Thank you." Jake nodded to the security guard posted at the corner of a door. Was he guarding someone inside the room? Or was that his normal post, just standing there watching the information desk? If it were Jake, he'd hope for the first option.

He walked down the short hall, slowing his steps. He couldn't appear too eager to get this over with, but at the same time it couldn't look like he was dawdling. He needed his best professional walking pace. Maybe put his hands in his pockets for a casual, yet focused, appearance. Not that he'd learned that with the SEALs. He'd learned that during his transition from the SEAL teams to the Human Intelligence division. They'd taught him the finer points of presentation and how people perceive others and that training had come in handy in so many areas of his life, especially in Homeland Security.

He took in the hall that led to a larger lobby on the end of it, the walls covered in art. The one closest to him was a desert scene and the color scheme blended in with the beige carpet and beige wall. All the beige reminded Jake of his last SEAL assignment overseas. He never thought he'd get the sand out of his hair and clothes after that one, or the scratchy feel of it off his skin.

The painting three paces to the right, though, was a large fractured snowflake. It looked so out of place with all the beige, its blue, white, and silver color scheme jumping out at him. That was how he felt today. Like a fractured snowflake that didn't belong in the sea of beige.

Continuing down to the lobby, his step slowed when he saw who was sitting on the couch waiting for him. *Ryan Smythe.* His gut tightened. Last time they'd been coworkers hadn't gone well and Ryan had transferred to Jake's old Human Intelligence Division in the CIA. Their friendship from serving together as SEALs had been severed as cleanly as their working relationship, and he hadn't seen him since. This was going to be awkward.

"Hey, Ryan," Jake said as he drew closer. He stood over him and folded his arms, knowing Ryan would stand. Ryan always preferred the eye-to-eye approach.

Ryan stood, but surprised Jake by holding out his hand. "Jake."

They shook hands and Jake could feel tension radiating from him, but that didn't necessarily have anything to do with Jake. It could have to do with the reasons why they were both being called to this meeting.

"What's going on?" Jake sat down on the couch next to where Ryan had been sitting. Maybe if he didn't mention what'd happened between them, they could go back to how it was before. Or, at least a version of it.

"I'm here for the meeting with Admiral Moore." Ryan sat next to Jake, but didn't meet his eyes. That didn't bode well.

"I haven't seen the Admiral in a few years. What about you?" Was Ryan working on something with the Admiral? Why would the CIA be involved in this?

He glanced over at Jake. "Yeah, I've seen him." He ran his hands through his blond hair. "It's not like anyone has a choice about that. When he wants to see you, you show up. I think you're the only person who might've had a chance to turn him down. You were always his favorite. Our whole team thought so."

Jake smiled at that, the tension draining away. "No way. Admiral Moore doesn't have favorites. And I always got extra PT and grunt work while you were getting your beauty sleep."

"That's how I knew you were his favorite." Ryan sat back and settled into the couch like he wasn't planning on getting up again.

Jake's phone buzzed and he took it out of his pocket. *Tyler*. "Sorry. I need to take this."

He walked a few paces down the hall. "Tell me good news, Ty."

"I have good news and bad news." Tyler's voice sounded far away and Jake knew the phone was between Ty's shoulder and chin. He was probably coordinating all his resources while talking on the phone. His fingers rarely left his keyboard when they were on a case.

"Just tell me we found him." Jake lowered his voice, in case Ryan was eavesdropping. Knowing the CIA, though, they were probably being briefed simultaneously with Jake. Their agencies had been better about communication in recent years, but in this moment, Jake wanted to be the first to know.

"We got his port of entry," Tyler said. "Our guy in the Gulf cartel got it firsthand that they were paid a pretty penny to bring Nazer in through the Laredo crossing. That's the good news."

Laredo. The word sank through Jake's consciousness. He'd suspected that all along, but it was pretty gutsy to go through there. It wasn't the easiest way for sneaking into the country, but when did Nazer do anything the easy way? "What's the bad news?"

Everything in the background on Tyler's end quieted. That's how Jake knew that whatever Tyler was going to say was important. It was a quirk he had, but it always alerted Jake to listen closely to whatever Tyler was saying. "That's also how Nazer got out. We were about an hour too late."

Jake closed his eyes and gripped the phone. So he'd possibly had a chance to take him into custody if he'd made it to Texas today. It was a slim one, but it was there. "Can you confirm that?"

"Confirmed. He was spotted getting on a private plane just outside of Tamaulipas, Mexico an hour ago."

A ball of discouragement lodged in Jake's chest. He'd gotten away. Again. "Ty, how are we supposed to fight these guys when our borders have more holes than the beginner targets at the shooting range?" He leaned against the wall in front of the fractured snowflake painting. "Did the informant hear what the end game was for being in the U.S. at least?"

"No, he didn't have anything else, but I have everyone on the ground listening for even a whisper of Nazer or what's going on. We'll figure this out." The keyboard clacking in the background resumed. He sounded sure, but Jake wasn't as optimistic. They'd been close too many times now. Nazer al-Raimi was always one step ahead no matter what Jake tried to do. He sighed. "Thanks, Ty. I'll let you know when I'm on my way back to the office."

He hung up and two other men came around the corner, headed right for him. Neither of them paid any attention to Jake, so he turned and went back to Ryan, giving him a tight smile as he sat back down. Ryan didn't ask what the phone call had been about and Jake was glad. He didn't want any affirmations from Ryan that the CIA already knew what Jake had been told. That would add insult to injury at this point.

The other men nodded a greeting to Ryan and Jake as they approached, but didn't miss a beat in their conversation about the waffle they'd gotten from a food truck. Jake's stomach rumbled. There was one waffle truck in particular he loved to go to whenever he was in New York and he hadn't eaten yet today. Yeah, he was jealous of these guys. He watched them fold themselves into small uncomfortable chairs across from the conference room doors. He was glad they weren't right next to him. They probably still smelled like waffles and that would be asking too much of any hungry man.

He watched them smile and laugh together, but even with their casual air, they had a military bearing. They were obviously part of this meeting somehow, but acted like they were here to shoot the breeze.

"Hey, Ryan," Jake nudged him in the side, his voice low. "You think those guys are Army?"

Ryan looked at them, then back at Jake. "Nah. They look too happy to be in the Army. Probably Air Force or something. Those guys are always happy with their heads in the clouds."

Jake gave an amused chuckle at the dig, but he wasn't looking at the other men anymore. A woman was coming down the hall, her professional pace a little faster than Jake's. She was dressed in business casual with a white blouse and black dress pants. Her jet-black hair was swept back from her face, accentuating her long neck and bronze skin, but when she looked at them, her eyes were mesmerizing as she measured each man she was approaching. Even from this distance Jake couldn't look away. A quick glance to the corner showed him that the other two men watched as well. She had captivated them all.

Ryan nodded toward her. "She's gorgeous, but from the looks of it an unhappy diplomat. How could you not smile with a cushy U.N. job?"

Jake didn't answer. The woman had stopped in front of the other two men and he was shamelessly trying to hear what they were saying to her. They stood and shook her hand, greeting her just softly enough that Jake couldn't hear what she'd said.

At that moment, Admiral Moore opened the conference room door. He was thinner than Ryan remembered, a little gray at the temple, but still a commanding presence. Ryan and Jake straightened immediately. "Sir."

"This way, gentlemen." Admiral Moore's tone was abrupt and brooked no argument. He barely spared a glance at the other three people waiting near them, but gave a curt nod. "We'll be with the rest of you shortly."

Jake's eyes slid back to the woman, her mouth tightening in annoyance at the Admiral's words. *She wants in.* That much was easy to see. Did she know what was going on? Or was she looking for answers like him?

Whichever it was, hopefully they both got what they came for today. He squared his shoulders and cracked the knuckles on his right hand. *Let's do this.*

CHAPTER TWO

Mya Amari did not want to be here. She wanted to be in that conference room, hearing what the latest was on the hostages, and making sure she had a voice in the mission they were all about to embark on. But instead, she was left in the lobby, politely dismissed.

She tucked a few stray hairs from her homestyled chignon behind her ear, hoping she still looked presentable. She'd been detained longer than normal at security and had practically sprinted here. At least she wasn't out in the lobby alone to stew in her own thoughts and wonder if her banishment were because she was late. Captain Hughes and Captain Mitchell were just across the way discussing the pulled pork they'd had on a waffle. She didn't know how they did it. How could they act so casual when all she felt was tense?

The only other person she'd seen who'd seemed tense in the least was the taller American with the blue eyes. He'd stood when she'd come down the hall, imposing and unflappable, watching her movements carefully. If she had to guess, she'd say he was career military or law enforcement for sure, and not someone low on the command chain. He just had that assertive air about him. But she couldn't let that intimidate her. She needed to think of him like an opposing counsel—they both had roles to play if this was going to work at all.

Mya ran her hands down her blouse, hoping all the wrinkles had come out. When she realized what she needed to do and she'd be leaving for New York and Algeria, there hadn't been much time to pack or organize her things like she normally would. Her suitcase had been too full since she didn't know how long she'd be gone or exactly what kind of clothes to bring, and so everything was smushed in tight and mostly wrinkled. She'd spent extra time on her appearance this morning, though, and hoped her efforts showed.

She wandered over to the couch the two Americans had been sitting on, trying to calm her nerves. She'd recognized some sort of tension between the two of them by the way their bodies angled away from the other, which suggested they weren't co-workers, but that's about all she'd been able to see right off. Usually it wasn't hard for her to read people, which made her good at being an attorney, but today she hadn't been able to read much about either of the Americans, except that she'd been drawn to the taller one. His lighter blue eyes contrasted with his dark hair and he'd had an intensity about him. Yet, she hadn't been able to draw any conclusions beyond he looked like the stereotype of every U.S. military man she'd ever seen—tall, dark, and muscular. Hopefully, he was the kind who didn't have any problems with women being a part of a mission.

She sat down and put her hand on the armrest, making sure she wasn't tapping her foot. Hiding her nervousness was a priority. She wanted to look in control, especially when she wasn't feeling it. Focusing all her energy, she stared at the closed door. Was eavesdropping in the U.N. a crime? And if she were arrested here would that affect her Oath of Barrister and Solicitor? It seemed like something she should know, but hadn't come across in law school.

She sighed. If she hadn't had that knock at her door three days ago asking her to help in the rescue of the hostages, she'd be starting her new job as an Immigration Law attorney at McKennon, Deveratt and Bank. She'd worked hard to land the position, but as soon as she'd heard the name Yasmine Dorval, she knew there wasn't anything in the world that she wouldn't do to be part of this rescue attempt.

Staring a hole in the door, she tried to imagine what was going on. Were they talking about Yasmine in there? Or were they still calling her the translator? Was that all she was to them? Her fists clenched. She needed to be in there. Mya wanted to make sure Yasmine was considered someone as worthy of rescue as the diplomat she'd been with. Which brought her back to her favorite questions since this whole thing started. Why was Yasmine in Algeria working as a translator? Was it by choice?

Mya was pulled out of her thoughts when, out of the corner of her eye, she could see Captain Hughes get up and head toward her. He was the younger of the two and the definition of happy-go-lucky. He was only about 5'9" with brown hair and brown eyes. Some might describe him as average, but his smile was the feature that made him stand out. It lit up a room. Captain Mitchell was older, maybe mid-thirties, tall and trim. He reminded her of her favorite law professor—calm and steady. He definitely had no time or inclination to deal with shenanigans. She pasted on a smile. They'd both been a friendly bright spot on the plane ride here from Toronto and she could use all the friends she could get right now, especially ones who might have information on Yasmine.

"Mya, why don't you come and sit with us? I'm sure it won't be much longer." Hughes gestured toward an empty chair near them. "I can't let you sit here all alone. It's not right."

Did she want to be alone? Part of her said yes, but the polite part knew she couldn't refuse. "I didn't want to intrude," she murmured. "Or hear about any more disgusting things you can put on a waffle."

Hughes laughed at that. "You sound like Colt."

At the mention of his name, Colt Mitchell stood and crossed the room to them. Mya had to look up to meet his eyes since he was so much taller than her. "I hope you'll take that as a compliment," he said to her. "Sounding like me, I mean."

She held back a grin. "Of course." With a glance at the still closed door, she looked back at the men standing in front of her. "To tell you the truth, it was nice to have something else to talk about besides the . . . besides what we're here for." She couldn't even bring herself to say it. The kidnapping. The only thing she'd been able to think about for three days.

"Well, that waffle gave us something to talk about for months. You wouldn't believe the choices we had," Hughes said with an enthusiastic smile.

Mitchell looked down at her, like a prosecutor getting ready to make his case. "Did you get some breakfast this morning?"

She was too stressed for that. The smell of the food had made her stomach queasy so she'd skipped it. "I was still feeling a bit airsick." She held her palm over her middle. "I'll be sure to grab some lunch."

He made a small noise of disapproval in his throat, but didn't give her grief about it and changed the subject instead. "Did you have a chance to go over the documents from the safe deposit box last night?"

"Yes." It was still odd that they knew so much about her. Her mother's safe deposit box had had a lot of documentation, even including school grades starting from the year she was granted asylum in Canada, but it had some priceless personal items as well, like her mother's journal. Mitchell had been poring over it on the plane and had barely even looked out the window. After reading the documents herself, she knew the danger to her was more than her mother had ever let on when she was alive. There were so many things she wished she could ask her mom, especially now. She still hadn't stopped picking up the phone to call her to just talk before she remembered her mom was gone. Six months ago. The familiar pain pushed into her heart, but she locked it away. Some days were definitely harder than others.

She focused on Mitchell's eyes. "The protocols for contacting my father were very clear and I didn't get the feeling they would ever change or expire." But the thing that had stuck out to her the most were her mother's warnings before she'd laid out how to get in touch with her father. *Going back to Algeria was too great a risk. So many sacrifices had been made for her safety. Stay in Canada.* Those three things had been the theme of her mother's journal entries to her, in between how much she loved Mya.

But her mother couldn't have foreseen that Yasmine would be taken. She couldn't leave her half-sister in the hands of kidnappers when she had the means to help bring her home, could she? She had to get to Yasmine before the kidnappers realized who she was. If her connection to their father were discovered, she would be killed or used as leverage. Mya couldn't live with herself if she sat back and did nothing while Yasmine suffered.

Mitchell reached out and patted her shoulder like an older brother would. "Then it's just a waiting game for us, eh?"

She smiled at him, knowing he meant well. It was an excruciating waiting game for her. The one thing their files hadn't told them was that Yasmine was her half-sister and she'd kept that detail to herself for now. She didn't want anything preventing her from being part of this hostage negotiation. Even if it meant she'd have to face her father. "Hopefully not much longer now," she said, her gaze drawn to the closed door like a defendant waiting for her jury to come back with a verdict.

"Can I get you anything?" Hughes asked, looking down on her with kind eyes. His face was so open, easy to read. She liked that about him.

"No, I'm fine." Her toe was beginning to tap again, though. What was taking so long? "Have you heard anything new since last night?"

"No. Just the same details you were given on the plane." Hughes moved to sit next to her and she scooted over so he could have more room.

"So, Ms. Dorval met Mr. Edwards at the plane as planned. They were headed straight into the mediation meetings, when they were rerouted down a side street. The caravan was ambushed, with the lead car bombed." She grimaced. "At least we know from security cameras that both Ms. Dorval and Mr. Edwards survived. They were hooded and hustled into another car." Yasmine must have been so scared. "Had Ms. Dorval and Mr. Edwards worked together before?"

"Yes, they met at the last U.N. summit in Algeria." Hughes gave her the information as if they were talking about the weather, which made it easy to ask the questions.

From the tidbit he'd just given her, apparently Yasmine had been working as a translator for a while then. That was a surprise. "When was that?"

"About six months ago." Hughes leaned back, but his eyes never left hers. "But that's all we know, really."

Captain Mitchell glanced down at her tapping foot with a quirk of his lips. "I know you're anxious, but Colonel Kenby is in there and if there's anything new he'll let us know."

He had a mild air about him, as if nothing could ever faze him, and Mya needed that right now. She forced her feet to be still. "I want to make sure we're all on the same page."

"That was the deal." Mitchell's eyes danced with laughter. "Did you really tell the Colonel that if he wanted you to help then he had to make your security clearance as high as his for the mission and be kept updated in the same manner he was?"

She smiled as she remembered the Colonel's stoic face trying to hide a grin at her demand. She had a feeling he wasn't as rigid as his men believed he was. "And I wanted it in writing."

Mitchell laughed at that. "I wish I could have been there."

So far the Colonel had kept up his side of the bargain, but the U.N. was asking for the support of the U.S. and that changed the game. From the look of the men that went into that room, they weren't used to bargaining or being second-chair. But she needed to be kept apprised and in control or Yasmine wouldn't have a chance. "Do you think I could make the same bargain with the Americans?"

Mitchell gave her an apprising look. “If I didn’t know about your deal with Colonel Kenby, I’d say you have no chance. But since he doesn’t make deals, you must be driven and convincing. A woman who knows what she wants. And you just might get it.”

Mya folded her arms. “Thanks, Captain. I intend to.”

CHAPTER THREE

Jake and Ryan followed Admiral Moore into the conference room leaving the woman and two other men in the reception area. Part of him felt sorry for the woman out there who so obviously wanted to be in here, but the other part just wanted to figure out why he'd been called here.

The room was just as he expected with a long conference table in the middle, microphones in front of each seat and the U.N. flag prominently displayed. It was definitely a room for talking and planning. Planning was necessary when he'd been a SEAL, and it was something Jake had been fanatical about, but right now if he had his druthers, he'd rather be in the field working on his Homeland Security cases.

Another man was waiting inside for them, his hands behind his back, and a serious look on his face. Admiral Moore stopped in front of him. "Gentlemen, this is Colonel Kenby from the Canadian Army." Admiral Moore motioned them to seats nearest the front of the table.

"Nice to meet you, sir," Jake said before he sat. Ryan echoed him.

"You as well. I've heard a lot about both of you," Colonel Kenby said. He looked young for a colonel, but his navy blue uniform was laden with all the ribbons and medals a man of his rank should have.

Why would a Canadian colonel hear about me? Jake smiled politely, but his mind was churning. What was this about?

When they were sitting down, the Colonel turned to the Admiral and a look passed between them. The Colonel finally nodded as if their silent conversation had come to an end.

Just tell me what's going on. Jake squelched the urge to say anything. The Admiral had always been the type that you waited to be spoken to and didn't ask questions. The Colonel looked just as forbidding.

Finally, Admiral Moore leaned forward. "Well, I wasn't surprised to see where you two ended up after you left the SEALs." He turned to Jake. "Although I heard there was a rift between you recently. Has that been cleared up?"

When the Admiral said it like that, it sounded more like a command to clear it up than a question of whether it was. Jake looked at Ryan. "No, sir."

"That's going to be your first assignment then." He looked between them as if that would be something easily done.

Ryan wouldn't meet Jake's eyes and was staring at some point on the wall. He also didn't look too excited about that assignment, but what could he say? "Yes, sir."

Admiral Moore folded his hands on the table and leaned forward. "Jake, I know it's been over two years since you left the SEALs and then Special Ops for Homeland Security, but something has come up and we need your expertise with it."

"What kind of expertise?" Jake asked, curiosity getting the best of him.

"What I'm about to say is classified information and I expect you to treat it as such." He looked Jake in the eye, before he turned to Ryan who merely nodded. Whatever the Admiral was about to say wasn't news to him. A little kick of resentment shot through Jake, but he squashed it so he could focus.

"Colin Edwards was in Algeria on official duty for the U.N." The Admiral looked down at the table for a moment, as if choosing his words carefully. "He was there to discuss options over stabilizing the situation in Mali when he was kidnapped."

Jake's heart rate sped up. He'd worked on a detail for Edwards' security team when Edwards was the Deputy Assistant to the Secretary of State. "Has there been a ransom demand?"

The Admiral leaned back in his chair. "Yes." He shook his head. "One hundred million dollars and three prisoners from Guantanamo. And we all know what happened to the last country that didn't pay up."

Jake inwardly shuddered. The video of that man's torture and eventual death had haunted him for weeks. "You know, that's exactly what Starks was asking for when he kidnapped former Vice-President Chalmers." That abduction a few months ago had shaved years off Jake's life. He'd been lucky and got the Vice-President out before he could be killed, but that had been touch and go for a while.

"We know. And since Nazer al-Raimi was behind that attack, when the ransom demand came through as almost the exact same as the Vice-President's, it made us take a harder look, but nothing's adding up."

Ryan leaned over the table, his eyes on Jake. "It adds up if Nazer is working with Haji al-Awani."

Jake folded his arms, meeting Ryan's hard stare. "People like Nazer will team up with anyone who can further their agenda. Homeland got the intelligence memo last week that al-Qaeda in the Arabian Peninsula is trying to unify with al-Qaeda in the Islamic Magreb." Jake's mind was racing. "But Nazer's been in Texas."

"Well, he doesn't run a one-man show," Ryan said with a condescending tone, turning his torso toward the Admiral. "Nazer has been associated with AQAP and he would want a higher position in leadership if AQAP and AQIM terrorist organizations were combining."

Jake tamped down his annoyance at his former friend. This wasn't a competition between them and he wasn't going to play games. He needed to focus on the issue at hand. "If he was trying to curry favor in a terrorist organization restructure, why was he in Texas?"

"If it is him behind the kidnapping, why would he be asking for ISIS leaders in exchange for Mr. Edwards? We all know AQIM is openly rebelling against ISIS." Ryan raised a brow as if he'd just check-mated Jake in their verbal chess game.

Jake held up two fingers. "First of all, if I was in a terrorist organization and had a chance to kill three of my rival's leaders, or even just take them prisoner myself for leverage, I'd do it. Second, Nazer might be trying to wrangle a position in ISIS. He doesn't have any loyalty and it would score him a lot of points with Fadel and his crew by arranging their freedom. Nazer is all about power and prestige." He turned to the Admiral. "What's the ransom deadline?"

The Colonel finally spoke up, but didn't answer Jake's question. "You've been chasing Nazer al-Raimi for the last six months. AQIM, AQAP, and ISIS all have very different agendas. Do you think Nazer could change loyalties that easily?"

Jake kept his eyes on the Colonel. "Yes, I do. I know he's got a personal vendetta against the U.S., though, beyond any organization, and it was confirmed today that Nazer used the Laredo border to enter the U.S. three weeks ago. He was spotted less than two hours ago leaving the same way and getting on a plane that flew him out of Mexico. We're still working on the reason why he was here at all. I just don't want to jump to any conclusions."

The Colonel steepled his fingers on the table. "So the three Guantanamo people Nazer wanted Starks to get for him are ISIS leaders?"

"Abdul, Adnan, and Fadel. Not only leaders, but the three most trusted advisors of Omar al-Zahiri." Ryan didn't need to recite their whole names. Everyone at the table would recognize the heads of the ISIS terrorist group.

"Nazer wanted them and kidnapped former Vice-President Chalmers, but didn't get them and now here we are with another high-level American kidnapped and al-Awani is demanding them. Coincidence?" the Admiral asked. "I don't think so. And that's why we've come to you, Commander Williams."

Jake looked at the man who'd been more like a mentor to him than a commanding officer. "Sir?"

"We believe Nazer is behind both kidnappings. You have insider knowledge of Nazer and how he works. He's been building up his terrorist organization to do everything he can to hurt the U.S. and having a lot of success lately. We need to get to this guy sooner rather than later. You know him. You've studied him."

"And none of it is good, sir." *Which doesn't bode well for Colin Edwards if Nazer really is behind his kidnapping.* "I'll tell you everything I know about Nazer, but how does this relate to Edwards? Is there a rescue op planned?"

The Colonel glanced at Admiral Moore. "We have a possible lead on someone that al-Awani trusts and Nazer has negotiated with in the past. We're hoping to use him to not only get our people free without any fuss, but lead us to Nazer and give us the opportunity to take him into custody."

"You have some bait." Ryan put in.

"A crude way to put it, but yes." The Colonel didn't seem impressed with Ryan's choice of words and his gaze shifted to Jake. "You want Nazer, we want to free the hostages."

"So what do you need me to do? Be a consultant of some sort?" Jake asked.

"The negotiator won't speak directly to us since he's in a delicate position of trust with these people while keeping himself distant from them at the same time. But we do have his daughter and we think he'll talk to her. She was granted asylum in Canada some years ago, which brings us to the issue at hand. If she helps us, her safety would be at stake."

Jake's mind flashed back to the serious looking woman sitting in the waiting room. No wonder she didn't look like she wanted to be here. "I'm still not sure how I can help. And I'd have to talk to my boss at Homeland."

"That's already taken care of if you accept." The Admiral didn't even blink as he said it and the 'if' sounded more like a when. He'd been pretty sure of Jake's answer, then. "This mission was custom-made for you, son. You've been in Algeria before so you know the lay of the land and are passable at the French language. You know Colin Edwards. And you are a SEAL." Admiral Moore held up a finger for each point he listed.

"And with our help you can get Nazer." His gaze drilled into Jake's.

The Admiral had him there. "So, you want us to take the negotiator's daughter to Algeria and get her to talk to her dad in our behalf and hope he'll be able to meet with Nazer? Then I grab him?" He shifted to look at Ryan. "There's more than just the two of us in this operation, right?" If there wasn't, this was over before it began.

The Colonel furrowed his brow. "Actually, Mr. Smythe is working with CIA assets in Algeria and coordinating intelligence. Your job would be to get Ms. Amari to the Canadian safehouse in Algiers and keep her alive and well until we get a location on her father. Then report it."

That pronouncement knocked him back a little. He'd be reporting to Ryan who was helping with the rescue op while he was a glorified bodyguard? "What aren't I getting here? You don't need a specialist for that. And I'm not a babysitter."

Admiral Moore took over, his tone as gentle as a commanding officer's could be. "Jake, you're a people person. You were a calming influence on any mission. We need that quality now. Ms. Amari is a little skittish about helping us and she's our only lead in a rescue attempt for Edwards. We need you to keep her calm and to keep her safe until she can make contact with her father. So you wouldn't be a babysitter, you'd be an integral part of a mission to save an American diplomat and capture a wanted terrorist."

When he put it like that, how could he refuse? He couldn't live with Edwards' death on his hands because he couldn't get over some petty disagreement with Ryan. It was a done deal the moment he'd been pulled off the plane. Squaring his shoulders, he got down to business. "What do we know about the negotiator? Is he even reliable?" Jake asked. "And how does he get access to people that most of the world has been hunting for years?"

The Colonel stared out the window behind them for a moment, gathering his thoughts before he spoke. "Ibrahim Amari started out leading rebels against the ruling party in Algeria in the early '90s, but he was always willing to negotiate peace, even when his ultimate plans failed. He made contacts with the extremists and gained their trust while at the same time keeping ties with government officials who also want peace. After things stabilized with the government, the rebels started using kidnappings to fund themselves, Ibrahim saw how he could use his contacts to help negotiate hostage releases."

"So he does this out of the goodness of his heart?" Jake knit his brows together. "What's in it for him?"

"He takes his cut as well. A large one. It's a lucrative business and he has a high success rate. He's elusive, though. The only way we even know about him is through third or fourth hand accounts. But it was him who negotiated the release of that French national last year. He's very, very, careful who he deals with." The Admiral tapped his finger on the table. "And he's Edwards' best chance of getting out of this alive."

He pushed back from the table, but didn't stand, his eyes flicking from Jake to Ryan. "You won't report to anyone but me and Colonel Kenby, if the chain of command is what's bothering you." He pointed his finger at Ryan. "But I meant what I said, your first assignment is to figure out your personal issues. We can't have that affecting this mission in any way."

"Yes, sir," they both said simultaneously.

"Good." The admiral pushed a folder with a dark plastic package on top of it toward them. "The details of the kidnapping investigation are there, as well as background on both Mr. Edwards and the translator that was captured with him. You're expected to be on a plane this afternoon. The U.N. is ultimately overseeing everything, of course, since Edwards was there on official U.N. business." He pointed to the bag. "There are secure phones in there for the five of you so you can have a way to be in contact at all times and the pertinent files have been encrypted and downloaded to them for easy reference."

"Five of us, sir?"

"Because of the international and delicate nature of this operation, my two top men will be joining you," the Colonel supplied. "This is to be a joint task force and you'll have access to all the Canadian assets as well."

"So we've got two Canadians with some assets, a CIA officer and me heading over to Algeria to spearhead finding the negotiator." Jake opened the folder and saw a picture of a smiling Edwards on top. His gut twisted. Edwards was a good man. Who knew what they were doing to him.

"That's right. And when Ms. Amari has made contact, you report where the negotiation is taking place so the team can grab Nazer and extract Edwards and the translator." The Admiral narrowed his eyes as if trying to read Jake's mind. "Once we have a location, the rescue team can be in and out quickly and quietly."

Jake closed the folder, pulling his face into a professional blank. Once upon a time, he would have been on that rescue team. Part of him wished he still was, but he clamped down on that feeling and focused on the Admiral's instructions. "Did you say there was a translator? There are two prisoners then?"

"Yes. Edwards was with a local translator. We're hoping to get her out as well." The Admiral's tone was confident, something Jake had always appreciated about him. No matter what, he had faith in his men.

"Where was Edwards' security team?" Jake asked softly, knowing the answer in his heart.

"His convoy was on a side street when they were ambushed. It was very well-executed and he was gone in under five minutes." The Admiral looked at the table before he met Jake's eyes. "Edwards didn't have a chance then. We can give him one now."

"We won't let you down, sir." Ryan said with a nod.

"I know you won't." The Admiral stood. "I think that's all."

"There's one more thing," the Colonel said as he stood next to the Admiral. "We needed to choose a leader for this mission. While Captain Mitchell and Captain Hughes are equal to you in rank, we've decided that with your experience heading up the Homeland Security task force, you were the natural pick for this one. But Captain Mitchell will need to be consulted and kept apprised of every part of the mission."

Jake glanced at Ryan as they pushed back their chairs. His jaw was clamped tightly. Was he upset they hadn't picked him to head the task force? Or was this a pity assignment to make Jake feel better because he was only there to protect Ms. Amari? "Yes, sir." The one silver lining was that they were working with Canadians. The few he'd come across had been polite and competent.

"Let Ms. Amari in." The Admiral turned toward the door and the two men that had been in the waiting room ushered in Ms. Amari first and they brought up the rear.

Jake's gaze turned to the young woman who stood before them now, her unusual light brown eyes piercing every man surrounding her. Up close it was hard not to stare. She was stunning. But with her arms folded and a guarded expression on her face it was easy to see she was upset about something. He pulled his eyes away. *Keep it professional,* he reminded himself.

"Captain Mitchell, Captain Hughes, thank you for joining us. I know you've been briefed on the situation. This is Commander Williams, a former Navy SEAL with Special Operations experience. He'll be the commanding officer of this task force." The Admiral's eyes were sharp, as if he expected them to contradict him, but they were silent. Jake was surprised he was being addressed by his former military rank, but he let it go. It wouldn't matter what his title was as long as he could get the job done.

Colonel Kenby stepped in. "I apologize for making you wait outside, but Commander Williams hadn't yet been briefed on the situation." He turned to Ms. Amari. "Can I offer you a glass of water?"

"No, thank you," she murmured. "But I need to know you will be keeping our agreement."

Her voice was low and she had the trace of an accent. Jake wanted to ask her what agreement she was talking about, not only so he knew what was going on, but also to hear her voice again. *Don't focus on her.* The last thing he wanted was to make her uncomfortable around him.

"Yes, the agreement is in place and I know how to get hold of you. And you will be present at this briefing which should answer some of your questions." The Colonel stepped back.

The Canadian who was at least as tall as Jake's 6'2" frame cut into his thoughts. "Colonel, do we have orders yet?" He wasn't the guy laughing with his friend over a waffle anymore. He gave Jake a once-over and Jake returned his stare. He was used to military types that took your measure with a look. This Canadian had a little bite to his tone, though. Jake looked to the Admiral, but the Admiral held up his hand. The Colonel would handle it.

"Captain Mitchell, I know you and your capabilities. You're qualified to lead this team, but Commander Williams has a unique knowledge of the man we believe is masterminding the kidnapping. I know you'll be a valuable asset to the mission and a credit to your country." The Colonel glanced at Ms. Amari. "Everyone will work together for the safety of Ms. Amari and the rescue of the hostages. That is our priority. We must do everything we can to contact Ibrahim Amari and have him negotiate their release."

The Colonel stepped toward the door. "I'll leave the logistics for your team leader to brief you on, Captain Mitchell. Captain Hughes. Ms. Amari. Thank you all. And good luck." He stepped out the door with the Admiral following close behind.

Jake sat back in his seat and sucked in a breath. Four pairs of eyes looked at him, and none of them were exactly friendly. *Time to introduce myself to my new team.* Jake walked around the table and stuck out his hand to the first man. "I'm Jake Williams. I didn't catch your first name."

The man shook it, his grip firm. "Colt. Colt Mitchell."

The man to Mitchell's left offered his hand. "I'm Nate Hughes."

"Good to meet you." He looked between them. "Do you prefer first or last names?" Sometimes the military men got so used to being called by their last names, they actually felt more comfortable.

"First will be fine." Colt gave a sideways glance to Nate, who nodded. "What should we call you, Commander?"

"Jake is fine." The air was starting to thaw a little. At least they were on a first name basis now. "The Admiral listed my background, and I'd like to hear more of yours. Do any of you have any experience overseas?" Jake asked.

Nate spoke first. "I served two tours in Afghanistan under Colt before I was promoted to Captain myself." He jerked his thumb toward Colt. "He's served four and is the captain of our troop in Joint Task Force 2."

Colt nodded his head in acknowledgment. "I believe our troop's equivalent in JTF2 is a SEAL team."

Well, at least they're qualified, Jake thought. "Mr. Smythe and I have served overseas together in the SEALs, but now he works for the CIA and I'm with Homeland Security." That summed it up without going into any detail.

Ryan gave him a sardonic smile. "You can call me Ryan. Mr. Smythe sounds so formal."

Jake resisted rolling his eyes and instead opened the bag the Admiral had given him and took out the phones to pass them out. "These are secure so we can be in contact with each other from now on."

Taking the last one, he started to approach Ms. Amari, but her folded arms and the irritated look in her eye made him pause. *What could I possibly have done to offend her already?* He left the phone on the table and stepped back, flipping past the first few pages in the folder to find the contact protocols. "Looks like we have a transport plane that will take us to Algeria leaving in three hours. We'd better get going."

Ryan nudged him, his eyebrows raised as his head tilted toward the woman. "Not to be rude, *Jake*, but you seemed to have forgotten one introduction." His tone was borderline mocking, especially when he'd said his name, but Jake decided to let it go. He'd just told the Admiral he'd try to figure out a way to put their personal issues behind them and he was going to keep his word.

The woman shook her head as she reached for the phone he'd left for her on the table. Sliding it into her pants pocket, she crossed the room toward the door. "The only thing you need to know is no matter what your name or title is, I'll be the lead on this team. And I expect to be included in every briefing from now on." She turned to face him with a nod. "Commander." And then she walked away, closing the door behind her with a soft *snick* in her wake.

Jake stared at the door. *Well, that's a wrinkle I didn't expect.*

CHAPTER FOUR

Every muscle in Mya's body was tense. Her fists were clenched so hard her nails dug into her palms. Not surprisingly, no one approached her as she stalked back the way she'd come toward the exit. She'd thought the Americans were probably going to be arrogant, but hadn't realized how right she was until the Commander had barely even given her the time of day. *Forgot an introduction.* The frustration burned in her belly. If they thought she'd be relegated to a pretty face in their little mission, they could think again. She was the only reason they even had a "mission."

She walked down the long hall, passing several security checkpoints. Colonel Kenby had assigned her a security guard named Darrell, but she didn't see him and frankly, she didn't want to look for him. She needed to get out of here, to cast off the claustrophobic feeling she'd had since she walked in. The Canadian military men had tried to put her at ease from the moment they'd met and she was grateful for that small kindness. If there was one thing she'd learned from Canadians it was that they were generally good people at heart. But she'd had all she could take today and just needed to be alone for a bit.

She took a deep breath before she reached the exit of the building, stopping in front of a painting of an African landscape to gather herself. It looked a little like her homeland and she wished she were in Algeria right now. Not to visit or look up relatives and old family friends. She wanted this thing underway, to be doing something, not cutting through all this red tape and putting a team together from different countries. They only needed her, why couldn't they see that? She could get through to her father, they could get Yasmine and the diplomat back. At the thought of Yasmine, tears pricked the back of her eyelids, but she quickly blinked them away. Her mind froze if she let herself imagine what might be happening to her half-sister and she couldn't let herself go there. This was no time to show weakness. She had to be strong and get this done.

Heading for the exit, she hailed a cab, seeing Darrell about a hundred feet behind her. Well, at least she wouldn't have to share a cab with him and she could be alone with her thoughts for a minute. She'd go straight to the hotel and then up to her room. There wasn't any harm in that, especially if Darrell was right behind her.

Giving the cabbie her hotel name, she leaned back in the seats. She couldn't remember the last time she'd slept and she was starting to feel it. Her eyelids were scratchy and heavy. She rubbed them, even though it would probably smudge the eye makeup she'd so carefully applied this morning. Since she was already packed, maybe she could use the time to catch a little nap. She knew she wouldn't sleep on the plane since she had to be on her guard constantly. Commander Williams was the poster child for arrogance, barely looking at her while he introduced himself to everyone else and chatted them up like old Army buddies. Well, she'd make him understand how it was going to be on this mission. If she'd been allowed into his briefing, she could have made that clear to all of them and had Colonel Kenby back her up. Why had they excluded her? She sighed. It just made everything harder.

When the taxi stopped she got out and paid the cab driver, anxious to get to her room and lie down. She'd be on a plane in a few hours where she'd be in close proximity to everyone she'd probably offended in that conference room. The adrenaline was starting to wear off and she could feel a headache coming on. Rubbing her left temple, the fire of anger fizzled inside her. She hadn't helped her case. If only she could get a redo, where she came in and was chatty and bright, someone Commander Williams would have smiled at and wanted to include. But, instead, she'd been like a bull in a china shop and ruined whatever chance she'd had. Why hadn't she taken deep breaths and calmed herself? Focused on the Colonel and used him to help her cause? She knew the answer. She'd been intimidated by Commander Williams from the get-go and tried to get some sort of upper hand by staking her claim. It was a rookie mistake. She should have finessed them all and now the judge and jury had come back and found her wanting. Well, she wouldn't repeat her blunder. She'd win them over yet.

Walking quickly into the large hotel lobby, she headed straight for the elevator, but the concierge behind the desk spotted her and headed her off. "Miss, miss, you got a message while you were out."

Mya closed her eyes. She didn't want to know what it said. All of her messages over the last forty-eight hours had been from government entities with mostly bad news. "Thank you," she said as she took the envelope. He stood expectantly, like she should open it in front of him. She wasn't about to do that. Snapping the clasp on her purse, he realized what she was doing and his eyes got wide. "No, ma'am, no tip. I just wanted to make sure it was safely in your hand."

She nodded and tucked the envelope inside the purse instead of getting out her wallet. "Thank you." She couldn't deal with one more thing right now. She had to lie down.

Heading for the elevator, she was glad to hear it ding. She was one step closer to her bed. The elevator only had one other passenger on it and it was almost a palpable feeling of relief for her. She didn't have it in her to smile or exchange any more inane pleasantries today. The man inside didn't even look up, just stared at his phone as she stepped toward him. She got in and turned her back, pressing the number 5. Touching the bridge of her nose, she let her shoulders slump. The only reason she'd agreed to any of this was Yasmine, but would they be too late?

Seconds later, before the doors fully closed, the man behind her moved and instinctively she tensed, her intuition screaming for her to get out. She reached out her arm to keep the doors open so she could run and the ding told her they'd opened again, but before she could even take a breath to scream he had his arm around her neck in a headlock. He scooted them to the corner where he wouldn't be readily seen and red spots danced in front of her eyes.

She grabbed his arm, trying to open even a small space so she could catch a breath, but he tightened his grip, cutting off her airway. Frantically she whipped her head backward, hoping to connect with a nose at least, but he moved out of her reach too fast. Switching from a headlock to his hand squeezing around her neck so tight she had no hope of breath getting to her lungs, she was scrambling to remember anything from her self-defense classes.

Mya put her chin down and twisted to the side to try and get some pressure off her carotid artery so she wouldn't pass out. *Please, let someone see.* The doors were open, but they were on the side so no one walking by would see unless they looked in the elevator car. She was oddly alone in a busy hotel lobby elevator. She pressed her foot forward to make sure that door stayed open. Being seen might be her only chance.

He bent closer to her and she threw her head back again. He only squeezed tighter until the pain was too excruciating to bear. Her attacker bent close to her ear and she could hear him sniff her hair. A shiver went through her and she tried to twist away from him to no avail. His sour tobacco breath across her cheek made her want to gag. "Did you think you could hide forever?" he grated.

That voice would haunt her dreams for the rest of her life. "Just know we can get to you at any time," he continued. "Kill you. Kill your family." He shook her until her teeth rattled in her head, but she had a small respite from the pressure on her neck. She tried to pull in a breath before he had a good grip on her again. "Remember that. There isn't anywhere you can hide, anyone who won't betray you."

Betray me? What did he mean by that? The doors were trying to close again, but she stretched to make sure her foot was still jammed in and would keep them open. It was easier this time and she realized when he'd readjusted their position, she was slightly forward and to his left now. With their height difference, and the way he was holding her, she knew she had to make the only move she could. She grasped his arms with one of hers for leverage and with a quick step to the side, she opened up just enough room where she could slam her fist backward and punch him in the groin.

When he grunted in pain and instinctively bent over, she scrambled out of his reach, falling out of the elevator onto the lobby floor, her purse spilling its contents everywhere. Anger and fear mixed in her veins but even gasping for air, she managed to croak out loud enough for him to hear. "You'll never get near my family."

He looked murderous as he took a step toward her. “We already have, *thameen*. You will pay if you interfere.”

“Hey!” Someone called out. Her attacker glanced behind him and immediately took off, but Mya couldn’t even turn her head to see which way he’d gone her neck hurt so badly. She tried to stand, but the oxygen she needed wasn’t filtering in. She couldn’t catch any air, it all just felt like suffocating sludge she couldn’t breathe. *In, out*, she told herself.

From her vantage point on the floor, she had a front row seat to Darrell rushing past her to give chase to the man that had attacked her. *How could I be so stupid?* She knew she’d become a target the moment she left Canada. Why had she tempted fate? She wasn’t safe anywhere.

A man’s voice hovered above her. “Are you okay?” The owner of it crouched down to her eye level and she recognized Captain Hughes. He reached for her, helping her stand. “Who was that guy?”

Mya couldn’t speak seeing the concerned look on his face replace his ever-present smile. Tears welled in her eyes. “I don’t know,” she whispered.

Captain Hughes had taken out his phone and was dialing a number. “This is Nate. Mya was attacked at the hotel. You better get down here.”

“Which floor is yours?” Nate asked solicitously once he’d put his phone back in his pocket. He bent to pick up the contents of her purse and handed it to her.

“Five.”

Darrell came back, his breath coming in puffs. "He got away. I've never seen anyone run that fast. Are you okay?" He looked down at her and when she nodded, his face turned into an angry frown. "Why didn't you wait for me?"

"I'm sorry," she rasped, holding back tears. "I didn't think anything would happen in a crowded hotel. And I couldn't find you when my meeting was over."

"Colonel Kenby said you were in a briefing and I thought I had more time." Darrell sucked in another breath. "I didn't think you'd go off alone like that."

"Well, it's over now, so let's just get her upstairs." Nate took her arm and Mya tried to steady her legs. The security guard stuck to her like glue as the elevator whisked them upstairs. Once the doors opened, she directed them to the left. Her guard's anger was rolling off him in waves. She'd been so stupid and he had every right to be mad. "My room is just six doors down," she said, her voice small.

Nate took her elbow again and let her move slowly down the hall. Her legs weren't cooperating and her bones had turned to jelly. She wordlessly gave him her key and they stepped inside, leaving the guard outside the door. Nate turned on the light, even though afternoon daylight streamed into the room. There was a small table and chairs near the window and he headed for that. Without a lot of extra movement, he closed the curtains and pulled out the chair for her. She sank down in it.

Putting her hand to her neck, she looked up at him. "Thank you." She was a bit light-headed from the lack of oxygen and she knew a full-blown migraine was likely in her future.

Nate shook his head. "I wish Darrell could have gotten him. He was faster than a Canadian snow melt in August."

Mya smiled at that. "Where are you from?"

"Originally from Manitoba. I've been based in Ontario since I joined the military, though."

He walked back to her mini-fridge and took out a bottle of water. Handing it to her, he sat down in the opposite chair. "What did he want?"

"He said he's going to kill my family." Her voice was scratchy, and she opened her water and took a sip. Those words squeezed her emotions as hard as he'd squeezed her neck. She'd lost her mother to cancer less than six months ago. She couldn't bear to lose her father and sister, but he also said he already had them. Was that true? Did he have her father? Was this all for nothing?

"Did he say anything else?" Nate asked gently.

He'd said that there wasn't anyone who wouldn't betray her. Well, there were very few people she trusted anyway, so his words just validated her reasons for that. Before she could answer Captain Hughes, though, there was a knock at the door.

Nate got up to let them in, checking the peephole first. "Colt, Jake," he said as Captain Mitchell and Commander Williams came through the door. Mya groaned inwardly. She didn't want to deal with the commander just yet. Deep inside she was hoping Captain Hughes had only called Captain Mitchell.

"We were still at the U.N. together, so Colt filled me in and we came right over. What happened?" Williams demanded, the moment he'd cleared the threshold. With his long stride he was at her side in three steps.

"She was attacked in the elevator," Nate said gently as if that would soften it for her somehow. He stood on the other side of her. Captain Hughes was smaller and stockier than Commander Williams, but he had a caring air about him that was easy to like in the face of Commander Williams' high-handedness.

Mya forced her hands away from her throat and clenched them in her lap, wishing now she hadn't let Captain Hughes call anyone. "I'm fine."

Williams snorted, but leaned down a little to look at her. "Ms. Amari, you've practically got that guy's fingerprints in a necklace around your throat. Whoever did that was sending a serious message."

Mya thought back to the man's sneer and the way he'd called her *thameen*, or precious. Suppressing a shiver, she met Commander William's eyes. "Message received."

"What did he say to you?"

Mya couldn't sit still any longer and stood to cross the room. "I don't want to talk about it." *At least not to you.*

She looked back at the three men in her room. Hughes gave her an apologetic smile. "This fell out of your purse."

He held out the envelope the concierge had given her, but Commander Williams snatched it and opened it. "It says, *Don't come.*" He narrowed his ice blue eyes at her. "What's that supposed to mean?"

"How dare you open that!" She marched over and ripped the envelope out of his hand. "That's my private correspondence."

"Ms. Amari, you are under my protection. You need to let me do my job." He stood over her, his legs braced apart like he was some super-hero come to life. Well, she didn't need him.

"I'm under your protection?" she asked incredulously. "Well, you're doing a terrible job." Her hands waved toward her neck area where the bruises were. At least it was what hurt the most besides her head. A bit of guilt chased her anger when she saw him wince, though. It was a low blow and not like her. Closing her eyes, she could feel the adrenaline seeping out of her and she just wanted to be alone and have a good cry. "Please leave."

Commander Williams folded his arms. "No. Where you go I go from now on." He turned to Mitchell and Hughes. "Colt, I'll keep an eye on her. We'll meet you at the airport."

Mitchell looked at Hughes, then at her, but nodded. "See you there."

Hughes put a hand on her shoulder and gently squeezed in a show of support as they left the room and she appreciated that. He seemed so nice. But once he was gone and the door shut behind him, she straightened her spine. Commander Williams was not going to intimidate her and she couldn't let down her guard even for a moment.

Commander Williams didn't even give her a second glance. He walked around the room like he owned it. "Are you packed?"

"That's what those closed suitcases by the door usually mean." She eyed the bed, her body longing to lie down and rest on it, to nap for just a minute. But Commander Williams blocked her view.

"Good. Let's go then. You can come with me to pack my things." He hefted both her suitcase and carry-on and headed for the door.

"I'm not going anywhere with you. You can pick me up when you're done." She sat down on the bed watching with satisfaction as he turned to look at her like she'd grown two heads. "Whoever that was isn't coming back. Like you said, he was delivering a message and I got it. Don't worry, I'll lock the door." The more she talked, the better that sounded. Away from him. Alone for a moment behind a locked door. And surely Darrell wouldn't mind standing outside if she promised not to leave without him ever again.

Commander Williams put down her suitcase and bag and slowly walked toward her. He crouched in front of her so they were nearly eye-level. "Ms. Amari, my job is to keep you safe until you can meet with your father and I take my responsibilities very seriously." He glanced down at her throat and she could only imagine how bad it looked when she saw him flinch slightly. "I didn't think my job would start until we got to

Algeria, but this mission just got real. From now on, you'll be in my sight 24/7. Okay?"

"No, it's not okay." She glared at him. "I don't need a babysitter."

He stood and held out a hand to her. "Think of me as a bodyguard."

When she didn't reach for him, he leaned down to catch her eye. "Please? If not for me, for the two people we need your father to help us save."

At the thought of Yasmine, Mya's heart twisted with worry. The last few days had been the worst of her life and the attack in the elevator had topped it off. Her emotions were at a breaking point, and tears filled her eyes. She turned away, trying not to blink. Crying was the last thing she wanted Commander Williams to see. She was tired. So tired. And the fear and adrenaline wearing off were just too much. "Okay," she said, trying to put conviction into her voice, but failing when she heard it hitch on the word. She struggled to get herself under control and when she was ready, she put her hand in his outstretched one. It was strong and warm, everything she wasn't at the moment. Looking up at him, she felt a zing of awareness go through her as he helped her up. Caught off-guard, she stumbled against him, but he caught her, his hands lingering on her waist.

"Are you okay? Really?" He didn't pull away, but stepped back to look at her. "Maybe we should get you checked out by a doctor."

"I'm fine. Sorry," she murmured. Could this day get any worse? Yet, part of her wanted to just close her eyes and let him hold her and offer her comfort. To bury her nose in his dress shirt that smelled like her favorite laundry detergent. But if she did that, he'd never look at her as anything but a damsel in distress and she would never be that. She took another step back. "Really. I can take care of myself."

"I'm sure your security guard would beg to differ." He tilted his head, knowing she couldn't dispute that. Embarrassment flooded her face and she wanted to put her hand to her cheeks, but wouldn't give him the satisfaction. He really was the most aggravating man.

"You're being presumptuous now." She folded her arms, cursing her weakness just a moment before of wanting him to hold her. If folded arms were the only barricade she had against the force of Commander Jake Williams, then she'd use it.

He ran a hand through his hair, the gesture giving away the frustration he was feeling. It gave her a small amount of satisfaction to see that he wasn't as cool and collected as he wanted her to believe. "Okay, we've obviously gotten off on the wrong foot." Smiling down at her, she could almost believe it was genuine. "Since we're going to be spending a lot of time together, you might as well call me Jake."

His smile revealed a dimple in his cheek and her stomach flipped. She'd always had a thing for guys with dimples. But in this case, that wasn't good. She didn't want to fight an attraction battle with Commander Williams. She already had enough on her plate with this guy. She mentally shook herself. They weren't going to be friends. He was a means to an end in getting her sister back. That was it. "You can call me, Ms. Amari."

He stared at her for a full thirty seconds as if he couldn't believe what he'd just heard. Finally, he said, "Ms. Amari, I need to go grab my clothes, then we can head for the airport." He picked up her suitcase and bag again. "Are you ready?"

She shoved the envelope into her pocket. No, she wasn't ready. That message of *don't come* was plain and simple, but was it from her father? Who else wouldn't want her in Algeria? And whoever was in the elevator had sent a clear message that she was a target wherever she went and wasn't safe even in a busy hotel lobby. But if all this meant she had a chance to save Yasmine, she would do it. She would do anything.

"Ready," she said, and she walked over to open the door.

CHAPTER FIVE

Jake directed the cabbie to his sister's address in Brooklyn and settled back into his seat. He gave the woman next to him a sidelong glance. Her arms were folded again and her vibe was definitely ice queen as she looked out her window. He rubbed his hand through his hair. Seeing her injuries had thrown him. Whoever had done that meant business. It galled him that she'd faced that alone. Granted, he'd been told she had security until they were on the plane, but she was his responsibility and he'd let her down. He should have followed her to her hotel, been there when she needed him. He'd been asked to protect her and failed in the first hour. That was hard to take, but he wouldn't let it happen again no matter how many protests she made.

She didn't seem in the mood to talk and Jake was just fine with that. Wasn't like they had to be buddies so he could protect her. He took out the new phone he'd been given and tapped the screen to get to the files on the kidnapping. The Midtown tunnel had traffic this time of day and they were making good time, but he still had a few minutes to go over some things. Skimming over the high points, the urgency to get to Edwards increased. These guys had to have high-level help. The Edwards grab was too clean, too precise. It had to be Nazer trying to build power and connections in both the AQAP and AQIM terrorist groups.

Putting that away, he took out his own phone and texted Chivonn. *Change of plans. Heading to your place to pick up a few things. Sorry! We'll catch up when I get back.*

When he was finished he caught Ms. Amari looking at him. For just a moment her eyes were filled with curiosity and not mistrust and he smiled. "Letting my sister know I'm headed to her place."

She didn't reply, just narrowed her eyes before she turned back to the window.

Wow. Apparently she hadn't lived in Canada long enough for the legendary politeness to rub off on her.

His cell phone buzzed and he took it out. It was a text back from Chivonn. "Meet you there." He smiled. She was in such a better place now. She had her job, which was time-consuming, but gave her purpose. She always worked through lunch, but she'd drop everything for him. Always had. Just like he'd do for her. Although it'd been too long since he'd been to visit her. The thought had crossed his mind at the U.N. that since he was in New York, they might have a small chance to catch up, but now he'd have to make time for her when this was over. Be a better brother.

They pulled up in front of the apartment building and Jake got out to help the driver with the bags. He kept an eye out, his gun holster within reach. He wasn't taking any chances, but it didn't seem like they'd been followed and no one out of the ordinary was on the street. He paid the cabbie before he hefted the bags for the trek up the stairs. "After you, Ms. Amari," he said, emphasizing her name. Hey, if she wanted him to call her that, he'd make sure he did.

He followed her as they went in the door of the walk-up. "Third floor," he told her, nodding toward the stairs.

"This is where you and your sister live?" she asked. The way she was looking around bothered him. Did she think this place was too nice for him? Or not nice enough? He couldn't tell. When they'd moved Chivonn to Brooklyn three years ago, they'd looked at every rat-trap available. They'd almost given up when they found this one. Yeah, it wasn't the best looking place on the block, but Chivonn was happy here, had great neighbors who looked out for her, and was close to her job. That was all Jake cared about. Not what *Ms. Amari* thought of it.

"No, just my sister lives here." He made the first turn on the stairs, juggling the luggage more comfortably under his arm. They slowly made their way up to the top floor and Jake set down the bags and got out a key to let them in.

The door opened before he could get the key in the lock and a smiling woman was in the doorway. "Jake."

"Chivonn, did you look through the peephole before you opened it?" Jake chided.

"Of course. I'm not an idiot." Chivonn waved them inside with one hand, a sandwich plate in the other. "And I was expecting you."

Jake glanced back at the woman standing next to him. "Chivonn, I'd like you to meet Mya Amari. Ms. Amari, this is my sister, Chivonn."

Mya walked into the sunlit living room and Chivonn gasped when she saw the injuries on Mya's neck. "Oh my goodness, what happened to you?"

Mya put a hand self-consciously to her throat where her bruises were obvious. "It's nothing. I'm fine."

It was obvious Mya was uncomfortable with explaining to Chivonn and Jake didn't know how much he could really reveal, either. "Don't worry, sis, I've got her."

"Well, you did the right thing bringing her here." Chivonn took Mya's hand and started drawing her toward the couch.

Mya let herself be led, but looked back at Jake, her brow furrowed in confusion. "You're brother and sister?"

Jake joined them before they got any further and put his arm around Chivonn. Her dark skin's healthy glow made even his tan look pale and her long, tightly curled hair was the exact opposite to his short straight haircut. "Yep. I'm her big brother."

Chivonn looked up at him and smacked his shoulder. "We were foster kids together and it was us against the world so we claim each other. Most of the time."

Jake snagged a bite of Chivonn's sandwich before letting her go. "Ah, now why'd you have to go and ruin it? I like claiming you as my sister."

"Can I make you a sandwich?" Chivonn asked Mya, ignoring Jake. "Sometimes when you've been through something, a little comfort food can help. I have peanut butter and jelly or bologna? Or would you rather just have some chocolate? I can break into my stash."

"I'm fine," Mya said, taking a step closer to Chivonn. Jake wasn't surprised to see a smile on Mya's face. Chivonn had a talent for making people feel at ease around her, to instinctively trust her with their deepest secrets. That gift had magnified after she'd lost her husband, as if her grief had sensitized her somehow to the people who needed her most. Mya had seemed a tough nut to crack, but even the ice queen melted in Chivonn's presence.

His eyes found Mya's. Her whole face was transformed with her smile, those unusual golden brown eyes lighting up like it was Christmas. It was something he could get used to seeing. He pushed that thought aside. She had to be a job, nothing more.

He nudged Chivonn's shoulder. "What about me? You could make me a sandwich or get me some chocolate. But it has to be quick, we've got a plane to catch." He walked through her small sitting area to the pristine kitchen. Chivonn always liked things to be clean.

"How about you make a sandwich for yourself while I talk to Mya," Chivonn called from the living room. Jake could see it now. Chivonn was probably offering Mya a seat in front of the fireplace and they'd be best friends in no time.

This could work to his advantage. He had a lot of traveling to do with Mya. If Chivonn could soften her up a little, that might make things easier. He liked that thought. Once that was settled in his mind he opened the fridge and got out the jam to quickly make a PB&J. If this job was as hectic as he thought it was going to be, this might be the best meal he got for the foreseeable future. Making one more for good measure, he leaned against the counter and listened to try and make heads or tails of the murmurs floating in from the living room, punctuated by laughter. Jake shook his head. If only he could bottle Chivonn's charm.

He walked back in and leaned against the doorjamb, seeing the scene he'd imagined with Mya on the couch in front of the fireplace, her shoes off and legs tucked up under her. "I'm just going to grab my stuff and we can head over to JFK."

"If you don't live here, why do you have stuff here?" Mya asked, looking at him with the friendliest face he'd seen all day.

His gut tightened as the full force of her beauty was turned on him. With her shoes off and her hair down now, she looked like someone he'd like to get to know better, open and pleasant. "Chivonn lets me leave some of my stuff here, in case I'm ever just on a layover or have a quick overnighter where we can visit. Good thing, too, or I'd have to fly home to Virginia before we left." He smiled, drawn to the warmth of her gaze and the coziness of Chivonn's living room. Maybe he could sit down and join them. A few minutes to relax wouldn't hurt, would it?

"If you leave in the next five minutes, I can drive you," Chivonn offered, transferring her plate from her lap to the coffee table. Her words broke the spell and reminded him he wasn't here to relax and visit. He didn't sit down.

"Are you on a lunch hour? I wouldn't want you to get in trouble for helping us out and taking too long." Concern laced Mya's tone, with no trace of her irritation and brusque demeanor he'd seen since he'd met her at the U.N. Chivonn was truly a miracle-worker.

Jake rolled his eyes good-naturedly. "She works 24/7 for an advocacy group for the poor and homeless. Have you even seen daylight this week?" He turned to face Chivonn. Maybe seeing the friendly Mya wasn't a good idea. If he kept thinking of her as an ice queen, it would be easy to remember she was part of his mission. The classified one the Admiral had given him not two hours before.

"Long enough to let you in and see that you're still in one piece." She patted Mya's knee. "Knowing my brother and the likelihood he's helping you out of a situation of some sort, just stick with him and you'll be all right. Jake's the best."

She smiled up at him and Jake's heart warmed. Chivonn had been the one person who had encouraged him, told him he could do better, and he'd wanted to make her proud. "Us against the world." Jake could feel Mya's gaze on him and when he turned to look at her, she dropped her head. Embarrassed? Angry? Who knew? And he didn't have time to figure it out. "Thanks, sis. I'll just go get my stuff."

He walked back to the small guest room and grabbed his duffel out of the closet. A long time ago it had been his go bag when he was with the SEALs. Now it was more of a weekend bag for quick visits and stuff he'd left behind in previous visits. With the bag on the bed, he checked over what he had, grateful he at least had a few necessities. Grabbing clothes off the hangers, he rolled them and packed them in less than two minutes. Done, and with all the precision that would have made the Admiral proud.

When he got back to the living room, Chivonn was hugging Mya who looked ready to cry. Was she more affected by the attack than she'd let on? When she'd been sitting on that bed in the hotel room, her eyes had a haunted look to them, and she'd been close to tears no matter how much she'd tried to hide it. At least she was getting some comfort from Chivonn since there wasn't any way she'd accept it from him. Part of him wanted to offer it to her anyway, to help make things better for her. He squelched the thought quickly. He wouldn't get that close. He couldn't. "Ready to go?" he asked softly, not wanting to be the one to end whatever was going on with her and Chivonn, but knowing they had to leave.

Mya straightened. "Ready." She patted Chivonn's arm. "Thank you so much. You don't know how much I needed that."

Chivonn gave her another side hug. "Anytime you need to talk to me, just ask Jake to call. He can get hold of me day or night."

Mya smiled at her, but it died on her face when she looked at Jake as if just now remembering he was there. He held up his hand, strangely wishing she'd smile at him like she had for Chivonn. "It's true. I do know how to get hold of her."

"Thank you again." Mya stood and looked down at his duffel bag. "That's all you've got?"

"It's all I need." He walked to the door and hefted her suitcase again. "When you travel as much as I do, you learn to travel light." He looked pointedly down at her heavy suitcase.

"I wasn't sure how long we'd be gone," she said in her defense, walking past him to open the door. She stepped through, but waited for them.

Ice queen was back and Jake suppressed a sigh. It was probably best, but it didn't mean he had to like it. Chivonn passed by and gave him her best what-do-you-think-you're-doing look. "What?" he asked, keeping his voice low.

"Why do you sound like Randall? Be nice to her."

Chivonn's comment stung. Randall had been their foster father and no one could do anything right when he was around. He was constantly lecturing them on the right way to do things. He'd never want to be a Randall. "Ouch. That's low."

"Well, knock it off."

"Fine." He ducked his head as he joined the ladies in the hall and Chivonn locked up. He walked to the stairs first, making sure they were alone in the hallway. He hadn't noticed anyone following them here, but he couldn't be too careful and wouldn't ever risk Chivonn's life. But it seemed they were the only ones in the entire building and they didn't meet anyone else on the way to the car. After all the bags were stowed, Chivonn got in the driver's seat and Jake opened the door to the passenger side for Mya. "Thank you," she murmured, giving him a half-hearted smile. She slid in and looked up at him. The sun on her face gave her a light that drew him to her like a moth to flame.

He nearly slammed his own hand in the door as he shut it, cutting off the connection he was starting to feel toward Mya. "You're welcome," he said gruffly.

He'd never had a reaction to a woman like this before. Ever. She was attractive and he was assigned to protect her. That alone could get anyone in trouble if they weren't careful. He needed to remember her prickly side and hold that memory close, but getting that small little smile out of her felt like a victory of some sort.

The women chatted up front about some TV show they both watched, while Jake texted Ryan to make sure he'd been able to get hold of Elliott and they were both waiting at the airport. Elliott Burke was the best medic he knew and a competent teammate. Jake wanted him with them on this job and Admiral Moore had okayed it. Call it intuition or foreboding, but for whatever reason, Elliott needed to be there.

Mya turned to talk to him and he put his phone away. "Can I ask why you two were in foster care?" She glanced over at Chivonn. "You don't have to tell me if it's too personal."

Jake didn't mind telling her his standard answer. "I was the only survivor of the car accident that killed my parents. My grandmother took care of me until I was eight, but then she died, too, and I was put in foster care."

He'd explained that so many times it was almost rote. Kids at school had always been curious and it didn't bother him to talk about it. He caught Chivonn's gaze in the rearview, though, and knew she was debating telling her story.

"My mother was homeless and couldn't take care of me anymore," Chivonn finally said. It was the truth, but a severely watered down version. Jake didn't blame her for not wanting to get into it. Her story was long and twisted and not something you told complete strangers.

"That must have been so hard for you both," Mya said softly.

"It was, but it's sort of what drives us now. Jake is out to save the world and I'm out to get homeless people off the streets." Chivonn glanced over at Mya. "Some things just set you on a life course and you have to see where it takes you."

"That's been true for me, too." Mya didn't elaborate, but turned to look out the window.

He didn't know much more about her story, but resolved to ask her. Turnabout was fair play, right? Although Chivonn would probably get more answers out of her than he would.

Didn't mean he wouldn't try.

Traffic was heavy and it took nearly an hour before they made it to the airport. Jake got out to get the bags and Chivonn got out with him. "I can get it," he said as they walked around to the back of the car.

She didn't answer, but pulled him into a tight hug. "I don't like this, Jake. I've got a bad feeling about it."

"Now don't go getting superstitious on me. You know what I do for a living." He looked down into those chocolate brown eyes, knowing he didn't want to see fear in them. Not from Chivonn. "It's going to be fine."

She leaned closer, her long braids brushing his arm. "I'll never forget what you gave up for me, you know that. And I have no right to comment on your life. But this seems like you're getting pulled into something. Is Homeland Security really asking you to do this?"

"You have every right to comment on my life, you're the only family I've got, but I can't talk about this," he murmured, hating that he couldn't tell her. He busied himself with opening the trunk.

"That sounds like your old life when you were on SEAL assignments." She took his hand. "I know you've missed that life just a little bit and I don't want you to have any regrets because of me. You know I'll support whatever you decide to do."

He put his arm around her and drew her close to his side. "I'll never regret coming home to help you after Abel died, remember that. Us against the world. Always." He kissed the top of her head.

She squeezed him tight and glanced into the car where Mya was still sitting in the passenger seat. "One piece of advice, though. Be careful. And be gentle with her. That girl's been through a lot, too."

"What do you mean?" His gaze followed hers to Mya. As if she could feel them watching her, she turned.

Chivonn waved and Mya waved back, but didn't get out, obviously giving them a bit of privacy for their goodbyes. "A woman just knows these things. She's got a lot of hard defenses around her and needs some softness."

Jake knew Chivonn was up close and personal with hard defenses in all the homeless people she tried to help. "I'll do my best, okay?"

He bent to grab the luggage, but Chivonn held his arm. "I love you, you know. And I'm so proud of you." Chivonn bit her lip. "One more hug and I've got to go."

Jake hugged her again, holding her for one moment longer than normal. "Love you, too, little sister. I'll be back before you know it."

Chivonn chuckled, as he knew she would. "Little sister? You're only six months older than me, Jake Williams." She kissed his cheek. "Be safe."

"Us against the world," he repeated one more time. That phrase had gotten him through some really bad times. It always helped to know he wasn't alone. He had Chivonn. "I'll call you when I get back."

Mya got out and stood on the curb as Chivonn got back into the car. He didn't watch her go, suddenly feeling more emotional than he had in years. "We need to get to the gate. We're running late."

She stiffened at his words, any softness and light she'd had draining out of her right before his eyes. "My, my, Commander Jake Williams is back. For just a minute I thought you might have a human side to you, but I see that's only for your sister's benefit." Mya walked double time to keep up with him, her heels clicking on the floor.

He let her go ahead of him by a few steps, wishing he could call the words back. He was no Randall and he needed to be more careful that he wasn't coming across like that, but it didn't help she was so stubborn. "At least after taking you to meet my sister I know you can smile," he said just loud enough for her to hear.

Her step faltered a bit, but she didn't turn around, her back straight, her fists clenched at her sides.

Jake groaned at her obvious anger. He wasn't doing himself any favors by riling her up. As it was, this was looking like it was going to be a very long trip with Ms. Mya Amari next to him every step of the way.

CHAPTER SIX

Jake wasn't surprised when Colt and Nate met them just inside the airport entrance. An airport employee appeared to take their luggage and another escorted them to a restricted area of the airport. Mya had stayed a few steps ahead of him, keeping up a conversation with Nate. Every now and then Jake felt her glance back at him, but he didn't meet her eyes. He was keeping an eye on the crowds. Airport security had also joined them. Was that because of her attack earlier? Or just routine? Even with their presence, he didn't want to let his guard down at all with Mya in public. The attacker earlier today certainly hadn't hesitated to deliver his message in a very public lobby.

They were ushered into a private gate area and Elliott Burke was there talking to Ryan. Jake thought about taking Mya to meet his old teammate, since he'd be part of "her" team, but she probably wouldn't appreciate being interrupted. From the looks of things, she was enjoying whatever story Nate was telling her.

Jake turned his attention back to Ryan and Elliott. It was like a SEAL team reunion. Last time they'd all been together was on a mission in Afghanistan. He never thought he'd serve with them again, but it felt good to have them here now. With Ryan, Elliott, and himself rounding out the Canadians, he was feeling better about this mission.

As if his thoughts conjured him, Colt came into view. "Everything a go?" he asked, as he drew near.

"Yep." Jake kept his eye on Mya, who was laughing with Nate, and he frowned. She was pretty comfortable with Nate to be so unguarded and laughing. How had he won her trust so easily?

"How did it go with Mya?" Colt pressed. Jake was starting to get that big-brother vibe from Colt. He was a caretaker-type, which could work to a team's advantage, especially on this team where they hadn't served together before and the trust hadn't been built yet. Caretakers made it easy to get things done because they were generally always double-checking everyone.

"Fine. Nothing out of the ordinary." Except watching her lean closer to Nate. They were both smiling now. "Did you guys know her before this op?" Jake asked, his curiosity about their relationship getting the better of him.

"No. We met her briefly on the plane down, but she mostly kept to herself. She seems pleasant enough and I felt bad for her with the situation she's in." He followed Jake's gaze to Nate and Mya. Jake wanted to look away, to not give Colt the wrong impression, but he couldn't take his eyes off her. "Why do you ask?"

From the carefully arranged blank look on Colt's face, he'd gotten the wrong impression. Jake sighed inwardly. "I was assigned to protect her and I want to get to know our team better." Jake turned his attention back to Colt to meet his eyes. Maybe if he said it enough, he'd believe it. Mya was like a magnet to him, more than a mission assignment should be, but he needed to keep those feelings in check.

Colt shrugged, as if he could hear Jake's inner turmoil, but wisely decided not to say anything about it. Jake liked him already. "Have there been any other orders before we leave? Anything I should be aware of?"

Jake's shrugged a shoulder. Colt didn't know him or he wouldn't have asked. Jake was the first to disburse information, especially when they were on a mission. "No, but I read through the file. If this hostage situation follows the same timeline as the others al-Awani has been a part of, we're definitely going to be under a time constraint." Their eyes both strayed back to Mya. "She's already been told not to come. You think she can persuade her father to help us?"

"She seems determined," Colt said, folding his arms across his chest. He had a black hoodie emblazoned with Canadian Armed Forces and a Canada flag to top it off that reminded Jake of one he had at home, only with U.S. Navy on it. "Every now and then I get the feeling she's holding something back, though."

"Like what?" Jake frowned again. He hadn't gotten that vibe from her, but then they'd spent most of their time being frustrated with one another so he might have missed it.

"I don't know. It's just a feeling." He let out a breath and his arms fell to his side. "I hope she'll trust us with whatever it is at some point."

Chivonn's words ran through his mind. *She needs a gentle approach*. "Me, too."

He didn't have time to say anything else to Colt as Admiral Moore approached them. "Williams, I need to talk to you. In private."

Colt stepped forward, his eyes on the Admiral, looking as if he might salute. He didn't. "Sir, if we're going to work as a team, shouldn't we all be privy to briefings?"

"This isn't a briefing," the Admiral barked. "And when I have one, I'll let you know." He turned on his heel and walked away. Jake followed, shooting an apologetic glance Colt's way. Hopefully the guy knew that Jake would share anything pertinent with him.

The Admiral stepped into a tiny room that was obviously someone's messy office. "I'm told Ms. Amari was attacked at her hotel, but she was able to give him a punch to the groin and got away."

A punch to the groin? That was the first he'd heard of it. Somehow it made things better in his mind to know she'd fought back and done well. "Yes, sir. She was also given a note that said don't come, but it wasn't signed."

The Admiral's eyes flashed. "Well, that has to be from her father. Who else could it be?" He paced a little before coming back to stand in front of Jake. "At least he's tracking her. Maybe making contact won't be as hard as we thought."

"Yes, sir."

The Admiral leaned against the desk, nearly sending a pile of papers teetering on the corner to the floor. "They're pretty bold to do that on American soil. Did they say anything to her beyond that?"

"Only that they were going to kill her family."

The Admiral cursed at that. "The girl's mother died six months ago, so they could only be talking about her father." He ran a hand over his face. "It's a complicated situation. Her father wants to protect her from his enemies. That's why he sent her and her mother to Canada, so it's not good that she's already been attacked while under our care. And if he doesn't want her to come and she goes in spite of that, will he still help us?"

He let out a breath. It was obvious he was merely thinking out loud, but Jake answered anyway. "I don't know, sir."

"This mission could be over before it starts," he muttered. "We've got to be on guard at all times. The Canadians have a safehouse in Algiers that no one knows about, or so they say. It's all set up. You just need to stick with her."

"Does she have contact protocols or something? Should I be putting a tracker on her?"

"She was given instructions on how to get to her father if anything happened to her mother. They're old, but she thinks they're still good. We're going with that." He glanced back at the others through the office window before focusing on Jake. "She's a long shot, but we don't have a choice."

Jake met his gaze. "You know I'll keep her safe, sir. I won't let her out of my sight." *Even if she hates me*, he added silently. "But sir, it's been brought to my attention that she might be holding something back."

"Of course she is. She doesn't trust us. That's where you come in. Gain her confidence. Make her feel safe." The Admiral folded his arms and looked at Jake with his signature you're-going-to-do-this-no-matter-what face. Jake suddenly flashed back to all the times he'd seen that face before and while he hadn't been sure at first, whatever the Admiral had asked had made him stronger and better. He trusted this man with his life.

"Sir, you know I'll do my best, but she doesn't like me." It was a little humiliating to admit, especially to him.

The Admiral snorted. "Williams, you're a SEAL and not a bad-looking man. If you need advice about the ladies from me, then I've underestimated you."

"Yes, sir." A flush was creeping up his neck. *Why did I bring it up at all?* "You haven't underestimated me."

"Okay then. Your first check in is tomorrow after you've landed and are at the safehouse. Don't be late." He nodded and exited the office without looking back. Jake looked at the ceiling and groaned. Why did this feel like mission impossible already?

Ryan leaned up against the open doorway, appearing out of nowhere like he'd been trained as a spook from the beginning. "Is everything okay?"

No way was Jake going to let on that anything was wrong. "Of course. Just last minute instructions."

"Like what?" Ryan raised his eyebrows, shoving his hand into his pants pocket.

"Making sure we all know our assignments." He cleared his throat. Maybe it was time. They were alone, the mission hadn't officially started, and the Admiral had said to get this worked out. "We're going to have to talk about what happened before you left Homeland." Adrenaline stuttered through his body. This confrontation had been a long time coming and they needed to clear the air.

"Not today." Ryan straightened, suddenly not as casual as he appeared.

"Why? The Admiral's right. We don't want anything taking our focus away from the mission." Jake resisted the urge to take a step toward him. He didn't want to come across as pushy, but for some reason he couldn't let it go. Maybe he needed to talk it out more than he'd thought.

"I won't if you won't." He backed up a step as if he were going to walk away.

"It's not that simple, Ryan, and you know it." Jake matched him step for step. "We're on a pretty tight time schedule before we start getting videos of Edwards that we don't want to see. Not to mention we're not even sure if Mya can contact her dad to help us." He looked at Ryan, hoping his sincerity was coming through in his words. "We're betting against the odds, in more ways than one and we're going to have to work together."

Ryan shook his head. "I'll work with you, but not under you. Ever again." With that, he turned to go back to the group.

"Ryan there's more to it and you know it." Jake quickly caught up to him and put a hand on his arm, not willing to let that comment go so easily.

Ryan pulled away, taking a step back until he was out of Jake's reach. "That is *all* it's about. You purposefully held me back."

Jake stopped where he was. He didn't want to escalate it, but if they could discuss what happened rationally, he knew they could move past it. The trick was making sure they stayed rational. "That's not true. You were out of line. You didn't follow mission guidelines. I had no choice but to discipline you. No one goes off book without consequences. You know that."

Ryan's fists clenched and Jake wanted to mirror his stance, but deliberately kept his posture loose and as casual as possible to keep Ryan from getting even more defensive. "You know, Jake, you did me a favor. I'm in a job that will take me places professionally. You're going to be stuck in the same position a year from now," he taunted.

Jake held up a hand. Yeah, they weren't going to be able to discuss this today. A comeback rose to his lips, but he squashed the temptation to verbally hit back. "Apparently, we're both where we want to be. But for now, we're working together because there's a man out there waiting to be rescued and we're going to make sure that happens." He brushed by him. "And you better remember that."

Why was Ryan acting like it was entirely Jake's fault? So aggravating. He headed for Mya, the other person who'd been aggravating him all day. "You ready to board?"

He'd interrupted her conversation with Nate and neither of them looked too happy about it. She shot Nate a look and raised her shoulder as if to say, what-can-you-do? With a frosty glance back at him, she said, "Did they call us? I haven't heard any announcements."

"Since it's a private plane, they don't call us like they would on a commercial flight. They just let us know we can board." He saw the gate doors opening, proving his point.

Mya stepped back a bit to include Nate into their circle. "Captain Hughes has volunteered to keep me company on the flight, so you don't have to worry about babysitting me."

Jake could feel Nate's eyes on him, but he ignored it. "We'll be sitting together. You're not leaving my side, remember?" His jaw clenched on the smile.

"We'll be on the same plane," she pointed out. "We don't have to sit together."

He needed to soften his tone. Be gentle. He looked down at her. "We should probably take the time to go over the protocols and what's going to happen when we get to Algeria. Then you'll know what you're doing."

He inwardly cringed. That hadn't come out right and she looked madder after he spoke. Mya took a step toward him. "I think we need to get something straight. I know what I'm doing. *You're* the one who doesn't seem to know what their job and their place is on this mission."

He moved closer as well until the tip of his dress shoes nearly touched the toe of her high heels. "I know exactly what my place is. I'm the team leader."

She lifted her chin. "I'm not one of your military guys." She motioned to all the men in the room. "I'm not on your team."

Gentle, gentle. Channeling his best Chivonn, he shoved his hands in his pockets. "I need you to be." He kept his voice low, but let a bit of pleading into his tone.

Her jaw dropped slightly and some of the fire went out of her eyes. The tenseness in her shoulders seemed to melt away right in front of him. "Well, okay then," she said.

Jake moved back slightly so he didn't feel like he was towering over her. "What about this? Mya, I'd like to get to know you better. Could you sit with me on the plane?"

She hesitated and he could see the conflict inside her racing across her face. She bit her lip, but agreed. "Okay."

He let out a silent breath of relief. "Okay."

He had one chance to make this right. *Now don't blow it.*

CHAPTER SEVEN

Mya couldn't remember ever being so tired. Her entire body felt like a glob of lead, too heavy to move out of her seat. She rubbed her eyes to force them open again. Ever since she'd been asked to help find her father she'd felt the need to stay awake, stay on guard, figure out what came next. At one time in her life, it had been second nature to be wary, always looking over her shoulder, and that was coming back to her in waves now. Intellectually, she knew she was safe in the plane, surrounded by military personnel, but not-long-buried survival skills were coming to the surface.

She looked over at Jake, sitting in the seat next to her. His steady, even breathing sent a shaft of annoyance through her. *So much for getting to know each other better.* Jake had been asleep as soon as they got to cruising altitude.

She took the unguarded moment to study him further. He'd taken his suit jacket off and his white shirt was unbuttoned at the top, his tie askew. He looked like he'd been wearing that suit for more than a day. His hair was longer than most she'd seen on military personnel and curled a bit on the sides. There wasn't very much that could be called soft about this man, but she'd bet his hair was as soft as it looked. The rest of him was all hard angles and edges. And yet, she'd seen a softening in his demeanor at Chivonn's. Almost enough to believe Chivonn when she assured her multiple times that her brother was the best and she could count on him.

When it came right down to it, Mya wanted to trust Jake, but pushing down her fear for her sister and her innate wariness that had been drilled into her from birth made it hard. And Jake hadn't made anything easier for her in that department. He was so bossy. But right now, he looked more approachable, more of the Jake she'd seen with Chivonn, instead of the babysitter-with-a-bunch-of-annoying-children-to-take-care-of persona she'd seen since she'd met him at the U.N.

Jake shifted in his seat and opened his eyes to meet hers. "Can't a man get any rest around here without people gawking at him?" His low chuckle rumbled through her embarrassment, rooting her to her spot.

She quickly looked away, glad he couldn't read her thoughts. "Well, maybe you shouldn't pretend to be sleeping," she retorted, feeling a blush on her cheeks.

His voice got closer and she knew he'd leaned toward her without looking back. "You really should get some sleep, you know. We'll need to hit the ground running when we get to Algiers."

His voice was smooth and soothing like hot chocolate on a cold night. “I can’t,” she said, a shiver going through her. She glanced over her shoulder at him. How could she explain anything to him when he didn’t know about Yasmine?

He stared at her for a moment, as if he wanted to say something else, but he stood instead and headed for the back of the plane. “I’ll be right back.”

She rubbed her arms, the chill in the plane even more pronounced with the seat next to her empty. She looked around the cabin at the rest of the passengers. The U.N. chartered plane had grouped seating of four, with two seats facing each other and a small table in between them strategically placed around the cabin. Captain Hughes had tried to sit by her when they’d first boarded, but Captain Mitchell had quickly pulled him away to the seat across the plane from her. His head leaned against the window now and his eyes were closed. Captain Mitchell had reclined his seat back and also looked like he was sleeping. The only one she didn’t know well was Commander Williams’ friend who’d joined them at the airport. Elliott. He had stretched out over two seats sitting across from Mr. Smythe. Both men were also asleep.

Seeing everyone else sleeping made her feel more alone. She opened the window shade and looked out at the darkness, but they were still over the Atlantic and there wasn’t anything to see.

“When I can’t sleep, it’s usually because I need a midnight snack.”

She jumped at his voice and turned back to see Jake standing there with a blanket over one arm and a plate and mug in his hands. *A peace offering?* "Why doesn't that surprise me?" she said, but her stomach rumbled at the sight of the food and betrayed how right he was.

He laughed softly and handed her a plate. "I could only scare up some cheese, grapes, and crackers. But I got some chamomile tea. That'll take care of your insomnia."

He sounded so sure of himself, as if he had the answer for everything, but as she took the mug from him, she decided it felt nice to be cared for. That hadn't happened for a really long time. Maybe, just maybe, he wasn't so bad after all.

She wrapped her fingers around the warmth in the mug and took a sip. "Thank you," she murmured, the heat from the drink infusing her.

He sank down in the seat next to her again and started to unfold the blanket. She watched him put it on her lap, but moved her legs away when he tried to tuck it around them. "I can get that."

"We need to get you warmed up." He waited, holding up the edge of the blanket.

She relented, reminding herself she'd just been thinking he was a good guy. Another sip of tea took the edge off the cold and she watched him tuck her in. He had a look of concentration on his face as if there was a right way and wrong way to do it.

When it was finally even on both sides, he sat back, a satisfied smile on his face. "I had to cajole the flight attendant to give up that cheese. They're saving it for some breakfast thing, so don't let my efforts be in vain."

She popped the cheese square in her mouth trying to imagine the flight attendant's face at Jake's cajoling. Or did he mean commanding? "Come on, be honest. You just gave her your 'I'm the commander' look and she handed it over."

He turned in his seat to face her, leaning toward her with a tilt of his head. "I do have a charming side, you know."

Oh, she knew. His blue eyes alone would charm any woman. But she couldn't tell him that. She slowly ate a grape as if she were contemplating his statement. "I can't imagine it," she finally said, hardly holding back a smile at the offended look on his face.

"Ouch. You just don't want to admit *you* find me charming." He raised his eyebrows, daring her to contradict him.

He had her pegged. He'd be dangerous in a courtroom if he could accurately read people like that all the time. What would happen if she did admit she found him charming? What would he think? In this darkened space, sitting next to him it felt like maybe she could be more herself since the mission and the team weren't crowding them. She took another sip of her tea, stalling for time to think of an answer, then decided to just go for it. "Maybe just for tonight I'd think about admitting it."

He gave a half-smile at her admission, which showed his dimple and made her knees weak. *Good thing I'm sitting down.* "Truce tonight then." He reached for her now empty plate and set it on the little table in front of them. Had she finished all that food? "Tell me about yourself. Something that isn't in the file."

"What do you want to know?" The tea, combined with his voice, had relaxed her. "I'm just like any other girl. I love sunshine and daisies and my family." Her voice trailed off. She didn't have much family left.

"How long has it been since you've seen your dad?" His voice was hypnotic, calling to her secrets.

"Since I was twelve." She thought back to that last day, to how tight her dad had held her when he said goodbye. She hadn't understood then that it was meant to be permanent. "He couldn't keep us safe anymore so he sent us away." And even with their banishment, someone had still kidnapped Yasmine. Why had she returned to Algeria? Mya thought she'd stay in Britain.

"Do you have any brothers and sisters?"

His question jolted her back to the present. Could she tell him about Yasmine? The words came to her tongue but she swallowed them back. Not yet. Maybe not ever. "No."

She finished off her tea, wanting to change the subject. "What about you? Anyone in your life besides Chivonn?" She leaned closer to him, their shoulders touching. He was right, the tea was making her sleepy. What would he do if she put her head on his shoulder and used him as a pillow? With a mental shake, she put that image out of her mind. She couldn't be that tired. But the darkness and the fact that they were the only two awake in the cabin made it feel cozy and safe.

"No. Just Chivonn." His brow furrowed slightly as if he was trying to figure out her motives for moving closer. When he couldn't, he reached over and took the mug from her. "My job doesn't leave enough time for anyone else."

Mya looked up at him, his blue eyes darkening when he returned her gaze. Was he feeling it, too? "Being in hiding doesn't leave much time, either." He pulled up the armrest and her heart skipped a beat. There were no barriers between them now and his body drew closer to hers, as if that arm-rest had been the only thing holding him back from contact. He reached out and time seemed to stand still. Would he kiss her? His hand hovered above her collarbone, and she held still, waiting to see what he would do. Instead of touching her, or drawing her close, he only grabbed the corner of the blanket and put it up over her shoulders. But his fingers brushed her neck and she let out a breath, trying to calm her racing heartbeat.

"I'm sorry about what happened today. I wish I would have been there," he murmured, nodding toward her throat. His voice was soft, but it wasn't whispering sweet nothings. Thinking back to the attack sent a shiver through her.

"It's my fault for not staying with my security guy. It won't happen again." She pulled the blanket tighter around her. "The last few days have been a lot for me to deal with and I thought being alone for a minute would be okay."

"Which is exactly why I don't want you to be alone again." He let his hand rest on her forearm as if he was emphasizing his words with his actions.

She looked down at his hand. Strong, capable. Like him. *Chivonn's lucky to have him to watch out for her.* "You really are charming," she admitted with a yawn.

"Get some sleep," he told her, that same half-smile on his face that showcased his dimple. He obviously had no idea what that dimple did to her insides as he nonchalantly leaned his head back.

She drew her eyes away from his face and closed them, resting her shoulder against the window. "Thanks, Jake."

He shifted his weight until she felt his body warmth at her back. "You're welcome, Mya," sounded close to her ear. He'd used her first name and she didn't mind. *Definitely not so bad after all*, she thought.

And she knew it was safe to sleep.

CHAPTER EIGHT

Jake had mastered the ability to sleep anytime and nearly anywhere when he'd been in the SEALs. It came in handy, especially right before a big mission where you might not get a lot of rest once it started. He looked over at the woman who was cuddled next to his side, using his shoulder for a pillow, her arm tucked around his waist. She would probably be mortified if she woke up and found herself in that position. But he was going to enjoy it a little longer.

Their chat last night had been eye-opening. She'd called a truce and admitted she found him charming. That was a huge step forward from the ice queen in the taxi. It was hard not to ask what her change of heart had been, but he didn't want to look a gift horse in the mouth. He was just glad she was letting her guard down with him a bit. He hadn't worked so hard to earn someone's trust in a very long time.

She shifted slightly and her hair fell over her cheek. Jake pushed it back over her shoulder, not surprised at how soft it was. Even in sleep, everything about her had a refined air about it from her eyebrows to her chin, but she had a tough spirit and had proven that yesterday from the first team meeting. He tilted his head back, knowing he should take his phone out and look at the files again or something. Anything to get his mind off the woman nestled next to him.

Hearing some murmuring coming from his left, he glanced over to see Colt watching him while Nate said something near his ear. Jake gave Colt a slight nod, then looked down at Mya again. She definitely wouldn't want everyone to see her sleeping on him. He stretched his arm back over his seat and grabbed his suit coat. Folding it up, he gently lifted Mya's head and slipped his jacket under it, as he scooted out. She only sighed, but didn't awaken. Pulling the blanket over her, he sat down in the seats across the table. Still close enough to keep an eye on her and within arm's reach if she needed anything.

Glancing out the window, he knew they'd be landing in Geneva soon to refuel. He hated to cut her rest short. If the dark smudges under her eyes were any clue, she needed more sleep than she was getting. At least they didn't have to change planes and they'd be back in the air fairly quickly.

He pulled out his phone and brought up the encrypted files Admiral Moore had given him. He'd read them so often now that he'd memorized some passages, but he wanted to be prepared in case some detail would make the difference between life or death. He always liked having a contingency plan for field ops where anything could happen.

He settled on the security detail's report of Edward's abduction, but it wasn't long before people were moving around the cabin and breakfast was being served. He debated waking Mya up, but decided to let her sleep. For now.

He looked up as Ryan sat down next to him, tilting his head toward the phone. "Are you looking for something specific? Maybe I can help you." When Jake didn't answer right away, Ryan glanced over at Mya. "Were you up babysitting all night?"

Jake followed Ryan's gaze. She hadn't moved except to pull his modified suit jacket/pillow closer. He really ought to ask the flight attendant for one of their pillows. That might be more comfortable than a suit coat. "I slept." He shut off his phone and put it back in his pocket.

"We got some intel this morning on Nazer." Ryan was smiling that annoying cat-got-the-cream smile.

Jake pinched the bridge of his nose and closed his eyes. "Yeah?" He suddenly needed more sleep than he'd gotten if this was how the day was going to begin. "What intel?"

"Nazer got on a private plane headed to Kabylia." He sat back and waited for Jake's reaction, but Jake was determined not to give him one if he could help it.

"Was that confirmed?" Jake gave Ryan a sidelong glance. Now they were getting somewhere.

"Confirmed."

"If Nazer is in the Kabylia region of Algeria, where he has known strongholds for his smuggling operation, maybe that's where they're keeping the hostages." He lowered his voice, making sure Mya was still asleep. "If we can get a solid location, they send in some drones, get the rescue team in there ASAP and they're rescued long before we need to contact any negotiator."

"Yeah, I know. That's why I thought you needed to be aware in case your mission was over before it started." Ryan held up his phone. "You might want to let the Admiral know this new detail."

Jake nodded at that, surprised Ryan was giving him that courtesy of telling the Admiral when it would be just as easy for the CIA to do it. No matter who said what to whom, though, the quicker they got a fix on Edwards and got him back, the better. "I knew we'd get Nazer sooner or later."

"Even if you had to use CIA intel to do it." Ryan smirked.

"I don't care whose intel we used. I just want this guy in our custody." He pulled out his phone. "I feel good about this one. Maybe we'll get him this time."

Before he could dial, the flight attendant came by. "We'll be landing for refueling soon. Make sure your seat belts are buckled."

Jake buckled his and Ryan stayed next to him, buckling his as well. "Things get sorted out between the two of you?" Ryan nodded toward Mya.

"We've called a truce." And he didn't want to talk about it. It felt new and fragile and she'd been tired when they'd talked. Maybe she wouldn't feel the same when she woke up.

The plane began its descent, but the landing was smooth and Mya slept on. While they were refueling, Jake checked in with the Admiral. The news about Nazer in the Kabylia region of Algeria gave him new motivation and the Admiral promised to reach out to all of his contacts there. If the hostages were in Kabylia, they'd be found.

Jake hung up feeling more optimistic about catching Nazer than he had in weeks. It was a cautious optimism, though. Nazer had eluded them more times than he could count and he wasn't going to celebrate just yet. He watched a still sleeping Mya on the seat across from him. If he could spare her having to use her father he would. When he'd asked her how long it had been since she'd seen him, it was easy to see the pain flicker across her face. Maybe if they didn't need her to ask him to do something, their reunion could be more natural.

The plane was getting ready to take off again, and Mya finally stirred, raising herself up to a sitting position. "What time is it?"

"We're still a couple of hours from Algiers. We're just getting ready to leave Geneva." She didn't respond to that with anything more than blinking at him. She was obviously still trying to get her bearings. "I'm glad you got some sleep," he said. "You needed it."

She ran her hands through her hair, trying to smooth out any tangles. "Hey, thanks for the tea last night. And the conversation." She gave him a smile and he relaxed.

She doesn't regret the truce.

But he didn't have time to pursue that thought or the feelings it evoked. Nate appeared carrying a breakfast tray. "Mya, you must be starving."

"Thanks, Nate." She smiled up at him.

Jake's own stomach rumbled, but he couldn't move to get his own tray. His entire focus was on watching them. *When had they gotten on a first-name basis?*

She looked down at the tray. "Look at all the cheese on this breakfast scramble. I'm glad there was enough for everyone." She met Jake's eyes with their little inside joke from last night and any irritation Jake was feeling toward Nate disappeared.

Nate just looked confused. "Yes, we all had enough cheese."

Jake smothered a laugh. "Thank goodness for that. I was worried there might be a cheese shortage."

"Who could be that charming?" Mya countered.

Nate looked between them. "I think I missed something."

Jake hoped he missed a whole lot more things. He liked this fun and happy Mya. But when the flight attendant came by to ask them all to take their seats, Nate immediately claimed the one next to Mya. "Better do as I'm told."

Mya concentrated on her food, not looking at either Jake or Nate, and Jake was trying his best to ignore the fact that he'd left the arm-rest up when he'd vacated that seat and now Nate was sitting very close to her. *Just concentrate on Mya.* She looked tousled from sleep, but still put together. Her eyes had a light in them this morning that he'd only glimpsed yesterday. And she was smiling. He'd hardly seen that since they'd left Chivonn's place. A new leaf had been turned and he was glad for it.

Nate leaned over her until there were mere centimeters between them and the happy thoughts fled Jake's mind. "So, we never got to finish our conversation."

The conversation they'd had at the airport where she'd been so engrossed in it and so annoyed with him? The memory wasn't pleasant for Jake. Why couldn't Nate go back to his own seat? "Hey, sorry to interrupt, but would you mind passing me my jacket? I think you're sitting on it." Jake pointed to Nate's seat where his jacket was half on the outer arm-rest and half under Nate.

Mya looked at him, her brows furrowed, but she didn't say anything and merely watched Nate hand it over. "Thanks." Nate started to say something else, but Jake interrupted again. "Oh and my files are under your chair. Could you hand me those as well?"

Nate was trying to maintain his smile, but his little huff told Jake he wasn't as happy-go-lucky as he appeared. Too bad he didn't have more stuff to ask for. Nate deserved to have his conversation with Mya paused indefinitely.

But of course Nate didn't let it go. Once Jake had his files, Nate leaned over her again. "So, do you know the restaurant?"

"Yeah, I think I know the restaurant you're talking about." She shifted and Jake thought she looked uncomfortable, but what could he do about it?

"If you're interested, the base isn't that far from U of T. I could pick you up. You've never tasted Indian food like this." Nate was completely focused on Mya, but Jake could hardly believe his ears. Was he asking her out? Right before a mission?

"You're a student?" Jake cut in, smothering his annoyance at Nate and making a mental note to talk to him about it later.

"No, I graduated from law school, but still live near campus. I was just about to take a position at a law firm in Toronto." Mya turned her gaze to him.

"You're a lawyer?" Jake raised his eyebrows. He never would have guessed that.

"In Canada, it's called a barrister, to be exact." She smiled and put another bite on her fork. "Don't look so surprised," she said before she put the eggs in her mouth.

"You just don't seem the type." Jake folded his arms. "I mean, most lawyers I know are stuffy and wear terrible suits."

Mya looked down at what she was wearing while she swallowed. "Well, my pantsuit has seen better days." She tried to smooth down some of the wrinkles. “All right, now that we’re in the air, I think I’ll take a trip to the ladies room.” She set her plate on the table and they watched her put on her shoes before heading to the back of the plane.

Jake made sure she was out of earshot before he turned to Nate. “Do you think it’s appropriate to ask her out when we’re supposed to be executing a mission?”

“She’s not the mission. Her connection is. And frankly, if I can give her something to look forward to, I will,” Nate replied. “You didn’t see her right after that attack yesterday.”

Regret filled Jake. He *should* have been the one there for her. “You’re right, I didn’t. But that won’t happen again.”

Nate crossed his legs. “After yesterday, I think she needs some reminders of home. The one place she’s felt safe and has a life to get back to once this is over.”

“We need her to feel safe with us here and now,” Jake pointed out, not liking where the conversation was going.

“I think she does.” Nate unbuckled and stood. “With me, at least.” He tilted his head toward Jake as if he’d just imparted some sage advice or something, before he walked down the aisle and met Mya on her way back. “Best Indian food you’ve ever tasted,” he said to her again. “And the company won’t be too bad, either.”

Jake listened closely, but she didn’t give him an answer, just smiled and shrugged before she came back to their seat. When had he started thinking of it as their seat? *The minute Nate sat in it.*

Her hair was in a ponytail, now, and she looked a lot more relaxed than she had before the tea last night. She took her seat across from him and pulled the blanket over her lap. “So, now you know I’m going to be a lawyer, are you still going to talk to me?”

“Does joking count as talking?” He crossed his ankle at his knee, spreading out a bit now that he was across from her. This seat had its advantages since he could see her body language. Not that he’d minded sitting close to her last night.

Mya rolled her eyes. “That’s why I like the word barrister. You never hear barrister jokes. But okay, let’s hear it.” She braced herself, as if he were about to set off a barrage of lawyer jokes on her.

He couldn’t resist at least one. “Why are lawyers never attacked by sharks?” He grinned.

“Professional courtesy,” she finished for him. “Yeah, I’ve heard that one a few times.” She crossed her legs and settled back in her seat, looking a little less burdened than she had last night. “Is that all you’ve got?”

“Yeah. For now, but I reserve the right to come back to it later.” She laughed at his attempt to mimic something a lawyer would say. “Why go into law?” he asked, genuinely interested in her reasons. With her background that seemed a little strange.

“I like the intricacies of it. And I want to be able to help others seeking asylum like I had to.” Her voice was quieter now. He was starting to learn her cues. When she was talking about something important to her, she spoke in low tones. Sort of like Tyler and his quiet times.

"Was that hard for you?" He could hardly imagine having to leave your country behind and start over.

"It was a process, that's for sure. Thankfully my mother had a good lawyer to help her." Mya folded her arms, her eyes pinning his with their intensity. She obviously had some strong feelings about what she'd been through. "We found a great place near Montreal. Since I spoke French, it made the transition easier at school. I didn't have much chance to use any Arabic, but I could understand the kids who spoke French at least." She traced the crease line in her dress pants. "But I missed being home."

A home she wouldn't see again for a very long time. Sympathy welled up in him. He knew exactly what it felt like to want a stable place to call home. "You know, I couldn't place your accent, but if you spoke French and Arabic, that would explain it," he said. He uncrossed his legs and leaned forward. "I'm glad you at least had a familiar language to help you re-settle. Did Canada ever start feeling like home?"

"Eventually. The people are welcoming, kind. The country is beautiful. But I'd be lying if I said I wasn't excited to see Algiers again." She sat forward, too, as if she were imparting important information, except her head was down and she was staring at the floor. "And my father."

The last bit was said so quietly Jake could hardly hear her. "Are you expecting a happy reunion?"

"I don't know what to expect, really. It's been a long time." She sat back again, her fidgeting giving away how truly nervous she was. She avoided his gaze and looked out the window. "I'm hoping for the best."

"We all are." He was mostly hoping they wouldn't need to use her, though, and they could track the hostages in Kabylia. "What do you remember most about him?"

She didn't answer for a long moment, then turned back to him. "I've talked enough about myself. What about you? You lost your parents at such a young age. What do you remember about them?"

He knew he'd pressed her too far and allowed the subject change. He hadn't thought about his parents in ages. "My dad liked to sing. My mom had a garden." He remembered a little red shovel he'd had. "I went out with her and dug in the dirt while she weeded." There wasn't much else to tell. Before he could say anything else, his phone buzzed. "Excuse me." He took it out of his pocket and looked at the caller ID. The Admiral. "Sir?"

"Commander, we have a solid lead on the hostages. Get Ms. Amari to the safehouse and wait for word there. You might be on a plane home by this time tomorrow."

Jake glanced up at Mya. *They* might be on a plane home, but she'd want to stay and reconnect with her father. He was sure of it. "Yes, sir." The call disconnected and he slowly put it away.

"What's going on?" she asked, her eyes focused on him.

"They have a lead on the hostages so we're supposed to go to the safehouse in Algiers and wait for word."

Mya sat up straight, her features suddenly wary. "What kind of word? What did he say exactly?"

"That's all he said." Jake was puzzled at her sharp tone. Just a second before they'd been laughing together. The relaxed atmosphere between them was completely gone.

"Would you tell me if there was more?" Her eyes narrowed and she looked every inch the high-handed force of nature he'd first met.

"If you needed to know." He tried to say it gently, knowing she wouldn't like it. He couldn't help the rules, but he was bound by them.

"So you decide what I get to know. That's not what the Colonel said. You heard him at the U.N. I was to be included in all briefings." She took the blanket off her lap and began to fold it, her movements jerky as she tried to get her frustration under control.

"Some parts of my job are classified. A need to know basis, but I haven't kept anything from you." He switched seats to sit next to her, but she slid all the way over to the window, looking at him like he'd kicked her puppy. "Mya, surely you understand that there might be some things that can't be talked about."

"Of course." Her voice was as chilly as Arctic ice. She turned from him and stared out the window. "Does it matter that I have the security clearances on this?"

"You were given a security clearance, yes. But there are possibilities of things happening or going wrong where decisions are made and that information would be above your security clearance given by a Canadian Colonel." He wanted their truce back. The more he talked, the more tense she became.

"Is it because it was given by a Canadian? Would it carry more weight if it was an American security clearance?" Her lips were pursed tight.

"Nationality has nothing to do with it. This mission is classified and there are several tiers of security to keep us safe. It's nothing against you." He needed her to understand. It wasn't about her, really.

She stared at him, like an interrogator waiting for him to break. But he was being honest with her, surely she could see that. "And I'm sure you understand that I am under no obligation to share information with you or your team. No matter what happens here, I'm still going to contact my father. I don't need any security clearances for that."

"I imagined you would." He put his hand on her arm. "Hey, I really hope you don't have a mission or anything else hanging over you so you can have a great reunion with your dad."

She didn't acknowledge his words and Jake let her have her space with a sigh. They were right back where they'd started. The truce was definitely over.

CHAPTER NINE

The plane landed in Algiers without incident and a rush of excitement surged through Mya. Would she remember more about her childhood by being here? She'd practically pressed her nose to the window on their approach. The Mediterranean Sea had looked so beautiful, but the city below is what she was anxious to see again.

She paused at the top of the stairs that would take her to the tarmac, just to take it all in. The air was salty and the humidity wrapped around her like a hot, wet blanket. It felt familiar to her, like a long lost memory and she smiled. A part of her had been missing her whole life and that was another reason why she'd come to Algeria. To find it.

She glanced at the building in front of her. This was the airport she'd flown to Canada with her mother from. The last place she'd seen her father so many years ago. Would he be here now? Did he know she was here? She looked around, but didn't recognize anything or anyone. A lump rose in her throat. What if she didn't remember anything? It all seemed so long ago. For the millionth time she wished her mother was here with her. She had so many questions.

She made her way down the stairs to the runway, anxious to get going, but Jake put his hand on her shoulder to hold her back. "Whoa, slow down. I need to go in front of you for security."

"I'm fine." But his touch sent a prickle of awareness down her arm. No matter what issues were between them, she was definitely attracted to this man and wished she wasn't. He'd watched over her while she'd slept just as he'd promised and she did feel a lot better after getting some rest. Her mood had improved considerably, that is, until he'd practically admitted he was going to keep her out of the loop. It put her guard back up and she hadn't realized how much she was enjoying the tentative trust they were forming between them until it evaporated. But it was important that she know what was going on with Yasmine the moment he knew something, and it sounded like that wouldn't be happening. She watched him lead them through the airport terminal, his stride sure and confident. She liked that about him, but his stubbornness was so frustrating. "Where's the car?"

"It's over there." He motioned to the exit on his right. The airport was busy, but it wasn't a crush and that made it a little easier to maneuver the team through. "But we'll be going straight to the safehouse, remember, while we wait for word."

"I remember." Mya pursed her lips in annoyance. She'd memorized case law, prepared closing statements, did he really think she'd forget something he'd told her less than an hour ago?

Either way, she wasn't going to wait for it to be a good time for the "team" to try to contact her father. She needed to find him right away, whether he would be happy to hear from her or not. When he'd sent her to Canada it was with strict instructions never to come back, but surely he would understand since her sister was in danger. The tiny voice inside her head told her he wouldn't. She was still going to hold out some hope, though.

They made it to the parking area outside and piled into an SUV. Colt drove with Ryan and Nate in the front seat next to him. She was squashed between Jake and Elliott in the back. Elliott looked kind, softer around the edges than Jake, and she shifted toward him. Jake brought up all sorts of warring feelings inside of her and the less physical contact she had with him, the better.

The cars drove toward the outskirts of the city, taking several turns through the neighborhoods. Mya watched the scenery with interest, hoping her memory would recall living here as a girl. The humidity and palm trees swaying in the slight breeze were definitely opposite of what she was used to in Canada. They passed a *crémerie* and her mouth watered thinking of the baked goods inside. There was an outdoor market, schoolchildren on the sidewalks, and she could occasionally glimpse a view of the bay, but she didn't remember any of it. Being here had been such a big part of her at one time. Her home, her identity. And now it was a struggle to even remember what it had been like.

Her shoulders slumped and she shifted, hoping Jake couldn't see her feelings on her face. She did her best to roll with the car's movements and not touch him at all, but the roads were bumpy. Finding it too hard, she finally gave up and just let her leg rest against his, ignoring the butterflies in her stomach the moment they touched. She folded her arms, trying to tamp down on her reaction to him. "How much longer?"

"Not long now," Jake answered, seemingly unaffected by the closeness between them, while emotions roiled through her. That fact was irritating in and of itself.

"Good, then I can shower and get out of these clothes." With as long as she'd been wearing it, she never wanted to see this pantsuit again. She spread her hands over the pants. At least they'd held up well. Maybe she'd keep them in case she was ever called to go overseas to save her sister and find her long lost father at the last minute again. She grimaced. That wasn't even funny.

With a sideways glance at Jake's infuriating profile, she pulled at her ponytail. It felt wrong somehow to just skip out on the team. Jake seemed so supportive of her seeking out her father without anything else clouding the moment, but she didn't feel like waiting was the best course of action. She closed her eyes. What else could she do? If she stayed with the team it might be too late. Yet, if she left to find her father she might not locate him without the resources of the team. There were so many variables to take into consideration. She needed time to think.

"We'll probably have some time on our hands while we wait for word on the hostages. I hope you brought some books or something." He tilted his head to look at her, quirking one eyebrow upward. Was he a mind-reader, too? Did he really know what she was thinking of doing?

"I'm sure I'll find something to do." She clenched her fists, wishing her choice to leave or stay were more clear. "If nothing else, Nate is a great conversationalist."

He looked down at her, his eyes flat and disapproving. "And just to be clear, you might want to tone it down with Nate. This is a mission, not a dating service."

She gasped at the outrageousness of his comment, twisting in her seat to confront him. "I haven't done anything to be ashamed of. He's just being friendly. Maybe you should take some notes." Pulling her legs away, she balanced in the center again, wishing she were anywhere but next to him. Elliott moved a little closer to the door. Was she crowding him? She couldn't help it. She did not want to have any more contact with Jake Williams.

"Commander," Elliott finally said. "Maybe we should table this discussion for now." He gave her a little nod, but the look he had for Jake was a silent conversation between the two men. "In this h-h-heat, I think we should be discussing how to avoid melting."

"Fine," Jake ground out, but didn't offer any other insights to Elliott's attempt to change the subject.

Mya folded her arms again, a bead of sweat trickling down her back. The humidity was already affecting her, or it could be the energy she was expending on the situation with Jake. There wasn't even any use glaring at him. It would probably go over his head so she didn't bother. At least Elliott had stepped in and helped bring her focus back to Yasmine and away from the commander or his attempts to get under her skin.

He'd been so different last night, she'd thought they'd finally found some common ground and that maybe he could be trusted. But she'd been wrong. Thankfully she'd kept her sister a secret. Who knew what Commander Williams would do with that information?

Yasmine. Six years older than Mya, she was the only daughter from her father's first marriage and the person Mya had idolized as a girl. Yasmine had left Algiers the year before Mya and her mother, to go to school in Britain. Mya's last memory was hugging her tight and hearing Yasmine whisper "We'll be together again, princess." Mya had waited for that day and now she might be too late. Yasmine had been gone four days. Was she hurt? Was she hungry?

Mya pressed her nails into her palms. This was where she needed to concentrate. Waiting for the military who'd pin their hopes on any bit of information would take too long. Her father had the contacts they'd need and could cut through any demands the terrorists threw up. With time running out and her sister's life at stake, she made her decision. She'd leave and find her father to save Yasmine before she ended up dead or her captors figured out who her father was and used her to get to him.

The car finally pulled up to a large two-story house. It had red decorative concrete stairs leading up to its gleaming white door. Potted plants were placed strategically around the entrance, making it looked lived in. It had a raised stone foundation and the boxy shape made it feel more familiar to her somehow. She stayed scrunched between Elliott and Jake as they got out and even as they walked into the house. "Stay behind me," Jake ordered.

This time she did glare at him and stepped out of line, just to his left. She hated his commander voice.

Jake took her arm and pulled her quickly inside the beautiful wrought iron gate in front of the house. "Listen, I'm not ordering you around. I just want you safe and that means staying behind me."

"Have you ever heard of asking instead of ordering?" She wanted to march past him, into the house, but he was a solid wall of muscle in front of her and his hand was still on her arm.

He stared at her for a moment and she willed herself not to squirm. Dropping her arm, his eyes traveled down to her neck, where she knew bruises could easily be seen, but she raised her chin at his perusal. Let him say what he wanted. She wasn't going to let it bother her. "Last night you said you were sorry you'd ditched your security and you weren't going to do it again. I need you to keep your word."

Except for that. She lowered her eyes and took a deep breath and let it out slowly. He had her there. But no matter what he said, he was still the most bossy man she'd ever met. "Okay, I'll keep my word, if you'll try harder to ask nicely."

He visibly relaxed, undoing his tie, but leaving it draped around his neck. "I'll do better. I wouldn't want Chivonn to be ashamed of me." He leaned down, close to her ear where no one else could hear. "Can we call another truce? Please?"

She stilled and bit her lip. She wanted a truce. Getting to know him last night on the plane had taken her thoughts down a path that included acting on her attraction to him. Yet being angry as a way of protecting herself from that attraction wasn't fair to either of them. She sighed inwardly. *Get control of yourself.* "I need some space to think, okay?"

He stepped back and looked around. The team was unloading gear from the car and wouldn't overhear whatever he was going to say. She looked up at him, his hair ruffled, his shirt wrinkled, his tie undone. He was tempting in every way. "Mya, I only have your best interests at heart. Truly."

She nodded, but didn't speak. His vulnerable expression and words of comfort blotted out the anger she'd felt earlier and she wanted to touch his face and tell him she was sorry. Sorry for thinking he was a bossy jerk. Sorry for not telling him about Yasmine. But she couldn't and so she stayed quiet. She had to stay strong until she had some idea of how exactly she might help get her sister back.

Nate and Colt were coming up the walk and after one look at her face, Nate lengthened his stride until he was next to Mya. "Is everything okay?"

She gave him a half-hearted smile. Nate was safe for her. He didn't make her crazy and he was starting to feel like a friend from home. Jake was mistaken about the flirting. Nate was friendly, that's all. "I'm just tired. Ready for a shower and a change of clothes."

Nate took her elbow. "I'll show you to your room." She glanced at Jake before they left. It was obvious he wanted to say something, but his jaw was clenched tight. He was wrong about Nate, but he just couldn't admit it.

Colt hurried from the front gate, through the covered patio area to unlock the door for them all. The traditional lock was coupled with an electronic keypad to unlock the second door, which was a nice touch for security. Once they were inside, Mya took a mental inventory of the interior of the house, surprised at how homey it felt. There was a small entryway, and it led to a larger sitting room. Beyond that were patio doors and an outdoor table and chairs took up most of that space. Brightly colored rugs covered the tile floors and they looked stylish and chic. The entire home was comfortable with lots of simple touches to make it feel less like a safehouse and more like somewhere she wouldn't mind staying for a while.

Nate led her through the sitting room to the kitchen beyond, talking the entire time about that Indian restaurant. Mya smiled politely, feeling Jake's eyes boring into her back. She knew he'd heard Nate re-issue his invitation to her and was glad Jake hadn't said anything.

She kept her eyes on the rooms, surprised at how modern everything seemed. The kitchen had all the amenities– stainless steel appliances, beautiful countertops, and a large fridge. Just looking at that fridge made her stomach growl. Her breakfast had been a few hours ago and it had been days since she'd had regular meals. Once she'd showered, she was going to come down and fix herself something to eat.

There was a small hall off the kitchen and Nate kept hold of her arm, leading her down it. "There are three bedrooms on the main floor and the stairs are through here."

The stairway was wide and near a back door. It was dark, but Nate flipped some lights to show them the way. She gave him a smile and he preceded her up the stairs. "Your room and the office are upstairs."

Before she could follow him into the stairwell, Jake caught up and put his hand at her back, the warmth of his palm seeping through her blouse. "Be careful," he said.

She nodded, not willing to intensify any more tension between them. Did he mean be careful with Nate or managing the stairs? "I'm fine."

She hurried up the steps with Jake on her heels. Once she'd made it to the top, Nate held out his arm. "Just a little more and you can rest."

For a brief second she wished she had something to hold so it didn't look bad if she didn't take his arm. But she couldn't ignore him without being rude, so she did. He led her to a large room on her right and walked through the door. A small bed with a homemade quilt was in the corner with a dresser and nightstand on the side. "You have your own private wash room," Nate said, pointing to the door in the corner.

"And the only other room up here is the office?" Jake cut in.

"Yes." Nate pushed back his shoulders and looked pointedly at Jake. "I'm sure we'll *all* be spending a lot of time in there, keeping an eye on things."

It sounded a bit like some sort of veiled warning and the energy between the men crackled. Mya looked at the younger man next to her and in that moment, knew Jake was probably right and he was taking her friendliness as something more. She dropped his arm, hating that she was going to have to have "that" conversation with him and define the boundaries of their relationship.

She closed her eyes briefly. What a day this had been. Emotions she hadn't expected were rushing to the surface, and tears pricked the backs of her eyes. She needed to get them out of her room or she'd be crying in front of them before she knew it and she didn't want that. "Thanks for the tour. I'm going to go ahead and get cleaned up."

The two men were staring at each other as if they hadn't heard her so she touched Nate's arm. "Thanks for the tour. I think I'll just lie down for a moment."

They moved to the hall outside and she shut the door behind them, wiping a stray tear away. She wasn't going to let her emotions get the best of her. She was going to focus on getting Yasmine back– and to do that she needed to contact her father.

Slipping her purse off her shoulder, she opened the zippered pocket on the side and took out her mother's journal. She'd given strict instructions to only use these contacts to find her father in an emergency. Well, this was an emergency. Flipping open to the first page, she looked over the first step. She needed to make a phone call. With the office right next to her room, there had to be a time when the phone would be free. Then she'd make her call.

A tiny part of her said she should trust Jake and let him help her. But his voice reminding her that she wasn't privy to all the information on this mission rang in her head. No, it was better this way. She had her own mission to accomplish and she was going to get started.

CHAPTER TEN

Jake blew out a breath, glad Nate hadn't followed him into the office next door. He definitely needed a break from the guy. Colt was already behind the desk, looking at a computer screen. "Hey," Jake said, glad Colt was here. The guy had a calming presence around him that Jake liked.

"How did the tour go?" Colt asked without looking up.

"Fine, but I'd like more than the company tour if you know what I mean." He sat down in the overstuffed chair against the far wall. He needed to take a shower and get out of this suit. It seemed like forever ago when he'd put it on. He couldn't wait to dress down a bit and put on a clean t-shirt and some jeans. As soon as he got the lay of the land.

"Sure. We have a safe room and a weapons room in the basement. The house next door is empty, so we don't have to worry about neighbors." He clicked his mouse a few times, then glanced over at Jake. "Have there been any mission updates?"

Jake crossed his ankle over his knee. "We have a credible lead on Nazer and the hostages, so we're sitting tight until we hear more. We're still supposed to keep Mya safe in case we still have to use her to contact her father." Although he had a feeling that wasn't going to be as easy as it sounded.

"That's the report I got from my superiors as well." He leaned his arm over the armrest of the office chair. "Do you have any ideas on how to do that? She doesn't seem the type that wants to stay inside for days at a time."

Yeah, she didn't seem like that type at all. Did she love the outdoors as much as he did? Jake ran his hand through his hair. "Hopefully it won't come to that. A day or two at most."

"Still, we're going to need to keep her distracted. She's got a lot of loose ends in Algeria that she'll be anxious to tie up."

That was an understatement. "Do you think she'd try to go off on her own?"

"In a heartbeat." Colt pushed his chair back. "She's a very determined woman and she's taking this mission personally."

"From the looks of things we've got a TV and movies. Internet connection. That should help. And, of course, our company." He still had a bitter taste in his mouth about Nate. What was it about the guy that was bothering him so much?

Colt raised an eyebrow. "I guess we'll just have to work with what we've got then." He looked back at the computer screen and Jake knew he had his opening.

"It might be a good idea to tell Nate to tone down the flirting. Treat this more like a mission." His jaw clenched as his mind went back to the look on Nate's face when he told Jake she felt safe with him. When he'd reminded Jake that he hadn't been there for her after the attack.

"I haven't seen anything untoward, have you?" Colt looked at him, his expression skeptical.

"I heard him ask her out." And she'd defended him as just being friendly. Why didn't Jake just take it at face value? Why was this such an annoyance? "You've got some seniority on him, right?"

"I'll talk to him." He powered down the computer and gave Jake his full attention. "Do you want to do the detailed tour now?"

"Sure." He stood up and tried to smooth out his pants, but it was hopeless. He'd definitely put their "wrinkle-free" status to the test. Maybe they should advertise that the pants stayed wrinkle-free for a day of meetings and a flight overseas, but wrinkled like an old paper bag after that. "Who has the combination to get into the safe room?"

"Myself and Nate. I'll give it to you if you like." Colt still looked pretty fresh for having been through almost the same activities the day before. Maybe his pants were forty-eight hour wrinkle-free suit pants.

"Thanks. I'd like Mya to have it, too, just in case." Not that anything would happen, but he'd like her to be prepared.

"We should probably include her in this discussion, let her know what her options are in the unlikely event we're attacked here. It's always good to have a contingency plan," Colt said, joining him near the door.

That statement alone endeared him to Colt since he thought the same way when he was on a mission. 'I agree. I'll go next door and invite her over."

He walked to her room and could see Colt leaning against the doorframe of the office, waiting patiently. The guy was like chamomile tea in human form. Soothing. He didn't seem the type that would ever go off half-cocked about something. At that moment, Jake was glad to have him on the team.

Jake knocked on Mya's door and heard some rustling before she said, "Come in."

He opened it carefully to find her sitting in a chair, looking out the window, but she seemed tense. What was that rustling sound he'd heard before he opened the door? What was she up to? "Hey, what's going on?" He kept his tone casual.

She stood and he could see that she'd changed into some cream linen pants and a loose flowing gold and white blouse that accentuated her eyes. Not that she was looking at him. She seemed to be looking everywhere but at him. "Not much. Just unpacking. What about you?"

Her smile was too bright and his eyes narrowed as he swept the room. Nothing looked out of place, but she was clearly up to something. "Did you get a chance to lie down at all?"

"I'm not tired, yet. The jet lag will probably set in tonight." She walked past him to the door, keeping her gaze on a point on the wall. "Did you need something?"

She was leading him out of the room for some reason, he was sure of it. He took one last sweep of the room, but nothing popped out at him this time either, so he followed. "Colt and I want to talk to you about the security measures for the house."

She turned around to face him in the doorway, but tilted her face away. "Great, let's go. Should we talk in the office?" She'd agreed quickly. Too quickly.

"Mya, what's going on?" He was about a foot away from her and could feel the nervous energy pouring off of her. When he looked closer, her eyes were a bit puffy and red. Had she been crying? Jake could feel Colt's gaze on them, so he took her arm and led her back into the bedroom and shut the door. "Are you okay?"

She gently pulled her arm away. "I'm fine. Just thinking. Remembering." She mustered another smile, less bright, but more honest. "I thought I'd have more memories of the city. I thought things would come rushing back, but they didn't. It's like that part of me is buried now. And I wish my mom was here."

The last sentence was little more than a whisper and Jake knew she probably hadn't meant to say it out loud. The anguish on her face was heartbreaking and he remembered all too well feeling the same way after his parents and then his grandmother had died. He wanted to take some of her pain away if he could.

"Mya." He clenched his fingers, wanting to reach out, but not knowing if he should. "It's going to be okay."

Choking back a sob, she pressed her face into her hand. He couldn't just sit there and watch her suffer. His arm went around her, rubbing her shoulder. She pressed her face into his shirt, letting out a small whimper. "It will get better, I promise," he told her. "I've been there. I know."

She didn't say anything, just cried into his chest and he let his hand move in a slow circle on her upper arm until the brunt of it had blown over. Glad that she'd let him comfort her in even a small way, he waited until he felt a shuddering breath go through her. "When did your mother pass away?" He knew the Admiral had mentioned it, but the exact time frame was escaping his memory just now.

"Six months ago," she said, not lifting her head. "Sometimes I feel like I'm doing okay, but coming back here just made me miss her."

Jake had to bend his head to hear her she was talking so softly. "Every time I see a garden it reminds me of my mom. I miss her, too." The pain had faded over the years, but never really went away. He'd just learned to live with it. Not that he would tell her that. "Memories and missing them helps keep them close."

She nodded and pulled back. "I– "

There was a knock at the door and Colt's voice came through. "Is everything okay?"

The moment was shattered. Mya closed her eyes and took a deep breath. "Coming."

She stepped back from Jake and he wanted to reach for her again. She was a bit like Chivonn, trying to be strong and holding everything in, but she didn't have to with him. He'd been where she was in so many ways. "Mya, I'm here if you need me."

She nodded and slowly turned for the door. "Thank you," she said softly before she walked away to let Colt in. "Sorry, Colt. Commander Williams was just telling me we needed to go over some security concerns."

Jake followed slowly, wishing they'd had one more minute alone. And that she wasn't back to calling him Commander Williams. Weren't they past that now? He exhaled, trying to let go of any frustration. Her eyes had looked so lost and he'd wanted to help make it better, to assure her she could trust him. But then going over security concerns and the fact that her safety might be compromised might not help, either.

They'd walked toward the office and when Jake joined them, Colt was behind the desk again and Mya was sitting in the padded chair in front of it. He took the overstuffed chair he'd had before and sat down.

"Nate showed you the main and upper floor of the house, but there is a basement area as well," Colt started. "We put in a reinforced safe room that you can go to where it's locked from the inside. There are enough supplies in there that you could live comfortably until it was safe to come out."

Mya was very still as she absorbed the information. "Do you think I'll need that? I thought this was a safehouse."

"It is. It's a just-in-case sort of thing." Colt steepled his hands on the desk. "There's a combination code to get in and Jake thinks you should have it."

She glanced at him then, her gaze skittering over his face before she quickly looked away. "Sounds like a good idea."

She looked like she was waiting for him to say something, so he went with, "Thanks." Wincing inwardly, he knew that sounded weird. But what else could he say? Glad I thought of it?

The word hung in the air until it was awkward and Colt finally stood. "Why don't we go down to look at it?"

"That sounds great." Mya was to the door almost before she'd finished speaking. Was she trying to avoid him? After what had just happened in her room, he could maybe understand that. She was obviously a woman who was used to taking care of things on her own. But one moment of weakness didn't make you weak. Hopefully he got a chance to tell her that next time they were alone.

Colt led the way with Mya in the middle and Jake bringing up the rear. They went down the back stairs and didn't see anyone on the way down, which was a little odd with so many of them in the house. Briefly Jake wondered if Ryan and Elliott had found their bunks. Should he bring them in on the safe room and weapons storage right now? He took one look at

Mya's back and could see how tense she already was. He'd find them later and show them.

Near the back door was another set of stairs that wasn't readily seen since it looked like a pantry door and not a door leading to a back stairway. Colt flipped a light switch and bent down to make it through the low door, but turned and waited for Mya and Jake to catch up. "It's a little steep, so watch your step," Colt said and proceeded down.

There was a bit of large space at the bottom of the stairs that led off to a hallway with two doors. Mitchell took out a key, and approached the closest door. He inserted the key into the keypad and then entered in a code. The door popped open with an airy whoosh and he pulled it wide. Mya stepped forward and Jake was right behind her.

"This is the weapons storage room," Colt said as he walked in. There was just enough space for a small aisle down the wall-to-wall weapons. Pistols and rifles of all shapes and sizes covered the wall and grenades were housed at the far end. It was a war room and Jake felt better just seeing it. If there were an emergency, they'd be prepared to defend the house and everyone in it.

Mya lifted down a 9mm from the wall and looked it over carefully, testing the weight in her hand. "Do you have a Glock 19? It fits better in my hand."

Colt nodded. "We do." He stepped over to the middle of the wall and took one down. "Do you know how to shoot?"

"My mother taught me to defend myself. I like the Glock 19 since the recoil is a little easier to handle as well." She handed the gun back to him. "Don't worry about me. If I need to use it, I can."

Jake's thought processes shifted as Colt showed her the compartment where the ammunition was kept. She wasn't some wilting flower that needed protection. She'd gotten away from one attack already. She'd relied on her instincts and so far they'd served her well. He needed to remember that.

"Are you ready to see the safe room, then?" Colt asked, as he waited for them to go back out the way they'd come in.

Mya turned and met Jake's eyes. The vulnerability he'd seen earlier in her room was gone, replaced by a steel he knew had gotten her through to this point in her life. She let her gaze fall to the door and repeated Colt's question to him directly. "Are you ready, Commander?"

Ready to figure out more about what makes Mya Amari tick. The more he learned about her, the more he wanted to know, but this wasn't the time or the place. "Of course." He turned around and went back out to the hall. Colt emerged and headed to the other door. "This one has an eight digit combination. 05041910." He punched it in with a smile.

"Do those numbers mean something?" Mya asked as he opened the door.

"It's the date the Royal Canadian Navy was founded. May 4, 1910." He opened the door with a flourish. "A home away from home."

The room was long, but not quite as narrow as the weapons room next door. There was a couch and chairs, monitors watching the outside door and main floor, as well as a table against the far wall. A cot sat in the corner. "The cupboards are fully stocked with food and water. The monitors will tell you when it's safe to come out." He turned and shut the door. "If you truly are in danger, as soon as you get in, punch in the same code to this keypad here and the door will be locked tight. There's no way in here at all, unless you open it."

"How long can I stay down here?" Mya asked.

"About two weeks." Colt walked over to the monitors. "We have the same monitors upstairs, but yours are on a separate system, so even if something happens to our feed, you'll still be able to see what's going on from down here."

The door behind them opened and they all turned. Nate poked his head in. "Is this a free tour?"

Colt waved him in. "I was just showing Mya what to do in case of an emergency."

Nate walked around Jake and stood next to Mya, smiling down at her. Jake resisted the urge to shake his head. Nate ignored him. "She won't have to worry about that. Not with all of us in the house."

"It's always good to have a back up plan," Colt said, mildly. "I think we're done here, though."

"I was just making something to eat. Are you hungry?" Nate asked as he shifted closer to Mya.

Her glance flickered backward to Jake. "I am a little hungry, but I have some more unpacking to do first. If you'll excuse me."

"Nate, can I talk to you for a minute?" Colt asked, as they exited the safe room.

"I think I'll head up to the kitchen myself," Jake said, relieved to leave them alone, especially if Colt was going to say something to Nate about his "friendliness" toward Mya.

He came upstairs and walked down to the kitchen, where Elliott was at the table, already chowing down on a sandwich. He thankfully finished chewing before he spoke. "Hey. How are things going? Everything okay?"

"As far as I know." Jake leaned closer and picked up a piece of bread, quickly making himself a meat and cheese sandwich identical to Elliott's. "I've hardly had a chance to talk to you."

"You have been a little b-b-busy," Elliott agreed.

Jake heard Elliott's stutter, but was glad to see how much more in control he was of it. When he'd first met him, Elliott hardly said a word because the stutter was so bad and it had affected how far he could go in his career. Now he'd controlled it and was much more confident.

Jake's thoughts went back to Mya like they had so often since he'd met her. There were so many contradictory feelings swirling in his head when it came to her. Hopefully she really was unpacking. "So, what do you think of our little task force so far?"

"The Canadians are well-trained. Professional. Polite." He smiled. "You and Ryan seem about the same. Annoying."

"We're the only annoying ones?" Jake raised an eyebrow at Elliott as he took a bite.

"Yeah, I'm g-g-getting a feeling you and Nate aren't hitting it off."

"You got a feeling?" Jake probably should hide that better. He did need to be professional and work with this man. "I just can't get a handle on this guy. Every time I turn around he's right there offering to help make Mya more comfortable."

"Is it bothering you more than it's bothering Mya?" Elliott studied him and Jake looked away. Was he that obvious? Elliott smirked. "It's been a long time since I've seen you flustered."

"I'm not flustered. I'm planning for every scenario." Jake stood up and took the last bite of his sandwich. "I'm going to go wash up."

"Sometimes s-s-scenarios come along you can't plan for," Elliott called out as Jake walked away. "You just never know with women."

And that was what Jake was afraid of.

CHAPTER ELEVEN

Darkness had fallen, but Mya still couldn't sleep. She paced the small room, her stomach in knots. The house was quiet. She needed to go next door and make the phone call, but something was holding her back. What would her father say? Would he let her help him find Yasmine?

She probably already knew the answer to that, but she still had to try. Her own safety took a backseat. If her sister died, Mya would always wonder if she could have saved her.

Moving back to the bed, she sat down, the images of the day running through her mind. Wanting that sense of homecoming. Missing her mom. Jake. He was so infuriating, yet had held her as she'd cried. Her face flamed remembering how she'd nearly melted at his comforting circles on her arm. As embarrassed as she felt breaking down in front of him, she'd had a sense of security with him. Those types of feelings were dangerous and could complicate everything, but she couldn't seem to help herself. He understood her in a way that few did and that was hard to overlook.

She got up and went to the door, listening for any movement in the hallway. She hadn't heard anyone in the office for over an hour, so whomever had been in there had probably gone to bed by now. She had to make her move.

Turning her bedroom door handle, she nearly jumped out of her skin when someone knocked on it. So much for her spy skills of not hearing anyone in the hall. She cracked it open to see who it was. "Nate?"

"I thought I might wake you." His eyebrows furrowed as he noticed she was still dressed in her clothing and not pajamas. "Were you headed somewhere?"

"Just downstairs for a midnight snack." She opened the door a little further. "Did you need something?"

"Why don't we discuss it over some fruit or something? The fridge looked pretty well-stocked."

She groaned inwardly. She didn't want to have an uncomfortable conversation with Nate right now. But what else could she say? "Sure."

He waited for her to precede him down the hall. "You seemed pretty quiet tonight."

"Just tired. It's been a tough couple of days." She glanced back at him. "I'm fine, really." She walked slowly down the stairs, wishing she were in the office right now making her phone call.

Nate turned on the kitchen light. "Do you want to get the plates and I'll get the fruit?"

She nodded and went to the cupboard. There would be plenty of time to make the phone call. She just had to make this quick. "So, did you need to talk to me about something?"

He set down some figs and prickly pears on the table. "I just wanted to check on you before I went to bed," he said.

She sat down at the table. "Really? You seemed anxious about it." Reaching for a fig, she raised her eyebrows. "I don't know how else to say it. I'm fine. You don't have to worry about me."

He sat down next to her and scooted his chair a little closer. "If you weren't fine would you tell me?"

She gently pulled back, putting some space between them. She didn't want to hurt his feelings. He'd been so nice to her. "Of course."

Leaning forward, he bent to catch her eye. "Is Jake bothering you?"

She took a bite of fig, weighing her words. "Jake and I got off on the wrong foot, but I think we're coming to an understanding." Sort of. When he wasn't busy being bossy. "Why?"

"He seems pretty territorial when it comes to you." Nate opened his palms on the table as if asking her to agree.

"I think he's concerned about everyone on the team. And ever since the attack in the hotel, he's felt more responsible for me, that's all." Even as she said the words, she realized that was probably true. Did he feel guilty for the hotel attack still? She needed to ask him.

"I've just noticed there are a lot of times you seem upset when he's around." Nate turned his face toward her. "And I heard there was an incident this afternoon. In your room."

Mya shut her eyes for a moment. This was exactly what she didn't want to have to deal with. But she'd had a weak moment and she needed to own it. "Nate, you're sweet to worry about me, but it was nothing. I just needed a moment to collect myself and Jake happened to be there." The memory of his arm around her offering comfort while she'd cried on his shoulder was fresh. He'd offered her a port in the storm of emotion she was feeling and instead of feeling humiliated, she was grateful. It was easier to confide in him about her mother's death since he knew what it felt like to lose a loved one. But how could she say that to Nate? "I'm just dealing with a few things, that's all, and Jake is trying to help. Honest."

"Did he say something to upset you?" He closed his hand and drew it back a little. "You can tell me."

She inwardly sighed. Nate wasn't going to let this go and Mya wished he would. "No, it wasn't like that." Mya reached for his hand that was still on the table. "Nate, you've become a good friend and I know you're looking out for me, but Jake hasn't done anything to hurt or upset me. In fact, he's been very kind."

Jake's voice cut in from the doorway. "You know, if you're so interested in my conversations with Mya, why don't you ask me about them instead of badgering her?"

Mya jumped and let out a squeak of surprise. "Do you make a habit of eavesdropping on people?" she asked, her hand on her heart. How much had he heard?

"My ears were burning," he said as he pulled out a chair and turned it around, sitting backward. "And here you are, talking about me." He grabbed a piece of fruit off the plate in the middle of the table, looking at Nate.

"Nate was just concerned about me, that's all." She bit her lip, feeling the tension coming off of Nate, but he was silent, wary.

"And he's asking questions about something that doesn't concern him." Jake held the fruit in mid-air, as if waiting for Nate to say something before he took a bite. "But I'm happy to clarify anything."

Nate leaned back in his chair, pulling his plate with him. "Mya made things very clear. But thanks for the offer."

Jake bit into the fruit, eyeing the other man. He took a moment to chew and swallow, but the atmosphere was still charged. "Nate, I know we don't know each other very well, but if you think there's a problem, you can come talk to me. Anytime. If we're going to work together, I'd prefer that."

"I'll keep that in mind." Nate scraped his chair back. "But just so you know, Mya has a lot of people here who care about her and will look out for her."

"Which is fine if it doesn't get in the way of the mission." Jake's tone was still friendly with a thread of warning.

"As long as we're all on the same page." Nate stood. "See you tomorrow Mya."

Mya grabbed another fig before she stood with him. "Thanks for the company," she said, not wanting Nate to leave like this. Nate looked like he wanted to say something else, but with a glance toward Jake, he didn't and walked toward the hall where the bedrooms were.

Mya put her hand on the back of the chair, suddenly tired and a little emotional. Nothing had gone right on this trip so far. "We should get to bed, too." As soon as the words left her mouth, she blushed, realizing how it sounded. "I mean I should go to my room and you to yours. Alone. To sleep."

He chuckled. "I knew what you meant." He motioned toward the unfinished plate of fruit. "But you didn't even finish your snack. Why don't you sit down for a minute?"

She was tempted. Her attraction to him was getting stronger the more she got to know him. Seeing him in jeans and a t-shirt, he seemed to have a different energy about him. When he'd been dressed in a suit, he'd had a careful, professional way about him. Now he had an indefinable magnetism that beckoned her closer. That alone was reason enough not to stay longer with him. She was here to do a mission. His piercing blue eyes seemed to read her thoughts with just a look, and she knew she couldn't. "I better not." She took a step toward the door. "But feel free to help yourself."

She headed for the stairs and didn't look back in case her traitorous-and- completely-attracted self overruled what she knew she had to do. The phone call. Her father. Yasmine. If everyone finally headed to bed, she'd catch her chance to use the phone in the office. Hopefully Jake was going to fall asleep in the safehouse as fast as he'd done on the plane. Time was of the essence and she didn't want any more emotional drama getting in her way. *Just figure out how to get hold of my father. How hard can that be?*

She walked quickly down the hall and went into her room, closing the door behind her. Back to pacing. She'd memorized the phone number and gone over every possible scenario she could think of in how this would go. Maybe her father wouldn't see her. Maybe he'd demand she come to him. But there was too much in between that could happen and she couldn't prepare herself for it and that's what was driving her crazy.

When she didn't hear any sounds on the stairs, she decided to make her move. After that scene in the kitchen, she was sure they'd leave her alone for the rest of the night. She opened the door quietly and peeked out. All was dark and quiet. Walking on tiptoe to the room next door, she turned the handle and slipped inside. The only light she had was from the security screen in the room and it gave everything an eerie blue sheen. Good enough for what she needed it for, though.

"Well, that didn't take as long as I thought it would." Jake rose from the chair in the corner.

Mya barely held back a scream, her heart jumping into her throat. "You scared me," she managed to get out.

"Good. Someone needs to scare some sense into you. You're going to break security protocol to contact your father without even a heads up for the team, aren't you? But did you think that your father's enemies aren't searching for you? And what if that call leads them here?"

Mya shook her head immediately. "These protocols were put in place by my parents. They would have been extra vigilant."

"Were you going to tell me? Tell anyone?" He spread his hands, frustration lacing his tone. "The least you could do is warn us so we're prepared."

"You wouldn't have agreed to let me do it." Her chin raised an inch. "You need to feel in control and you hate it when you can't control me."

"I need you to be safe. You're our only hope if this other intel doesn't pan out." He stood just a step away from her, but he was close enough she could feel his body heat, the appeal he exerted over her back in force. "Did you think of that?"

"Of course I thought of that," she snapped as she stepped back. She needed some distance from him right now. "But you are so set on this intel and we don't have the luxury of time. We've got to get to her now."

"Her? Who are you talking about?" His eyes narrowed as he closed the gap between them, not letting her breathe with his proximity stealing her breath.

Too late she realized her mistake. "Them. The hostages. We have to get to them as soon as possible. We don't have time to wait." The shadows of his face were more pronounced as he tried to find her eyes in the gloom. Her palms were beginning to sweat. Now was not the time to tell him about Yasmine.

"Is that all?" His voice held suspicion, but his question told her he'd at least partially believed her.

"What else would there be?" Her emotions were on a razor thin edge. She needed to maintain a tight rein of control on herself this time. If nothing else, for Yasmine's sake.

"What's your plan then?" He moved back toward his chair and she gave an inward sigh of relief at the breathing room.

"I need to make a call and the person on the other end will give me instructions on how to contact my father." It should be simple, but this was the most difficult call she'd ever had to make. What if no one answered? What if her father answered?

"What if the protocols don't work anymore? Or if they ask you to go somewhere?" His face was shadowed in the blue light, making him look otherworldly. But in the dark or the light of day, he was still acting like he knew everything. It got under her skin every time. *Don't let him get to you*, she chided herself.

She waved a hand. "I don't know. I don't know anything until I've made the call."

"Let me do it." His voice was commanding and it was like he was showcasing everything she didn't like about him. Did he do it on purpose?

"No. They're expecting to hear from me, not you. If they hear your voice, we might lose our only chance." Surely he could see the logic in that.

"So they're expecting you? When did that happen?" He folded his arms, pulling his t-shirt tight across his chest. The shirt looked well-worn, like it was a favorite of his. She tore her eyes away and pulled her mind back to the conversation at hand. He was still questioning her like she was a witness on the stand. "What aren't you telling me?"

She mirrored his stance, knowing the more confident she appeared, the easier it would be to throw him off his questioning. "What aren't you telling me? Have you heard anything new at all? I thought I heard a call in here earlier."

He looked at her for a moment longer before answering. "The rescue team is there and it looks like they might have found AQIM's hideout. They're sending in a drone strike to clear out the terrorists and we can move in and grab the hostages. We're waiting to hear whether it panned out or not." He leaned a hip against the desk. "So maybe we should save the phone call for tomorrow or after we know something."

At least he was asking instead of ordering, but her heart sank, knowing that his offer made the most sense. She didn't want to wait when she could be doing something, but at the same time, she didn't want to be distracted from what was already happening. At least they had an idea of where Yasmine might be and this could all be over if they were right. But what if they weren't? "Why don't we set a few deadlines? If we don't hear anything by noon tomorrow, then I make my phone call."

He reached his hands back to grip the edge of the desk. "How about we give them a little more time and say five in the afternoon."

"Done." She backed up a step. "And I expect you to keep your word."

"I always do," he assured her, looking a bit miffed she would even suggest that he wouldn't.

She pulled open the door. "We'll see about that." Heading back to her room, she shut the door and sat on the bed. At least she had a time frame for contacting her father and she didn't need to do it in secret. But with action to save her sister already underway, she turned her eyes heavenward. "Please," she whispered. She wanted a chance to heal her family and this was it. "Please let this work."

CHAPTER TWELVE

Jake slept in the office. It wasn't that he didn't trust Mya, but he didn't want her making any decisions in the heat of the moment that she'd regret later. He'd done that too many times himself during stressful situations. When Colt arrived bright and early, though, Jake's back was more than regretful after sleeping in an uncomfortable chair. "Hey," he said as Colt went around the desk and sat down.

"You slept in here?" Colt raised his eyebrows as he scooted his chair in.

"Yeah." He stretched his back and winced at the cracking sounds he heard. Someday he was going to pay the price for sleeping in places other than a bed. "How did you sleep?"

"Better than you probably." The computer whirred to life and Colt started to click through some screens. "You know, since being out in the field I appreciate a bed a lot more when I have one. I would have thought the same thing about you."

Jake chuckled. He was finding so many things in common with this guy. "I should be smarter, but just wanted to make sure everyone stayed where they were supposed to last night, that's all."

"Did you have reason to think otherwise?" Colt's attention was divided between the monitor in front of him and Jake.

"I caught Mya in here last night, ready to make a phone call to find her father, but I convinced her to wait to do anything. We need to see if the rescue team can do their job. If they can't, then we'll still need her and we don't want to burn any bridges." He ran a hand over his face. It was weird to feel whiskers again. When he'd been in this part of the world last time he hadn't bothered shaving, but since he'd been home in the U.S. he hadn't missed a day and he'd gotten used to being clean-shaven.

"There's no new update," Colt said, sounding a bit defeated as he turned back to focus on Jake.

"I should get a phone call this afternoon." At least Jake hoped he did. He didn't think he could hold Mya off much longer than that. She was determined to contact her father, and while he understood it, it still worried him.

"Why don't you go down and get some breakfast? The doc was cooking up some eggs when I went by."

The thought of food perked Jake up. Making plans was always a bit easier on a full stomach. He stood. "Thanks. I'll see you down there?"

"Yep. Just finishing my check-in." Colt turned back to the computer and Jake opened the door to find Mya standing there. She looked beautiful with her hair in a braid down her back, dressed in yoga pants and a t-shirt. His mind suddenly went blank, so he said the first thing that popped into his head.

"Did you hear anything interesting while you were listening at the door?" His voice had come out louder than he intended and as her pleasant smile turned to a frown, he quickly backed up. He probably looked exactly like his disapproving foster father, making accusations without all the facts. Even if she had been eavesdropping she wouldn't have heard anything important, so it wasn't a big deal. What was it with him? He couldn't seem to say the right thing whenever she was around.

"Good morning to you, too. Elliott asked me to come and find everyone and tell them the M'shewsha is ready." There was no warmth in her voice, and her eyes were like brown chips of ice looking at him.

Take it easy, he reminded himself. "Sorry if that sounded accusing. I didn't get much sleep last night." Her eyes softened a bit and he took that as a good sign. "I love M'shewsha." His mouth began to water at the thought of the Algerian egg dish. "I didn't know Elliott knew how to make that."

"He didn't. I did." She turned around, but gave him an over-the-shoulder smile. "And I guarantee you've never tasted M'shewsha like mine."

He quickly caught up to her, any tiredness he'd felt disappearing in the face of the smile she'd shot his way. "Oh yeah? The last time I had it, the guy who cooked it was the former chef to the Algerian president."

"Psh, he doesn't have my secret ingredients." She started down the stairs, her step light, but he kept up with her.

"Secret ingredient? Isn't it just eggs, semolina, and flour, all drenched in honey?"

She stopped and turned so fast he almost ran into her. "That sounds terrible when you put it like that. So, no, that's not all there is to it. Not for me, anyway."

He walked down a step and leaned to catch her eye, the pull to be close to her impossible to resist for long. She relaxed for a second, letting herself move just a hair closer to him. With him a stair higher, her face was nearly level with his chest, but she tilted her face up to look at him. Did she know how kissable she looked? "I can't wait to taste it," he managed to say, his voice low and his mind no longer on M'shewsha.

"It'll be better than the chef's I guarantee it." She bit her lip before she turned away, but he noticed she grabbed onto the stair rail as she went down. Did she feel as off-balance about what was going on between them as he did?

She entered the kitchen just ahead of him, and went immediately to the stove. Elliott was at the table, his eyes closed as he chewed a bite. "Hey, Elliott." Jake said as he joined Mya at the stove. His arm brushed against hers as she passed him a plate and he dished himself some food. The electricity crackling between them was palpable and he wished they were alone.

"How's it tasting over there?" He was still talking to Elliott, but his eyes were on Mya. *Please let Elliott be done eating.*

When Elliott didn't answer, Jake finally looked over at him. "El?"

"There are n-n-no words." Elliott looked down at his plate almost reverently. "This woman has created a culinary masterpiece."

Mya gave him her I-told-you-so smile, but he only held up his plate. "Is there a fork? I've got to try this."

She silently leaned forward and opened the drawer to Jake's right. Handing him a fork, she motioned to the chair. "You should always sit down and eat. It helps you slow down and savor your food."

"Maybe that's why the military always has us eating on the g-g-go. So we don't think to savor it." Elliott chuckled at his own joke. "Seriously, man, this is best M'shawshaw or whatever it was Mya called it that I've ever tasted."

"It's M'shewsha. And how do you know it's the best if you've never had it before?" Jake got some on his fork and gave one last look at Mya before he ate it. If it weren't the best he'd ever tasted, would he admit it to her? She looked so confident. But he knew as soon as he tasted it that he didn't have to worry about that. She was right. The chef's paled in comparison to this. There was just a hint of spice that mixed with the honey and it made him want to close his eyes like Elliott had done.

"So?" Mya sat down at the table with her own plate, her voice innocent.

Jake got another bite ready. “I owe you an apology. This is amazing.”

She looked pleased. “Thank you.” As she settled down to eat, Jake turned to Elliott. “Where’s everyone else? Or is this just for us?”

He shrugged. “I’ve only seen you two and Colt so far this morning.”

“No Nate or Ryan?” Jake took another bite. This stuff was addicting.

“Nope. Colt told some terrible jokes and went upstairs. Then you showed up.”

“Who tells terrible jokes?” Colt said as he walked in. “And what smells so good in here?”

“Mya made M’shewsha. Algerian eggs with a twist.” Jake motioned toward the stove. “Better get some before I’m ready for seconds. It’s incredible.”

When Colt was at the table and before he had taken a bite that would propel him to M’shewsha heaven, Jake pointed his fork in Elliott’s direction. “So, you going to share some of these jokes with the rest of us?”

“No,” Elliott objected, holding up a hand. “Please. No more jokes.”

But Colt paused with his fork halfway to his mouth. “You’re Navy, right, Jake?” When Jake nodded Colt put down his fork and smiled. “Why is there a flap on the back of the Navy uniform?”

Jake shook his head. “Why?”

"So the Marines have something to hold onto." He smiled over Jake's groan. "Good thing you're not a Marine, eh?" He put the bite in his mouth and all speech stopped for a full minute. "Oh, this is really good."

Jake finished off his plate and went to the stove for seconds before Colt got any more ideas. "Even though you tell terrible jokes," he said when he got back to the table. "Canadians are good friends to have."

Colt managed to open his eyes from the food nirvana he'd reached. "Oh yeah? How many Canadians have you run across?"

"You'd be surprised. My unit at Homeland has worked with Canadian Border Agents and Customs quite a bit actually." Jake enthusiastically dug in to his second helping.

"What made you transfer out of the military?" Colt didn't wait for an answer, just took another bite and closed his eyes again. Elliott and Mya were both staring at him, though, waiting for Jake's answer.

How could he explain how badly Chivonn had needed him after her husband died? That she was the only person who had ever cared about him and he would give up anything for her? "It's a long story." And not one he was anxious to talk about. Chivonn had healed, she was doing well, and that made it all worth it.

Elliott changed the subject and leaned toward Jake. "Now that I've had a chance to look at you over the b-bbreakfast table, what happened to you last night? You look terrible."

Jake shrugged as he put down his fork. "I didn't sleep that great." He gave Mya a sidelong glance. "How did you sleep?"

"Like a baby." She smiled and took another bite as if taunting him with that fact. Had she known he was in the office? Probably. Hopefully she knew it was for her own good.

"So what are your plans for today?" Jake asked, making sure to catch her eye.

"Just waiting on a phone call." She tilted her head at him, as if that was a silly question. "But while we're waiting I thought I'd make some cookies."

"Cookies are my favorite," Elliott put in.

"And these aren't your normal kind of cookies," Mya's whole face lit up. "My grandmother used to make them. They're called L'Arayechs and are like little works of art."

"I guess I'm a chocolate chip kind of guy," Colt said, finally finishing his breakfast. "But after this egg masterpiece, I'm willing to be a taste tester for you."

"Me, too." Elliott took his plate to the sink and started to run some water.

The mood in the kitchen was fun and happy and Jake couldn't help but smile. With only the two of them at the table now, he wanted to share a bit of that happiness with her. "You're in a cooking mood this morning," Jake said, watching her take her last bite. Had some Algerian memories come back? She'd been so worried about that yesterday.

"It's like cooking all the Algerian dishes my mom used to make for me helps me feel closer to her. And to Algiers." She looked pleased, all the distress from yesterday gone from her face. She pushed away from the table and handed her plate to Elliott. "Silly, I know."

"Not silly at all," he reassured her.

"And it helps that we have a deal. Before today ends, I'll have answers whether they're from you or from a phone call to my father." She leaned her elbow on the table and Jake noted how much more relaxed she seemed. If only he'd known earlier that setting a deadline would dissolve the tension between them, he would have done it the first day.

"Hey, if we get to reap the benefits, I'm all for it." Elliott turned the water off and started washing the dishes. "Anytime you want to cook, just let me know."

Mya laughed. "Okay." She stood and started to open the cupboards and took out a large bowl. "My grandmother would have liked you at her afternoon teas. She liked a man with an appetite."

"Your grandma would have loved me," Elliott said with a grin.

Mya was like a whirlwind, gathering ingredients out of the cupboards and setting them out. "These are traditional fare at an afternoon tea and my grandmother always took the time to make them into fancy flower shapes. I almost didn't want to eat them they were so pretty, but I couldn't resist they were so good." She stopped for a moment, her face turning wistful. "I haven't had L'Arayechs since my mom died."

The obvious enjoyment that had been in her face a moment ago faded. Jake stood, seeing the shadow of pain in her eyes. "She lives on through you. And cookies. And however else you remember her."

She gave him a small smile, acknowledging his words before she turned back to the array of ingredients spread on the counter. "You'll appreciate her, too, when you taste these cookies."

"If they're as good as the M'shewsha, I'll love them." He stepped back, glad to see a little happiness on her face again. "Can we help?"

Mya looked at him skeptically. "Do you even know how to bake?"

Jake folded his arm and leaned back against the cupboard. How did he explain his baking experience? "Well, they have this can of frozen dough at the grocery store that I have to put on a cookie sheet and bake in the oven. Does that count?"

She curved her lips, trying not to laugh. "I suppose." With that, she started measuring out some of the ingredients and putting it in a bowl. "I'm going to need you to shape these into balls in a minute. I don't know, though, it takes a gentle hand to really get the dough right."

Jake held up his hands for inspection. "I've got gentle hands."

With one glance at his hands, she looked into his eyes and quirked a brow. "I'll just take your word for it." His pulse picked up a bit at her saucy look. He wouldn't mind showing her how gentle they could be. Seeing her happy gave him a whole other perspective on her. And he liked it.

It wasn't long before all three men were rolling the dough into balls for her. Colt had to leave to do regular security checks, but that was the only interruption. "If anyone had told me I'd be baking cookies in Algiers this week, I would have called them crazy," Colt said.

Jake agreed. "I couldn't have even dreamed up this scenario. Baking cookies with Elliott and two Canadians wasn't even on my bucket list." He squished together another dough ball. "It definitely should have been."

Before he could roll it out to put the filling in, though, Ryan and Nate appeared, bleary-eyed. "What's going on in here?" Ryan asked.

"Making some cookies," Colt said. "Are you guys hungry? We had eggs earlier."

"I don't think we had any left over, though, did we?" Jake asked, finishing up one more little dough ball.

"I set two plates aside for them," Mya said, drying her hands on a dishtowel. "They're over there."

Nate looked at her gratefully, the tension from last night apparently gone. Hopefully Nate would be open to starting fresh with Jake and they could be on better terms. Jake resolved to make it happen. "Thanks," Nate said to Mya. "I'm starving." He sat down at the table, but Ryan moved next to Jake.

"Have you heard anything?" Ryan asked, leaning a hip against the counter. He was still dressed in suit pants and shirt and tie like he was going to the office. Everyone else was in jeans or sweats. What was he trying to prove?

"Nope." Jake turned back to the oven. "Mya, what temperature are we supposed to set it on?"

"311 degrees," she said. Her voice wasn't as bright as it was before and Jake wanted to kick Ryan out of the room. He hadn't needed to bring the phone call up. He would know if Jake got any news.

"Why 311? That seems odd. I'm used to 350." Jake was determined to keep things light. Hopefully Ryan would get the hint and either join in or go somewhere else.

"The Algerians have their own way of doing things," she said, turning back to the cookie sheet. "The almond filling is ready. Do you want to help me shape the cookies?"

"Sure." Jake turned his back on Ryan and faced the counter with her. "What shape are we making?"

"Starfish." She flattened one of the balls. "You make a nice round shape like this. I'll put the filling in with a "T" shape, and then we'll pinch it together to make a starfish." Her fingers were fast as she showed him what she meant.

"It's going to be okay," he said softly under his breath. "I know it's hard to wait for the phone call, but don't let it get to you."

"I'm trying," she whispered. She kept her eyes on the cookie dough. It was easy to see now she'd been doing all this cooking to distract herself. He hoped they got good news when that phone call finally came.

Elliott appeared on Mya's other side. "I'd like to help, too."

She passed him a little dough ball. "Just follow Jake's example."

Jake followed the instructions she'd given him, making a round shape so she could fill it and make the starfish. Soon they had a nice little assembly line with Elliott and Jake making circles as fast as she made a starfish. *They really are sort of pretty*, Jake thought.

Nate finished his food and brought his plate to the sink. "Mya, that was amazing. I'm glad you saved me some. I know that must have been hard with these guys." He jerked his thumb toward Elliott and Jake, but he was smiling. That was a good sign for team unity.

"If I'd known she had a hidden stash I would have commandeered it." Elliott laughed. "You are very lucky, my friend."

Everyone joined in the laughter and any residual tension dissolved. They all stood talking and working on starfish cookies. Once they were baking and Mya was making the icing,

Jake sat down at the table. Ryan hadn't said anything else and Jake was glad. He definitely sucked all the fun out of the room. "How'd you sleep last night?"

"Not great. I was up monitoring a few things."

Jake was tempted to ask what he'd been monitoring, but he held his tongue. That was exactly what Ryan wanted. "I always hate it when that happens."

Ryan pressed his tie down and got up to leave. "Let me know when you get that update."

Jake nodded. "Of course." Mya's back was to him, but he could tell by the stiffness in her shoulders that she was as anxious as everyone else.

After Ryan left, Elliott excused himself to get dressed, and Nate went to check in with Cole. Jake got up to stand next to Mya, liking the fact that they had a moment alone. "How's it coming?"

She'd made several beautiful vines in pink icing on the cookie. It was really artistic and totally out of Jake's league. "I think it's coming okay. Not as fancy as my grandmother's, but pretty good if I do say so myself."

"Mya, these are incredible." He picked one up to look at it more closely. "I can't imagine your grandmother's being more fancy than this."

"She made them look almost like real flowers," Mya said wistfully. "You almost didn't want to eat them they were so beautiful. But I always gave in, they tasted so good."

He held the cookie out to her. "Are you going to taste test yours?" He put the cookie close to her mouth and she opened and took a small bite, her eyes never leaving his. "So?"

"Not bad," she said, licking a crumb off her finger.

Jake couldn't turn away. He'd seen so many sides of her already from strong to vulnerable, upset to upbeat. But this playful chef side was pulling his feet out from under him, like a rip current he couldn't control. He ate the rest of the cookie, not surprised that it tasted as good as it looked. "You should give up the lawyer thing and become a chef. You'd have lines around the block for your food."

"Did I hear the word food?" Elliott said as he came back into the room. "I leave for one minute and you're already eating all the cookies?"

"That was my plan," Jake said, backing up a bit.

"How many has he had?" Elliott demanded as he walked over to the cookie sheet.

"Just one." Mya picked up the little toothpick she had to help her with the icing.

Elliott ate one whole. "Mya, seriously, is there anything you can't do in the kitchen?"

"A few." She looked over at Jake, an amused smile on her face that vanished when she heard his phone ring.

He pulled it out of his pocket, his stomach twisting in anticipation. *Please let it be good news.* "Williams."

"Commander Williams, we have a problem."

CHAPTER THIRTEEN

Mya's vision narrowed to focus on Jake and the phone in his hand. Her life could be forever changed by the words spoken on this call. She twisted her hands, suddenly wishing she hadn't eaten anything this morning.

"I understand," Jake was saying. "Yes."

He wouldn't meet her eyes and his mouth was a tight line. That didn't bode well. She wanted to close her eyes or walk away, but she was rooted to her spot. She had to know what had happened to Yasmine. Was she safe? She couldn't even think of the alternative.

He hung up the phone and slowly put it back in his pocket. Agonizing seconds ticked by. "Tell me," Mya said, her voice hoarse.

Finally his eyes met hers, but they were somber. "There was a firefight. The terrorists were backed against a wall, in the caves, and just before our men went in, a bomb was detonated."

Mya could feel horror and grief rising in her, but she pushed it down. That didn't necessarily mean Yasmine was dead. She needed details. "What about the hostages?"

"They're sifting through the rubble now, but so far they haven't recovered any bodies except Haji al-Awani's." His voice was flat, but echoed in her mind. *Recovered any bodies.* It wasn't a rescue operation any longer. It was a recovery mission for the hostages.

Her mind grasped for any alternative. "If there's no bodies except his, then they can't be sure the hostages were truly in there, right?"

"The intel was good, Mya. They had a positive ID of Haji al-Awani before they went in." He looked at the floor. "I'm sorry. I know you really wanted to help get those hostages out."

No one was more sorry than she was. Sorry she'd waited for a task force to be put together. Sorry she'd not been in better contact with Yasmine. Now she'd waited too long and Yasmine was dead. Her fists clenched and she wanted to smash all the cookies on the cupboard, the canisters, the dishes, everything she could get her hands on. She wanted everything to be as broken as her heart. Sensing all eyes on her now, she bit the inside of her cheek to keep from yelling her pain and anger at them and started toward the stairs. She needed to be alone and sort this through in her head.

Jake reached out and took her arm as she passed him. "Mya, what are you going to do?"

"What I should have done from the beginning. Find my father." She jerked her arm away. Why had she waited for the military? She should have just gotten on a plane and found her father the moment she knew Yasmine was involved.

"Mya, wait," she heard Nate call, but she couldn't. She just couldn't. Taking the stairs two at a time, all she could think about was there wasn't anything holding her back from leaving here, contacting her father, and figuring out her next step. Throwing open her bedroom door, she grabbed some capris and a loose flowy blouse out of the closet she'd hung all her clothes in yesterday and went into the bathroom to change. Once she was ready, she took her suitcase and put it on the bed, methodically packing her clothes in it.

Jake appeared in the doorway as she knew he would. There was no way he'd just let her go. "We need to talk about this."

She glanced at him over her shoulder as she bent down and put on her running shoes. "What is there to talk about? The hostages are dead. There's no mission anymore. You can go home." She marched into the bathroom and grabbed her toiletry bag and put it in the suitcase. "I kept my side of our bargain, Commander, and you need to keep yours."

"That's fine, you can make your call, but I don't want you to leave like this. At least let me make sure you get to your father's house safely."

There was no way she would depend on the military again. "I don't need any help. I'll make the call and he'll come for me." She zipped up the makeup bag. "You don't have to worry about me anymore. I'll be fine."

He stepped closer until he was right in front of her. "I *will* worry about you. You've already been attacked once and there are people still out there who would use you to get to your father. It makes sense to just see you safely to him." He gently took her shoulders and bent down to look her in the eye. "And to be frank, you don't know what kind of reception you'll get from your father. He might not let you stay or come for you in the first place."

His hands offered strength and comfort. He was standing so close all she had to do was take one step and wrap her arms around him. She knew he would calm her, but it was easier to let her anger at the situation surge through her. "Why do you care?" she said, folding her arms so they wouldn't betray her feelings and reach out for him. "I'm not your sister. I'm not even your mission anymore. I want everyone to leave me alone."

"No," he said firmly, his hands tightening on her shoulders. "You don't need to be alone. Not right now."

"You don't get to say what I need or want." She tapped her chest. "Only I get a say in that."

He stared at her, then let her go and walked over to the bed to stand next to her suitcase. For a second she thought he might start unpacking it, so she went to the other side to make sure her belongings stayed where they were. "You know," he said, looking down at her clothes she'd already packed in the suitcase, "I'm not really sure why you're so upset. I mean, wanting to help the hostages is one thing, and we're all mourning their loss, but you can still call your father. The hostage situation doesn't affect that."

The statement hit her hard, like his words were boulders against her battered soul. The "hostage situation" as he'd called it affected everything in her life. The fact that her sister had just been killed cut her off at the knees. "You don't know," she choked out, the loss of Yasmine slicing through her anew.

"I do know," he argued back. "Colin Edwards was a friend of mine. He's the reason I was in Algeria before, the reason I was even asked on this mission. And he's gone." He closed his eyes, sadness and frustration coloring his tone. "I wanted a different outcome just like you."

Seeing the pain on his face started an avalanche of feeling she couldn't control. The tears she'd been holding back spilled over, angry and grief-stricken. "You don't know what I've lost." She hardly recognized her voice. It sounded ragged and tortured to her ears, exactly as she was feeling. "Yasmine was more than a friend to me. She was my half-sister. My father is all the family I have left now because I waited and didn't contact him the moment I arrived in Algeria."

Jake looked so confused. Mya sat down on the bed, knowing she owed him an explanation. The tears and the pain were coming fast now and she was having a hard time talking. Discreetly, she tried to wipe her face and take deep breaths. "Yasmine Dorval, the translator, was my half-sister. If anyone had a chance to reach her, my father would have. Or me. But we waited too long."

The silence in the room was deafening. Jake stared at her. "The translator was your half-sister?" His words were full of disbelief. "How did intelligence miss that? And why didn't you tell me?"

"It wouldn't have made a difference." Tears continued to fall in a never-ending stream. "I hadn't seen her since I left Algeria all those years ago. She was sent to Britain and I don't even know why she was back here. I need to talk to my father. Find out what went wrong."

Jake stood and began to pace, stalking back and forth across the room. "This information could have changed the whole mission. Do you think she was targeted because of who she was and the ambassador was just collateral damage?"

Hot tears were replaced by cold anger pushing through her veins, numbing the grief for a moment. "This was not my sister's fault. Why would they target her? They didn't know who she was. If they had, they would have reached out to my father, not the American government." How dare he accuse Yasmine of anything!

"Who says they didn't? Maybe our government was the back up plan." He took another few steps away from her, then turned back, his face searching hers. "You should have told me."

She should have, she knew that now. But Mya had never trusted easily and by the time she'd realized Jake was trustworthy, it was too late. There was a wounded look in his eyes that she was sorry to have put there, but hindsight was 20/20, and there was nothing she could do now. It rankled a bit that it was somehow all her fault, though. "Maybe if you'd let me contact my father yesterday we would have had more answers to questions like that." She went to the window, staring out into the empty street, trying to calm herself. Why had she let him talk her out of that phone call?

"Well, as soon as you're calm, we'll go call your father," he said, his tone brusque and commanding. Again.

"I'm calm enough to call my father right now and who is this "we" you keep talking about?" She turned toward him, biting the inside of her cheek again to control her tongue and not let loose with what she really wanted to say. "And in case I wasn't clear, I don't need your permission anymore. For anything."

He came to the window, but he didn't look out, just watched her face until she squirmed under the scrutiny. He let out a long breath, letting his perfect posture sink toward her just a bit. "I'm sorry, okay? You're right. You don't need my permission, necessarily. But I hope you'll accept my apology." She didn't dare look at him, but nodded. "Tell me about your half-sister," Jake asked quietly.

Could she talk about Yasmine? She'd been a secret for so long it didn't feel like she should. But she needed to. "Her mother was my father's first wife. When she died of cancer, Yasmine was only six. It was hard when my father married again, but when I came along she said I made it all worth it. She was like my second mother." Mya gave him a ghost of a smile. "She was so grown-up and beautiful, I wanted to be just like her. I copied everything she did and even with our age difference she always had time for me. Being separated from her was so hard, but she still wrote me sometimes."

"When was the last time you heard from her?"

"About eight months ago. She was still in London then, so that's why I was surprised she'd been taken hostage in Algeria. What could have made her come back here? Did my father know she was here?" She looked at Jake. "Has anyone told him she's gone?" That thought started another round of tears. She did not want her first conversation with her father to be to notify him her sister was dead.

"As connected as he seems to be I'm sure he knows." Jake stood and grabbed a tissue off the nightstand and handed it to her.

"I hate crying in front of you, do you know that?" she said as she took the tissue. "I rarely cry, but since I've met you all I seem to do is cry."

"Most women say that about me," he joked.

"I doubt it." She wiped her eyes, feeling a little better. "Most women probably fall at your feet."

He brushed her hair back from her face. "I can't think of a time that's happened. Not a woman I wanted to fall at my feet anyway." His dimple was out again with his smile and Mya gave in and reached up to touch it. He held her wrist there, his eyes focused on her lips, but he didn't move. Her pulse was racing, but she couldn't read his reaction. Was he holding her hand close because he wanted her touch or was he making sure she couldn't go further? He let go of her and drew in a breath without giving away any answers. "Are you ready? Or do you need a few more minutes?"

She stepped back, not sorry for tracing his dimple. She'd wanted to do that since the first time she'd seen it. If only he'd give her a clue how he was feeling. Her usual powers of reading people seemed to have taken a vacation when it came to Jake. "Let's go." Whatever Jake was feeling, the ball was in his court now. When she reached out to her father, there was a good chance they wouldn't see each other again. Was she ready for that? Was he?

They walked silently to the office next door and Jake pushed the phone on the desk toward her. Inhaling deeply, she dialed the number she'd memorized. This was it. The moment she'd dreamed of for years. Someone picked up. "*Âllo*." The voice was gruff as it spoke the French greeting. Was it her father?

Should she speak in French or English? If she recited the phrase exactly as it had been on the paper her mother had left it would be in English. "The baby bird has fallen out of the nest."

There was an audible gasp on the other end of the line and the gruff voice said in accented English, "The baby bird must be taken back to the tree by 5 a.m. tomorrow. Wear a red scarf." And the line went dead.

She replaced the receiver and sank down into the chair in front of the desk. "He said I have to go back to the tree by five tomorrow morning."

"Where's the tree?" Jake took a seat on the couch closest to her chair, reaching for her hand.

Mya took it, liking the fact that he'd reached out to comfort her with just a touch while she searched her faded memories of Algeria. "There was a park I loved to go to with my parents near our old house. It had a very distinctive tree in the middle of it. That's the only thing I can think of."

"That's got to be it then. We'll get you to the park tomorrow, make sure everything is okay." His tone brooked no argument.

"You don't have to do that." As unsure as she was about everything right now, she wanted him to come with her, but didn't want him to feel obligated, either.

"It's no trouble," Jake said, as if reading her mind. "Honestly. Us against the world."

She smiled, remembering how Chivonn had used that phrase to describe them as foster children. "Would Chivonn mind you saying that to someone else?

"She'd be the first to say it to you right now. She's got a big heart. And it means you're not alone."

Mya liked the way his face lit up when he talked about his sister. "You're lucky to have her." She turned away, sadness filling her heart again as she thought about Yasmine. Had she died thinking no one was coming for her? That thought twisted the pain a little deeper.

"So, you'll stay here one more night? It's the safest option and you might as well. Our company isn't that bad is it?" His words hung in the air until she met his gaze. She wanted to say yes. She didn't want to be alone. Right now she wanted to stay in this office with a man who made her feel safe. It had been so long since she'd let her guard down with anyone and it felt exhilarating and frightening all at the same time, but that wasn't something she could confide in Jake Williams.

"Let's not push our luck." She dropped his hand and gave a little laugh to try and cover her feelings, to keep the mood light, but Jake seemed to see through her.

"Mya," he started, but the door behind them opened, interrupting whatever he'd been about to say.

Colt, Nate, and Ryan filed into the office. "Where's Elliott?" Jake leaned forward, his forearms on his knees as he watched them all come through the door.

"Cleaning up in the kitchen."

Nate hadn't looked at her when he said it, but Mya still winced. She should be down there cleaning up her own mess. She'd have to thank Elliott later.

"So, what's the plan?" Nate asked, getting right down to the point.

Colt went around the desk and took his usual spot. His hand went immediately to the mouse and he woke up the computer. Ryan sat next to Jake on the couch, while Nate perched on the edge of the desk.

"Mya got the meeting set for tomorrow." Jake shifted away from Ryan, like he wasn't comfortable sitting on the small couch with the man.

"Where's the meeting at?" Ryan asked, trying to act casual, but it came out a little too quickly.

Mya could hear a thread of stress in his voice and she decided she wanted to keep that detail to herself. Giving Jake a look that she hoped said, *don't say anything*, she turned to face Ryan. "It's a place only my father and I would know."

"No." Colt said on a long breath, oblivious to their conversation and engrossed in what was on the computer screen. He was frantically tapping at the keys.

"What's wrong?" Nate came around the desk, his gaze fixed on the monitor Colt couldn't take his eyes off of.

"Someone's tampered with the alarm system."

Jake stood and Mya could see he immediately looked at Ryan with an unspoken accusation. *What's the story with these two?* "Can you tell who?"

No one had a chance to say anything else before they heard breaking glass toward the front of the house. "We need to get downstairs to the safe room. Now." Colt stood up. "I managed a glimpse of the security feed before the system crashed. They're coming and we're definitely outnumbered."

"Is there any back up nearby we can call?" Jake moved next to her and Mya was glad for that.

"Nothing that will get here in time." Colt stood right behind Mya now. "We need to move. Fast."

She went immediately to the door, her heart pounding. Ryan was in front of her, but let her go through the door first. She didn't think twice and headed for the stairs.

"Let me go first, Mya," Jake said before she could get far. She turned and he had a gun at the ready.

She stopped to let him pass and sniffed the air. "Did they start the house on fire?" Her eyes began to burn. "What's the smoky smell?"

Jake took her arm. "It's probably just smoke bombs for cover. We'll be okay in the safe room."

She pulled away. "My mother's journal. I forgot it in my room." Turning around, she tried to go back upstairs. "I can't let it burn or let them get their hands on it."

"I'll get it," Ryan volunteered, just as the alarms started shrieking overhead. "Just get downstairs," he shouted as he disappeared down the hallway.

She bit her lip, but Jake didn't give her time to think about it anymore and rushed her the rest of the way down the stairs. Elliott was crouched at the bottom. "There's at least two working on the front door," he said.

"Let's get everyone to the safe room." Jake had a death grip on her elbow as they practically sprinted for the basement. Wrenching the door open, Jake reached around her to flip on the light when she heard the first gunshots ring out. She instinctively ducked and felt herself lose her footing. Before she could even scream, she was falling into the blackness below her.

CHAPTER FOURTEEN

Jake barely caught the back of her shirt and saved her before she fell down the stairs. "Are you okay?"

"Yeah." She looked behind them. "Can they see us through all this smoke?"

"No and that's to our advantage. El, we need to get downstairs." Jake tried not to rush Mya, but that had been too close whether it was a lucky shot or not. He needed to get her to that safe room. When they finally reached the bottom of the stairs, he nudged her toward Elliott. "Head to the safe room. I'll be right behind you." He tried to give her a reassuring look. "I want to get another gun. Just in case," he added.

Jake headed into the gun room and Colt was right behind him. He grabbed some smoke grenades of his own and the Glock 19 for Mya. "How long do we wait for Ryan?" Colt asked as he stashed the weapons in various places on his person.

"Until we can't anymore." But Jake's insides were already churning. Ryan should have been here by now. But no matter what, Jake had to keep Mya safe. He only hoped it didn't come down to having to choose one or the other.

The safe room door was open and Jake walked in. Mya, Nate, and Elliot were already glued to the security camera footage. Elliott glanced over at him. "We're definitely outnumbered. We should close the door. They'll be down here any second."

"We're going to wait a little bit longer for Ryan," Jake said, watching the grainy picture of six men go through the front room. This wasn't good. *Where's Ryan?*

Mya's eyes widened. "He hasn't come down? He was just going to grab my book. What if they . . ." She couldn't finish and her hand flew to her mouth.

"Don't worry," Jake said, but it didn't come out as reassuring as he would have liked. He walked to the door of the room, his hand on the knob. They needed to close it, but maybe if they waited one more minute, Ryan would show up.

"Jake," Colt called. "You need to see this." He pointed to the security camera that showed the door to the basement. Jake could see Ryan, his hands on his head, being escorted downstairs by a gunman. "We've got to close the door."

"I can't leave him behind." No matter what he'd done, they were still SEAL brothers. He looked at Mya, torn between responsibilities. Who could he leave behind?

Colt's gaze followed his. "Your mission was to protect her and I haven't heard any different. Let us go out there for Ryan."

"No." Jake shook his head immediately. "I'll go."

"We're a team," Colt said, moving toward the door. "Let's act like one." And before Jake could protest further, Nate and Colt were out in the hall. "Shut the door," Colt instructed. "And don't open it for anyone or anything." Elliott nodded and locked the door from inside.

"He's right," Elliott said as he returned to Jake's side. "We're a team."

Jake's chest felt like it was being squeezed in a vise, but he couldn't take his eyes off the camera that would show them exactly what happened out there. His fists clenched. He should the one standing at the bottom of the stairs, not Colt and Nate.

Mya slipped her hand into his and squeezed. "It'll be okay."

All three of them stood there in silence facing the security camera TVs. When Ryan and the gunman came into view, Jake turned up the volume. He didn't want to see or hear this, but he couldn't miss it, either.

Colt and Nate had taken defensive positions on either side of the stairway. When Ryan came into view, the gun at the back of his head was easy to see. So was the gleam in his captor's eyes when he saw Nate and Colt. "Put your weapons down or I'll kill him," he announced, digging his gun into the back of Ryan's head.

"It's okay. Do as he says." Ryan looked pained as he said it. Jake was so focused on the gunman, he'd nearly missed Ryan's comment. He turned the volume up as high as it went.

Every fiber of Jake's being protested Colt and Nate giving up their weapons. Terrorists never kept their word. But could they risk Ryan's life? Colt lowered his weapon, but still kept it at the ready. Nate followed suit. Jake held his breath.

"It's just one guy, I think we can take him." Colt took a step forward and the gunman retreated, keeping Ryan in front of him.

"I think not." The gunman looked back at the stairs and shouted something unintelligible. Footsteps almost immediately sounded, clomping down the stairs. "I'm afraid there's a lot more than just one."

Jake briefly thought about the idea of Colt picking them off as they came down the stairs, but the gun nestled at the back of Ryan's head would make anyone hesitate.

"Tell the people in the room behind you to come out," the gunman said.

Colt shook his head. "We don't need them. Let's make a deal. We'll give you the guns we have here and you let us go."

"I want all of you in front of me." The man forced Ryan to his knees in front of him. "And if they do not come out, I will shoot him, and then the two of you, and bomb them out."

"Why do you care about them? You have us and we can make a deal." Colt was trying to keep him talking and from the camera angle Jake could see Colt's gun half-hidden behind his back. Maybe the gunmen wouldn't notice. He could still take a few of them with him if this got ugly.

"You Americans, always making deals." The gunman shook his head, as if it were tiresome.

"I'm not American," Colt said, his eyebrows raised. "I'm Canadian."

The gun behind Ryan's head lowered slightly and Jake's hope rose. Could Ryan use this distraction to get away? Even if he could they wouldn't be able to fight their way out of this unscathed. The odds were nine to three if Ryan had a gun in his hand, but some of those gunmen looked pretty inexperienced with the way they were awkwardly holding their weapons.

There was a chance.

Mya's fingers wiggled in his and he loosened his grip, realizing how tightly he'd been holding her. "Sorry," he said, drawing her closer with his arm around her shoulder. She didn't say anything, just put her arms around his waist and held him as they watched and waited.

"Canadians are a little more reasonable than Americans," the gunman was saying as if he were thinking out loud. He gave Colt an appraising look. "Who is hiding in that room? I want the truth."

Jake's mind was racing at that comment. So they weren't here for Mya specifically if he didn't know she was in that room. But how had they found them then and what did they want? This strike had been too surgical to be random. He leaned forward trying to figure out what Colt was going to do. From the side angle, he was leveling his gaze at the gunman, indecision on his face.

"I'll tell you who's in there." Ryan turned and slowly got to his feet, his arms raised in a conciliatory gesture. "It's a doctor, a woman, and their bodyguard. No one important."

The gunman considered this for a moment, then shook his head. "You're lying. Why would they have all of you and a fortress of protection? They have money, obviously. Maybe I could hold them for ransom."

Jake's pulse rate picked up. They wouldn't get much ransom off Jake or Elliott, but Mya was a different story. He couldn't let that happen. His arm tightened around her. There was no way they were unlocking that door, no matter how much he wanted to be out there.

"Ransom takes so much time. Take the guns I offered. That whole room just behind you is an arsenal." Colt gestured toward the war room.

The gunman glanced at the door. "You protect them so fiercely I want to see them for myself. Tell them to come out."

"No. Deal with us." Colt was adamant. Using his height advantage over the gunman, Jake had to admire the way Colt was staring down the enemy. He looked fierce.

"I say what goes here." The gunman raised his weapon again, this time pointing it at the security camera above them and speaking directly into it. "I know you can hear me, doctor. Your friends will need your services very soon if you do not open this door."

As soon as the gunman was distracted with the security camera, Jake saw Colt make some sort of hand signal to Nate and he made his move. He threw the smoke bomb into the middle of the room. Ryan grabbed the gunman's weapon, turning it on the men closest to their boss. Nate rolled to the nearest doorway, the gunshots deafening in such an enclosed space. He picked off a man who'd trained his gun on Colt, then kept moving toward the corner of the room. Gunshots and smoke were all around him and Jake could barely see Nate scrambling for cover.

"Come on," he muttered under his breath. "Stay down." Jake wanted to crawl through the screen and help. He hated standing there, safe and helpless to do anything for his team.

After what felt like an eternity, the smoke began to clear, the room finally silent. Jake leaned forward, squinting at the scene. He counted six men down, including Ryan. He was clutching his leg in one hand and the gun in the other.

"Enough!" The man closest to the stairs shouted. He looked at the two of his men still standing, their leader on the floor, obviously dead. Speaking to Colt who stood near him with his gun raised, he said with a thick accent, "Hassan was greedy, but I will deal with you. What do you have beyond the guns held here?"

Ryan looked up from the floor. "There's a warehouse in Algiers full of guns and ammunition. It's yours if we all walk out of here unharmed."

Colt turned to face Ryan. "No. We're not supplying these people. They'll use it on us or your military!"

"Shut up," the new leader snarled. He crouched in front of Ryan. "Give me the address and my man in the city will verify it. Then you can all go if what you say is true."

The camera showed a brief, guarded look pass between Ryan and the leader. The hairs on the back of Jake's neck prickled when he saw that. Something wasn't right here. Did these two know each other? Was Ryan setting them up?

The new leader spoke to his man near the stairs who took out a phone from his pants pocket. Everyone listened as he made the phone call and the tension in the room ratcheted higher as they waited. After what seemed like hours, he finally got the news, and a smile spread across his face. "It's verified."

"You're free to go," the new leader said. He raised his hand magnanimously, as if he'd just granted them a huge favor.

"Put your weapons down then," Colt demanded.

The new leader looked at his two men and shrugged, putting their weapons in front of them on the floor. Easy to pick back up, but enough of a chance that Colt could get off a shot if they tried anything. Jake had to admire Colt's negotiating skills.

"It's time to go," he said softly, slowly releasing Mya.

She looked up at him, her eyes wide, unshed tears shining in them. "Thanks for staying with me. I know you'd rather have been out there to protect Ryan."

"I'm right where I needed to be." He kissed the top of her head and released her. There was no time to analyze what that kiss meant, but he knew it wasn't goodbye. He kept his gun at his side, ready to use, and handed her the Glock 19 from the side table where he'd set it. They checked the ammunition and made sure they were ready if they needed to be. "Let's go." He looked at Mya, her small hand on her gun. It was strange seeing her with one, but oddly comforting, too.

Elliott unlocked the door and opened it. The smell of gunpowder wafted in as they walked out. Jake kept a close eye on the newly disarmed gunmen and took Mya's elbow as soon as they reached the bottom of the stairs. Elliott went immediately to Ryan.

They made their way upstairs and headed for the front door, stepping over the carnage that was throughout the house. The canisters on the counter were broken into a million pieces on the floor. Plants were overturned and glass was everywhere. The smell of the baking cookies was now replaced with smoke and guns. It was a little surreal. Jake helped Mya navigate it all, grateful she'd put her shoes on earlier. The faster they were out of here, the better.

Their two available cars were waiting, just where they'd left them and Jake got in the driver's seat of the first one. Mya was in his passenger seat and Ryan and Elliott in the back seat. Nate and Colt took the car behind them. "Follow right behind me," Jake said to Colt before he got in.

He kept a close eye on his rearview as they cleared the compound and headed into the city. Elliott was hard at work in the back seat trying to stop the bleeding on Ryan's leg. "We're going to need to stop soon," Elliott said.

Jake pursed his lips, unable to shake the feeling that there was more to this whole thing. That look Ryan had shared with the gunman was out of place, unless . . . but Jake couldn't finish that thought. He didn't want to.

He took several turns through the city, taking some back roads and winding through to the main thoroughfares. As soon as he was sure they weren't being followed, he pulled into the parking garage of a deserted building. Slamming on the brakes, he turned in his seat. "You've got a lot of explaining to do," Jake said through gritted teeth to Ryan. "And I want some answers about what was really going on back there."

CHAPTER FIFTEEN

Mya glanced in the back seat and wished she hadn't. Elliott had cleaned Ryan's leg wound, but there was still quite a bit of blood that made her stomach queasy. She faced forward, guilt tagging along on her adrenaline rush. He wouldn't have been in that position if she hadn't asked him to go back for her book.

"Mya," Ryan said from the back seat. "Here."

She turned around again and kept her eyes on his face. He held out her book. "I managed to grab it for you. Thank goodness it was small enough to fit in my pocket."

She took it and clutched it to her chest. "Thank you so much." He was trying to keep his face neutral and not wince as Elliott cleaned the wound and it squeezed the guilt deeper into her heart. "I'm really sorry about all of this."

"It's not your fault." His voice sounded like he was drowning in pain and regret chased through her.

Jake broke in, unable to look at Ryan directly from his position. He didn't have any trouble with his voice echoing through the car, though. "You're right, it isn't her fault. You knew that guy back there, didn't you? Is that how he got our location? You gave it to him?" He waited, but when Ryan didn't answer, Jake got out of the car and slammed the door.

Elliott finished bandaging the leg wound and Ryan opened his door before he leaned his head against the seat. "Hear me out, Jake," Ryan said to Jake's back as he struggled to stand next to the car.

Since it seemed as if the team meeting was going to be outside Jake's door, Mya got out. What was Jake trying to say? That Ryan was involved in the whole thing? That didn't make sense. Colt and Hughes had joined them, their arms folded as they stared at Ryan. His jaw was clenched as he stood alone, propping himself against the car and gingerly stepping on the toe of his injured leg. She went to stand by him, so it would look less like he was facing a firing squad.

"Don't bother sympathizing with him, Mya. He could have gotten us all killed." Jake faced Ryan now, anger in every line of his face. "Did you give them our location?"

"Yes." He spoke clearly so they wouldn't be able to mistake his answer.

It was hard not to gasp at such a bald announcement of betrayal. "Why? Why would you do that?" Colt stepped forward now. "That was a clean safe house that our country graciously allowed you to use to run your op. It wasn't yours to burn!"

"There was a larger purpose." Ryan tried to straighten a little more, but grunted and hunched over again.

"You risked Mya's life!" Jake said, his fists clenched at his sides. "All of our lives."

"She was never in any danger." Ryan flicked a glance at her. "I made sure of that."

"There were bullets flying all over that place. She could have been hit by a ricochet, you had no control at all." Jake threw his hands up. "She nearly *was* hit as we were going downstairs!"

"I knew you'd get her to the safe room. And once she was there, she was fine, you have to admit that." Ryan's voice was fading, his face white.

"Jake, he needs to sit down." Elliott stepped forward on Ryan's other side. "He's lost quite a bit of blood."

"So getting shot wasn't part of your plan?" Jake asked.

"Of course not," Ryan snapped. "We were just supposed to make the exchange. They got curious and greedy, that's all."

"This was about guns." Colt was incredulous. "You used my country's hospitality to do a gun trade?"

"Those guns have tracers in it. We'll be able to track where they're going and more effectively figure out how AQIM and ISIS are recruiting and where. This was a golden opportunity." Ryan slumped lower despite his best efforts. "We couldn't pass it up when it could help us root them out sooner rather than later."

"But you didn't discuss it with us or warn us, you just did it. You tampered with the security system and let us all hang out to dry. That's what I don't get. You betrayed the team." Jake's voice lowered, but it was still laced with anger.

"Betrayed the team? He betrayed my country and could have jeopardized our position in Algeria! But who cares about that," Colt said, angrily. "Just stepping on everyone else to get what you want. Isn't that how you work?"

"The team was dissolved the moment those hostages were blown up." Ryan raised his chin. "And believe me, the people we're dealing with aren't going to be telling the Algerian government the Canadians have active operations going on. You're fine. So, in the end, I didn't betray anyone."

Mya took a step back from him, stunned at the cavalier way he dismissed everyone's concerns. He really thought doing a gun exchange in the middle of trying to rescue hostages was a good idea? Did he even care about the hostages? She turned away, her own anger rising.

"You acted without any regard for anyone but yourself." Jake took a step closer to Mya, as if reading her thoughts. "And whether the mission is over or not, you had no right."

"I was following orders just like you." Ryan limped back toward the seat of the car. "We need to get to the airport. We're all being called home. It's over."

Mya shook her head before Ryan had even stopped talking. She wasn't going anywhere. "You can just drop me off at a hotel. I have unfinished business in Algiers."

Jake nodded at her before he spoke to Ryan. "Colt can drive you to the airport. I'm staying behind with Mya until she's settled." He went around to the passenger side and Mya followed, relief in her heart. She hadn't wanted to bring up how much she wanted him to come with her, but was glad she didn't have to.

"I'd like to make sure Mya is okay as well," Nate said, looking over at Colt. "We haven't received our official orders yet, right?"

"No, we haven't." He glared at Ryan. "But with your injury, you should definitely be on that plane home to the states. Or wherever else the CIA is wreaking havoc in the world."

Ryan shrugged. "That's fine. You can just drop me at the airport. But you can't stay at any hotel. People are still looking for Mya."

"Do you have proof of that? Have you been the one giving out her location?" Jake shook his head, too angry to wait for an answer. "You probably just painted a target on her back with your little gun exchange stunt." Jake made sure she was inside before he shut the door and went around to the driver's side. "Let's get you to the airport. The sooner we're on our own the better." He shut Ryan's door for him as well.

The ride there was silent, but as they approached the airport, Ryan leaned forward. "If you could just look at the bigger picture, you'll see I'm right."

Jake didn't take his eyes off the road. "You never were a team player, Ryan, that's the biggest problem. And when you're in our business, if you can't trust your team members, you're dead."

"I protected you the entire time," he countered. "The only person who was even injured is me."

"But it could have gone either way. You should have warned us so we were prepared. You chose to go rogue." Mya could see how tightly Jake was gripping the steering wheel. Every muscle in his body was tense.

"I didn't go rogue. I followed my orders to the letter."

"Then the CIA betrayed the team and they should have to answer for it. Why is gun running more important than human life?"

"It isn't. We're trying to shut down terrorist groups and those guns will help us do it. We're trying to save lives." Ryan sat back with a small moan, grabbing his leg again. "And it was just supposed to be a simple exchange."

"That's a pretty backwards way of doing it. Putting guns in their hands isn't the best plan I've ever heard." Jake found a parking spot in long-term parking and got out. Ryan gingerly followed suit. "Do you need help getting inside?" Jake asked, eyeing Ryan.

Elliott stepped forward. "I'll help him." Mya stood by the car, unsure of what she should do. It looked like Jake was walking away as well, but he wasn't going toward the airport.

Ryan brushed Elliott's offer away. "Don't worry about me. I can take care of myself." He took a step, but turned back to face them. "Someday when we've got ISIS pinned down, you'll see this plan had merit."

"I doubt it." Jake stared straight ahead. "Tell the Admiral I'm staying on for a little while longer, okay?" Mya let out an inward sigh of relief. Wherever they were going, he wasn't going to leave her behind.

"He's not going to like that." Ryan glanced at Mya, then back at Jake. "There's a lot going on in this part of the world that you're not aware of, Jake. You need to follow orders."

"As you said, the task force was dissolved the moment the hostages were killed. I'm on my own time now."

Ryan shook his head and pointed a finger at Jake. "You think my problem is not being a team player? Well, your problem is being stubborn and unwilling to listen. You've proved that over and over." He started to limp toward the entrance to the airport and this time he didn't look back.

"You didn't even give me a chance to listen. Then or now." Jake folded his arms and they watched him go.

"Do you think you were a little hard on him?" Mya asked quietly.

"No." Jake turned around as Nate and Colt walked toward them. "But he's not our concern anymore." Once Nate and Colt joined them, he motioned to the cars they'd parked. "We need to leave the cars here in case they're being tracked. Those guys back there weren't stupid."

"What's the plan then?" Colt asked.

"I've got a contact who can help us, but he's pretty nervous. If all five of us descend on him, he'll bolt. I'll take

Mya with me, get another safehouse secured, and then meet you at Le Jardin d'essai."

"What's that?" Colt asked.

"It's a botanical garden in the city. It should be pretty crowded this time of day so you can just blend in. Stay together, though." He looked at Mya. "We're going to get you to your father."

"I know." She looked at the other three men, grateful they were willing to stay and help. After the hostage situation at the house, she felt bonded to them in a way she hadn't before. They'd all put themselves in the line of fire to protect her. That meant something.

The men walked beside her as they headed for the taxis. With a nod to Colt, Jake helped her into one and gave the driver an address. "Are we going into the city?" she asked.

"Yes." He shifted closer to her. "I've got a contingency plan in place."

That didn't surprise her. Jake liked to have plans in place so he could be in control, which was part of the bossiness side of him she didn't like, but in this situation, she was glad. "Does this contingency plan have a name?"

Jake glanced at the driver who seemed engrossed in the traffic and the music on the radio. "Annis. You'll like him. He owns a *crémerie*."

"How long have you known him?" She couldn't stop herself. She wanted to know more about Jake and his friends he'd made in Algeria.

He looked over at her. "Five years."

He didn't say anything else and even though she had a million more questions, she decided not to press him. Maybe he had a reason for being so mysterious. "At least we can get a pastry." She sat back in her seat, but couldn't stand the silence between them. "Did you enjoy your time in Algeria?" That was a safe question.

"I did. The people I met were friendly, anxious to preserve peace for their country and the ones surrounding them that were falling into war and chaos." He watched as the taxi driver turned into a business district. "I got a chance to brush up on my French, too."

"That was one of the best things about Canada in that I didn't lose my French-speaking abilities and it helped me communicate when I first arrived." She looked out the window at the stores they were passing. "Are we close?"

Jake leaned forward and spoke to the driver. "We're getting out here."

Mya looked around. "I don't see any *crémeries*."

He paid the driver and waited for her to join him on the sidewalk. "It's just better this way if anyone is trying to follow our tracks."

He kept up a quick pace as they walked two blocks, passing several restaurants with delectable smells drifting to the sidewalk. It made Mya's stomach growl. "Is this going to be a long walk? Or do we have time to stop for a snack?"

"I'll make sure we grab something before we meet the others, okay?" He was staring up at the storefronts and smiled when he saw the last one. "Here we are." The door had a little bell above it that jingled when they entered and the waft of familiar and exotic baking spices floated to her nose. The man behind the counter was helping a customer pack up his purchases in a little white box, laughing at something she'd said. As soon as he saw Jake and Mya, however, he sobered. Jake waited until the customer left. "Âllo, Annis."

"Qu'ést-ce que tu fais?" He looked at Mya before going to the door and turning his small sign from Open to Closed. "You cannot be here," he said in English as he turned to face them.

"Annis, you know I wouldn't come unless it was an emergency." He stepped closer to the man. "I need to call in my favor."

Annis was wringing his hands. "It's in the back. Let me get it for you." He lifted his eyes heavenward as if praying for strength. "Stay here."

Mya looked at his case of pastries while he was gone, her mouth watering to see the delicacies she hadn't had in years. "He has Makrout a Louz," she whispered.

Jake joined her. "I don't think I've had that. What is it?"

"It's like an almond cake." Now she was craving it. She had to have it. "Can I get one?"

Jake nodded. "I see my favorite over there on the end. Annis makes a hazelnut mshawek that's to die for. You have to taste it, too."

They both looked up when Annis came back in carrying a backpack. "We were just admiring your Makrout a Louz," Jake told him.

"Really? I would have thought you'd be after the mshawek." Annis set down the backpack and came to stand with them in front of the case. "I could never make enough mshawek when you were in town."

"I've missed you, Annis." Jake reached out and gave Annis a side hug. "I'm sorry to have to come to you, but you know I wouldn't have unless it was an emergency."

"I know." He glanced over at Mya, speculation in his eyes. "Is this your wife?"

Mya flushed, not daring to look at Jake to see his reaction to Annis's assumption. Suddenly she was very interested to see what else was in his display case. "No, he's helping me find my father," she said over her shoulder.

Annis looked back at Jake. "He is good at helping people. I wouldn't be here today, with my own shop and a safe place for my family without him."

Now it was Jake's turn to look uncomfortable. "You were a hero, Annis. You know that."

Annis waved his hand. "I did what I could." He pointed to the backpack. "There's money and keys inside, some documents, and the car is out back."

"I need a red scarf, too, if you have it." Jake went over to the window and looked down the street. Mya had totally forgotten that she was supposed to wear a red scarf to the meeting with her father tomorrow. Thank goodness he was detail oriented.

Annis plucked a red scarf off a hook behind the counter. "My wife left this one here and it's not her favorite." He handed it to Jake before he walked around to the back of the case. "Let me put some Makrout a Louz and mshawek in a bag for you."

"Thanks, old friend. I'm in your debt."

"Never." Annis gave him a box full of sweets. "But I've built a good life here and don't want anything from my past to ruin that."

"It won't. I'll make sure of it." Jake hefted the backpack over his shoulder. "But, this will probably be our goodbye."

Annis nodded. "Thank you. For everything." He motioned them toward the rear entrance of his store. "Be careful. Bonne chance."

"We will and thanks again." Jake reached for Mya's hand.

"Mérci, Annis." She said as they passed. He nodded, then went to help a lady who was knocking on the door and peering in. Mya and Jake walked quickly out the back and a very old four-door car was waiting. "Where to?"

Jake pulled open the passenger door for her before sliding into the driver's seat. "Annis has a place we can stay for a night or two. We'll go pick up Elliot, Colt, and Nate and head there." He started up the car and drove toward the street they'd come in on.

"How did you meet Annis?" Her curiosity got the better of her. "He seems nice."

"When I was with human intelligence, Annis was our man inside the AQIM recruitment sites. He'd give us numbers and training corps movements, but it got too dangerous for him. I got him out and relocated him here."

Mya took that in. "No wonder Annis is grateful to you then."

Jake nodded. "He saved a lot of people before we had to pull him out. He really is a hero." He turned his concentration to navigating the traffic and it took a lot longer than she'd thought to get there. That was one thing that she did remember about Algiers– the traffic was terrible. They finally pulled up in front of the Jarden d'essai. Elliott, Nate, and Colt were waiting near the fountain at the entrance and started making their way toward them. Once they were all seated in the back, Jake turned. "See anything out of the ordinary?"

"Yeah, I saw a giant rose tree." Nate was squashed in the middle between Colt and Elliott. "Where are we going?"

"I got us a safehouse for a couple of nights." Jake turned into traffic and headed away from the city. "Just long enough to make sure Mya's okay."

Mya looked out the window. She appreciated the sentiment, but as grateful as she was for their help, if tomorrow didn't go well with her father, she didn't know if her life would ever be okay again.

CHAPTER SIXTEEN

Jake pulled up to the address Annis had given him and was impressed that it was a nice villa and not a ground floor apartment like he'd expected. "Here we are," he announced. Elliott opened his door as fast as he could and the three men in the back seat got out and stretched their legs. There hadn't been much room for three grown men back there.

Jake led the way through the gate, across the small terrace and to the front door. The sun was setting and it added a little glow to the villa's white outer walls. "I'm sorry we had to leave your luggage behind," he said, turning to Mya as they walked in.

"I'm just glad we're all alive. Luggage seems unimportant after what we've been through today." She looked around the small living room. "Hopefully I'll be able to replace my clothes tomorrow." Her hands were fidgeting, though, and he knew she was trying not to think about exactly what tomorrow could bring after meeting with her father.

"Why don't you go sit down? Colt and I need to check the perimeter and the locks." She nodded and headed for the kitchen. He watched her go, then took Colt on a standard perimeter check. It was easy to see Colt needed to talk and the check would give them an excuse.

As soon as they were alone on the opposite side of the house, Jake turned. "I'm sorry about Ryan. I didn't know."

Colt clenched his jaw. "I need to check in with the Colonel and figure out what to do about the safehouse. I started the self-destruct protocols on the computer system as soon as I knew we were compromised, but we'll have to sanitize it, if you know what I mean."

He did. Leave no trace took on a whole different meaning in the military. "As soon as we get set up, you can make your call, okay?" He finished his room sweep, but put his arm out so Colt couldn't brush past him. "Thanks for what you did back there. I appreciate it."

"Even if it was saving Ryan's sorry hide, you're welcome." Colt smiled. "Glad to run point, but next time, it's your turn."

"Deal." Jake followed him back to the kitchen where they joined everyone else standing around the kitchen table, except Nate. He was sitting and examining a wound on his forearm.

"Let me look at that," Elliott offered, sitting down next to him.

Colt sat down as well and leaned his elbows on the table. "We need a plan."

Jake set the backpack he'd gotten from Annis down on the chair in front of him and pulled out a field medical kit. He handed that to Elliott. "Mya is going to meet her father tomorrow morning. I'll go along to make sure everything is smooth and once she's safe, we'll be on our way home."

"Where is she meeting him?" Elliott asked, as he opened the kit and started pulling out supplies.

"There was a park near my home when I lived here. The meeting is there." Mya stood just behind Colt.

"So what if things don't go smoothly?" Colt got back up and offered her his chair. She took it, shooting him a grateful look.

"It's hard to say. I guess I'll just go home with you." She bit her lip, as if she wasn't sure that would be feasible.

"Can you really put all of this behind you?" Jake asked, surprised. "Go on like this never happened?" He knew he couldn't do it. But what else could she do? It's not like she had a lot of ties in Algeria beyond her father.

"Of course not, but what choice do I have?" Mya lifted her chin, adding defiance to her words. "I've come this far, I need to see it through. No matter what the outcome is. That's what I can live with."

"What if he accepts you? Will you stay here?" Elliott asked softly.

"I don't know. I'll have to cross that bridge when I come to it." Mya closed her eyes for a moment. "I just want to see him. Whether we have a relationship or not, I just want to have one last memory of him, you know? He's my only family."

No one had anything to say to that. Jake knew all too well how it felt to want a connection to a parent. He couldn't fault her for it. Bending to the backpack, he removed a couple of small packages. "First of all, I'm sorry we don't have something better to eat, but we need to lay low." He pulled out some energy bars and the box from Annis's *crémerie*. "I know it's not much, but I do have something to tide us over." He passed the energy bars around and broke the pastries into almost equal pieces. Most of the men ate the pastries first before resigning themselves to opening the energy bars, but no one complained about a less than filling dinner.

Jake went on once they were all eating. "We've had a busy day and should probably get some rest. I'll go with Mya tomorrow morning and hope things go well. I think it's a good idea to tag her so you can track her remotely from here." He held up a couple of phones. "We probably shouldn't use the phones we were given in New York since they're likely compromised, but I have two here so we can at least stay in contact."

"Why would we need to tag her? What do you think is going to happen?" Nate asked, sitting straighter in his chair.

"I just like to be prepared for anything." He settled his gaze on Mya. "We've had some close calls since this whole thing started and we're not sure of the reception she'll get. After the last incident, I just want to make sure we have a location on her at all times, even if we're with her. Then if we're separated, we have a fallback plan."

Nate looked like he might protest again, but Mya held up a hand. "That's fine," she told him. "After today, I'd rather be prepared for the unexpected."

"So, I'll take first watch tonight and we'll all be ready by 4:30 a.m." Jake set the phones down on the table. "Anything else?"

Everyone shook their heads. "Colt, do you and Nate mind bunking up? The far bedroom has two beds in it." Jake pushed back his chair. "Let's get some sleep. We'll need everything we've got tomorrow." He watched Mya slowly rise and head toward the room closest to the kitchen. She looked tired and vulnerable. Hopefully everything went as well as she wanted it to tomorrow.

He opened the fridge and found some flat bread and dates, but nothing else. The cupboards were similarly bare, but he did find some canned soup and different flavored teas. Obviously Annis hadn't fitted the place out with groceries in a while, unlike the Canadian safehouse that had looked like someone lived there. Who knows, they probably had until their team moved in yesterday. At least the energy bars had been in the backpack. Not the greatest dinner, but it would do. Jake took out the tea and put the kettle on to boil. If nothing else, making tea would keep his hands busy and himself awake for first watch.

He was looking out the kitchen window when Mya came in. He could see her out of the corner of his eye, standing in the doorway, watching him. She looked undecided, as if she wanted to come in, but didn't know if she should. "Is everything okay?" he asked finally, turning his face toward her.

"Yeah." But she still didn't sound sure.

He moved to the table and motioned her toward it. "Looks like a pretty quiet neighborhood. I don't think we have anything to worry about."

"That's what I thought about the last place." She shuddered slightly. "Watching those gunmen through that camera made me feel so helpless. I thought they were going to kill them, then come for us." Her voice trailed off. "I've lost so many people in my life."

The vulnerability in her voice was unmistakable, the longing for connection. Jake saw himself in her statement, their similar losses forging an emotional bond he'd never felt with anyone else. He put his hand on hers, needing to touch her. "You won't lose me." The attraction that had been simmering between them flared to life. He lifted her hand, letting his thumb run over her knuckles. "I promise." She sucked in a breath, unable to keep her eyes off him as he flipped her hand over palm up and pulled it to his mouth, kissing the inside of her wrist.

"Jake," she whispered, leaning close.

He lifted his hand to cup her face and she nestled her cheek against it. He wanted to kiss her lips, to feel her mouth on his, but when the kettle whistled, he knew that was his wake-up call. This wasn't the right time or place. He took a deep breath to calm his racing heart. "I better get that." But he didn't move. Her skin was so soft and her eyes were urging him closer. "Right?"

She blinked as if coming out of a haze and sat straighter, the moment gone. "Right."

He got up to take the kettle off the heat, silently cursing his idea to make a drink. "Can I make you a bit of tea?"

"What is it with you and tea and late nights?" she said with a chuckle. "First on the plane and now here. It's your answer to everything when you can't sleep."

"When it helps, it helps." He got out a cup and saucer, grateful now for the distraction. What if someone had walked in on them? "Luckily there's even two cups here so we both can have some."

He got it ready and brought it back to the table. He sat down in the chair across the table from hers, in case he felt the need to kiss her again. Close enough to comfort, since she was still fidgeting and looked like she was in need of that, but far enough away he wouldn't be tempted to cross any lines. "There's not much food here, but there's plenty of tea. It's like Annis knew what we needed."

Mya smiled and swirled the liquid in her cup. "It did help last time."

"See? And you act like I don't know what I'm talking about." He sat back, unable to keep his eyes off her. Her braid wasn't as neat and tidy as it had been this morning, but the rumpled look definitely worked for her. "So tell me what's bothering you."

Rubbing her arms for warmth, Mya stared at the table. "My emotions are all over the place." She held up a hand. "Apart from anything to do with you and me." With a hand to her temple, she went on. "I'm nervous, angry, sad, frustrated. I want to get this over with, but at the same time I'm afraid."

"Afraid of what?"

"Afraid my dad won't want me." Her voice was small.

It was all he could do not to reach out and pull her to him. He took a sip of his tea instead. *Focus on her.* "I used to have dreams that my parents were coming back to get me, that it had all been a mistake."

"I just feel like I'm missing such a huge part of myself," she admitted. "I know I shouldn't feel that way, I mean, my mother did a great job of parenting me and I'm a grown woman now, but I need this connection to my father."

"He'll always be part of you, Mya. No matter what happens tomorrow. Remember that." He set down his cup, careful not to slosh any of the drink over the side. It was still too hot to really do more than sip. "And you're one of the strongest women I've met. You've lost so much, but you're not giving up. You're going after whatever you can get to find some closure. And maybe start a relationship with your dad. That's brave."

"Thanks." She took a small sip of her tea. "I don't feel very brave."

"No one does. That's why it's brave." He smiled.

"Do you have very many memories of your dad?" She looked at him over the rim of her cup.

Jake thought back. "Not really. I have a vague memory that he used to like to take drives. I'd be buckled in the back seat with the windows down and he'd say, "Hold onto your navel, Mabel," and then he'd floor it. I remember laughing and my hair flying in the wind. I loved that."

She laughed. "Why Mabel?"

"I have no idea." He leaned an elbow on the table. "It sounds so silly now, but at the time it seemed like something cool to say just because my dad said it."

"I bet you're glad you have some memories of your parents, especially where they died when you were so young." Sadness crept back into her gaze. "I have a lot of great memories of my mom. I'm glad I had her for as long as I did."

"Me, too." He gave in to temptation and reached over to squeeze her hand. "Is the tea working? Are you relaxed and sleepy?"

She gave him a half-smile. "Yeah. I think I'll go try to get some sleep. Thanks for staying up with me again."

"Anytime." And he meant it. "See you in a few hours."

Mya stood, but didn't step away. "Jake, I just want to thank you for being here with me. I know you didn't have to, but I'm glad you stuck around."

"It'll be okay, Mya. Whatever happens tomorrow, you'll get through it." He wanted to go to her, to hug her and tell her he knew how she felt, that he wanted to be there for her so she could have a different ending than he had and all the emotional support she needed. But he stayed seated.

She stood there for a moment more as if she were waiting for him to do something. Did she want him to close the distance between them? He couldn't tell and didn't want to overstep in case he was wrong.

Before he could decide whether to stand or stay, she turned away. "See you tomorrow," she said before she went to her room across the hall and softly closed the door. He ran a hand through his hair. This was going to be a long night.

His mind wouldn't be quiet as he made his security rounds, going over all kinds of scenarios of how this could end with Mya. If she stayed in Algeria. If she came home. If there was anything more between them than a dangerous situation that had bonded them together. The hours dragged with unanswered questions until Colt spelled him off. Falling exhausted into bed, it felt like mere seconds until Elliott was shaking him awake. "Time to go."

He rubbed his eyes, trying to clear his head. "I'm up." Going into the bathroom, he ran cold water over his face, looking into the mirror at his tired reflection. Doing his best to appear presentable with only water and no comb, he finally gave up and with a sigh, headed toward the kitchen. Mya was already there with some flatbread in her hand. "There isn't anything else to eat unless you want soup for breakfast."

"Bread is fine." He took the piece she held out to him. "Thanks."

She finished her bread, her eyes flitting to the front door every few minutes. As soon as he was finished, she headed toward the front entryway.

"Wait up," he said, grabbing the package and the scarf off the table as he passed. He had to quicken his pace to catch up with her. "I need to tag you."

He handed her the scarf and she quickly knotted it around her throat. He took out the kit and put a small tracking device just behind her ear, letting his fingers linger a moment. Being this close to her was intoxicating. Even without having a change of clothes, her hair hastily pulled back, and eyes that said she hadn't slept much either, she still looked beautiful to him.

She held his hand to her face, looking up at him. They were so close their noses nearly touched. "Thanks," she said, then softly added, "I'm scared."

She reached out for him and he pulled her against his chest. It felt so right having her in his arms, especially when the future was so unknown. He took a breath, pulling back slightly to tuck her hair behind her ear. "It's going to be fine. I'll be with you every step of the way."

"I know." She gave him a tremulous smile. "We've got this. Us against the world."

"That's right." He squeezed her hand and spoke loudly to Colt who was waiting in the living room with the rest of the tracking set-up. "Colt, is it working?"

"Yep," Colt said. "We've got you covered." He joined them in the entryway, his hands on his hips. "Good luck."

"Okay, we're ready." At least he hoped she was ready. Even he was starting to feel a bit anxious. It was good she'd let him hold her for a minute. They'd both needed that. He went out the door and she followed close behind and got into the car. "Do you know how to get to the Kouba district?"

"I had some time last night to map out our route." He flicked a glance to her. "The park is just by where you lived when you were little, right?"

"Yes." She settled further into her seat. "It had a statue of a woman and a large tree in the center."

"We're not far from it." He pressed the gas pedal a little harder.

She stared out the window, lost in her own thoughts. Jake couldn't blame her. This meeting would change things for her. Whether her father accepted her or not, both options changed things for her.

They made it to the park and left the car a block south. Walking toward the tree, the street was deserted at that time of morning. Mya kept pace with him as they approached the statue. Jake kept a close eye on any movement, but it didn't look like anyone was anywhere near the park. Had the guy on the phone given her a false lead?

Mya stood beside him, fingering her red scarf and looking around the park herself. "He's not here." Her voice was thick with disappointment.

"Let's go over by the tree before we jump to any conclusions." Jake walked purposefully over to the large tree across from the statue. A small bench sat in front of it and Jake could see a white envelope outlined starkly against the old wood. "There's something on the bench," he said to Mya.

She nearly doubled her pace to reach it and ripped it open the moment it was in her hands. "Stone, give me patience." She stared down at the words. "Is this some kind of game? Why would he give me a saying from an Algerian folktale?"

"Apparently, your father is very security conscious and only leaves clues to his whereabouts." But inside he was a bit annoyed. Was he playing a game with his daughter's feelings? "Do you have any idea what that means?"

Her eyes lit up. "I think I know where I'm supposed to go next." She started walking back to the car. "We have to hurry."

Jake worked to keep up with her. "Where are we going?"

"To the refinery." She was nearly running now. "It's a long story, but the short version is, when it was built, my father thought that it would be good for us, but some thought it was a stone around the neck of the people. The wealthy would steal the resources meant to make us all comfortable. My father often likened the refinery to the old Algerian children's story of Bab El Oued, that when the stone was returned to him, the gift of patience was given and justice would reign. When the oil and its wealth were given back to the people, their patience would bring justice and wealth to our land. That's got to be where he is. "

It made sense in a roundabout way he guessed. He'd trust her on this one since he didn't have any better ideas. "Wait." He reached for her arm. "First, we need to figure out a strategy for the refinery. We don't want to go in blind."

Mya shook her head. "I'm sorry. No more plans or strategies. I'm not waiting any longer. I'm going with or without you. I've got to do this now."

He looked down at her determined face. They could make up a plan on the way. "Okay, let's go."

They got to the car and called to tell Elliott he should just meet up with them at the bus stop near the villa. Mya was tapping her leg, as if she could make this go faster somehow. Jake swung by and picked up Elliott, then followed her directions outside of town. "How far is this refinery?"

"It's a ways." She was biting her lip again, her eyes showing her worry. "What if he's not there?"

"It can't hurt to check, right?" Jake began to regret those words the further they traveled. The road practically disappeared into a dirt path and the car bumped over so many potholes Jake thought his teeth would rattle out of his head. Now that they were going to an actual building, he knew security would be tight if her father was there. Meeting at the park had surprised him, but now it was starting to make sense. Someone like Amari would have layers of security. That's how he'd been able to stay alive for so long. But what would that mean for Mya?

He looked over at her. She was watching the road as closely as he was, holding on to the dashboard when the bouncing got to be too much. They finally reached a gate that led to an abandoned looking refinery. Yet, the gate was obviously new and had a manned guardhouse next to it. He rolled down the window as the guard approached.

"Give him this," Mya said, handing Jake the envelope. He handed it over to the guard who read it briefly, then gave it back.

"Go to that building there." The guard pointed to a small outbuilding that could use a little paint.

"Thanks." Jake accelerated and they made it to the front door in record time. Even though it looked deserted, there were eyes on them. He'd always had that sixth sense when it came to being watched and his personal radar was going crazy right now.

"I think I should go in alone," Mya announced as she opened her door. She was getting out before she was even done speaking.

"I don't think that's a good idea," Jake said immediately, not knowing exactly what was going on here and what kind of reception they'd get. "Look at this place. We don't know what's behind those doors. Let's stay together."

She nodded, and Jake was relieved she didn't argue with him. The longer they stayed in the open, the more something felt off. Glancing back at Elliott still in the car, he gave him the nod that meant keep the phone close and the car running.

He made sure Mya was slightly behind him before he opened the building door. He went through first, glancing around the poorly lit lobby area. A large man stood in the corner, his cigarette glowing brightly in the semi-darkness.

"Father?" Mya asked tentatively. Had it been so long since she'd seen him that she wouldn't recognize him?

"No. I have a few questions for you before you'll be allowed near him. Why have you come?" He flicked the ash off the end of his cigarette and stared at Mya. He reminded Jake of a large coiled snake, warily watching them, ready to strike.

"Does my father know I'm here?" Mya demanded.

"Answer my questions." His tone was hard.

Mya tossed her head, just as annoyed as the man in front of her. "My mother is dead. I need to talk to him. Please, bring me to him." She stood straight, but her shoulders hunched a little as if she were afraid of the answer. Jake put his hand at her back for support and to bring it in closer proximity to the gun at his side.

The man threw up his hands, but his voice wasn't emotional at all. "You should never have come. It is too dangerous for you here. That's why you were sent away." He stalked toward them and Jake gripped Mya's waist. When the other man was mere inches from them he stopped to stare, taking in Mya, and Jake's hand on her hip. Jake held his ground, but wanted to step back. The guy's onion breath mixed with tobacco was overwhelming. "You are a foolish woman."

He pushed his face into Mya's space and Jake moved between them, placing a firm hand on the man's chest. "Step away."

The man did as he was asked, shooting another scowl in Jake's direction. "Stay here. I will give your message to your father," he said, turning back to Mya. "But you have to respect the answer your father gives. And go home."

Mya lowered her eyes, but Jake felt her tremble under his fingers. "Of course." Hopefully her father would at least see her. If she'd come this far only to deal with Onion Breath, it would be a huge disappointment.

He didn't move from his spot, just glared at Jake before tilting his head in Mya's direction. "I have to ask, have you been contacted by anyone else?"

Mya gave a slight nod. "Before I left the U.S."

"Then you already see the danger. You could get everyone killed." He shook his head and let his cigarette fall to the concrete, smashing the butt with his heel. With one last annoyed look at her, he strode to the door, slamming it shut behind him.

Mya slumped against the wall and Jake went to her immediately, putting an arm around her. She had her hands on her knees, but looked up at him. "That didn't go so well."

"It's a wonder you were able to talk with his breath in your face." Jake knew she was close to tears and was glad to see a small smile on her face at his observation. He reached out to squeeze her shoulder. "I wouldn't say it went too badly. You still have a chance to meet your father today."

"If that's the reaction I get from his messenger, I can imagine what my father's will be." She arched her back before straightening again. "But you're right, I can't throw in the towel just yet."

"What did you mean when you said someone had contacted you?" Jake moved back a little, giving her some space.

Mya rubbed her temple. "That day in New York. At the hotel. The guy who attacked me said he could get to me at any time and he would kill me and kill my family. That there isn't anyone who wouldn't betray me and I better not interfere."

He was quiet. Did that mean Ryan had betrayed her location? He'd probably never know. "What did he mean about interfering? Was he talking about the hostage rescue?"

She shrugged. "I have no idea. I thought it was strange at the time. Maybe it'll mean something to my father." She leaned against the wall, her hands behind her. "How long do you think we'll have to wait?"

"Not long," Jake said as the door behind them opened. They stood together, ready to face him.

CHAPTER SEVENTEEN

"Come with me," Onion Breath said, holding out a hijab for Mya to place over her head. With everything happening so fast and the thought that she was about to meet her father, she didn't understand at first, so he unfolded it for her. "Cover your head. For respect."

She quickly put it on and he held the door open for them. They left the outbuilding and walked across a short walkway. Mya could see Elliott watching them from the car, but he didn't get out or do anything but watch them, the phone to his ear. She knew with the tracker on, they could see where she was at all times. How would they know if she needed help, though? Maybe she should have listened a little more when the men were discussing strategy. All she'd wanted to do was meet her father and that was about to happen. The butterflies in her stomach wouldn't stop flapping at the thought and she put her hand to her middle. *Stay calm.*

They went into another building, a larger one, and the door inside was much heavier, like it was reinforced. Once the man got it open for them, they stepped through and were met with an even more burly guard than Onion Breath. They didn't get close enough to smell the new guy's breath, though, and Mya was glad. He didn't say anything to them, just searched Jake and confiscated his gun and a knife he had strapped to his ankle. Jake grimly let him take it, but it was easy to see he wanted those items back.

They walked down a long hall, the fluorescent lights above making little popping noises as they walked. Windows into rooms showed empty tables waiting for people to man them. The air of desertion made her more nervous. This refinery had been a hope for the people and look what had happened to it. What if Mya's hope for having a relationship with her father ended the same way?

When they finally reached a closed door at the end of the hall, their escort opened it to reveal a tall thin man sitting behind a desk. He looked up at them, his eyes a familiar golden brown as he gave Jake a once-over before his gaze rested on Mya. How could she have ever mistaken Onion Breath for her father? He was so familiar. Her heart began to pound and she wanted to reach for him, but was rooted to her spot. What if he didn't want her? "Father," she said, trying to find her voice.

"Chérie?" The endearment was said in a whisper, a dazed look on her father's face as he took her in. "You are as beautiful as your mother."

At that, Mya couldn't hold back the tears. She'd waited so long for this moment and wished with all her being that her mother was here to experience it with her. "She died six months ago."

"I know. She wrote me when she knew the cancer was advancing." He came around the desk and slowly walked toward her. He stopped and tentatively reached out to touch her shoulder. "She talked only of you and how proud she was."

"Why didn't you contact me?" Her voice sounded small and hurt, but she didn't care. She had to know.

"I couldn't, chérie, or it would have put you in danger. Like you are now," he said his thick eyebrows coming down in a disapproving frown. "You should not have come."

"When I heard about Yasmine, I couldn't stay away." She looked up into the face that was so familiar and yet strange. He'd gotten older, gray streaking through his hair and beard. He wasn't quite as tall as she remembered, but he still had a strength about him. "Did you know about her kidnapping?"

"I'm aware of the situation and I'm taking steps to get her back." Her father spoke quietly and glanced at Jake when he said it, as if he didn't want to talk about it in front of him.

Mya wiped away the tears on her cheeks and patted her father's hand resting on her shoulder. "Father, there was a firefight during an attempted rescue and a bomb went off. Yasmine was killed." Her father's face didn't change at all at her words. It was like she hadn't spoken. "Did you hear me?"

He let out a breath. “Yasmine is not dead. Nor is your ambassador. But the negotiations to free them are very delicate and I don’t want any interference from the U.S. government.” He turned to Jake. “Thank you for bringing my daughter to me safely. My men will escort you back to the gate.”

Jake stepped forward with a sharp intake of breath. Mya knew the shock on his face was a mirror of how she was feeling. How could they be alive? “Mr. Amari, if what you say is true, I’d like to help recover the ambassador and your daughter,” Jake said.

“I’m sorry, but your government is part of the reason we’re in this mess.” He took Mya’s arm and started to walk toward the door.

“What do you mean?” Jake took two steps and planted himself in front of them, unwilling to let this go.

Mya looked up into her father’s face. He looked tired, mostly, but there was a trace of anger in his expression. He closed his eyes briefly, then faced Jake. “Since ISIS has emerged, the U.S. has been looking for any foothold they can get among the different terror groups. There was some infighting when AQIM publicly denounced several ISIS policies and attacks, so the CIA sold guns to them, to supposedly help them fight ISIS. Only it backfired when the guns ended up in the hands of ISIS anyway. AQIM isn’t equipped or trained to mount the kind of insurgence against ISIS that is needed.”

"So, you're telling me the U.S. sold guns to an al-Qaeda affiliated group, in order to try to start a war between them and ISIS?" Jake ran a hand over his face. "That's not a great plan."

"You and I agree on that point." He stared at Jake. "The diplomat who was kidnapped was trying to alert the CIA that AQIM was actually selling the weapons to ISIS and they shouldn't make any more exchanges. AQIM grabbed him and my daughter before he could. They don't want to lose their source of income." He shook his head. "That's why the CIA is trying so hard to cover things up right now. How would it look to the world if it was broadcast that Americans had armed anyone associated with al-Qaeda?"

What had happened back at the safehouse with Ryan and those men was starting to make so much more sense now. Mya covered her mouth with her hand. Those men had been the very ones holding her sister and had come close to taking her as well. "We met those men in Algiers," she whispered.

Her father turned quickly. "What do you mean?" His tone was terse and she flinched slightly. This was a side to him she hadn't remembered.

"There was a CIA man with us. Our location was compromised and he exchanged guns for our freedom." She was trembling now. "This whole thing is over guns." It was hard to believe, but it rang true.

"How can we trust what you're saying?" Jake's face was stony. "I don't believe for a minute my government is totally to blame for this or that our president is aware of what's going on."

Her father snorted in derision at the question. “You had a mole on your task force from the beginning, you were given no real mission or information, and you were watched from the moment you landed in Algeria. Do you still think your government is innocent in all this?”

Jake grimaced. “The task force was put in place by the U.N. They could be the ones directing this whole thing. If it was the U.S. government, wouldn’t they want to keep this as limited as possible?”

“They did. They only involved you and a few Canadian men that don’t have strong family ties. They didn’t expect you to come back.” He took Mya’s hand, and his eyes that looked so much like her own, showed disappointment. “That’s why I sent you far away from this life. You can trust no one. I didn’t want that for you.”

“So you’re saying this was a suicide mission from the start? That we’ll all be killed and no one will be the wiser?” Jake shook his head, his entire body tense. “I don’t believe that.”

“Then how do you explain all the coincidences I just explained to you?” Amari’s voice was rising as he waved his hand as if trying to wave away Jake from before him. “I don’t have time to argue with you. You will go home and everyone will clap you on the back for a job well done. Count that as your success if you make it back alive.”

Jake narrowed his eyes and folded his arms. He obviously didn’t like her father’s dismissiveness. “If what you’re saying is true, there should be consequences. At the very least, the CIA should be held accountable or anyone else involved, including the U.N."

Amari laughed as if Jake had just told him the funniest joke. "Who will testify against them? The terrorist groups that enjoy the guns and money they received? The only witnesses were the diplomat who is supposedly dead. If we can successfully recover him, there might be a chance for justice, but we only have seventy-two hours."

"Why would the CIA want everyone to think their only witness is dead? That doesn't make sense." Jake frowned.

"They didn't. They're still searching for bodies and hopefully they keep searching long enough to give me a chance to save my daughter. Now, I really must go. As I said, our time is limited." He swept past, bringing Mya with him. She looked back at Jake. Would this be the last time she saw him? There was so much to say now that the moment was here.

"Let me help you." Jake backed up nearly to the door, making sure they couldn't leave. "I *need* to help you."

Her father didn't have a chance to answer Jake's plea before they heard shouting in the halls, punctuated by gunfire. A helicopter's rotors suddenly roared overhead. Amari raised his eyebrows and pointed at Jake's chest. "You led them here," he accused.

"No. I made sure we weren't followed." Jake jutted out his chin as he shook his head. "I swear, it wasn't us."

"Obviously it was." Amari's face was grim and he ran a hand over his beard. "Now we have no choice."

Before Amari could reach for the door, it opened and the burly guard ran in, shouting. "We must go. Hurry."

Amari didn't even look back at Jake, just pulled Mya with him into the hall. He walked quickly to the door at the end of the hall and stopped in front of it to touch Mya's cheek. "I didn't expect our first meeting to go like this, but your safety is now, and has always been, my only concern."

She leaned into his palm, feeling tears well up in her eyes. She'd only just found him and now they were being separated again. "I know."

He looked at her for a heartbeat longer, then backed away. "There is another hallway beyond this door. Go two doors down on your left. It leads to the tunnels. Head down the stairs and walk to the shelter a few hundred feet in and wait for me there. I'll find you when it's safe."

"Can I get my gun back in case I need to protect her?" Jake asked, standing next to Mya.

"Go, go." He waved them back toward the door he'd led them to. "There's no time."

Jake was about to protest, but Mya took his hand and did as her father asked. Lightly running, she could hear gunshots pinging outside and picked up the pace. Had she put her father in danger by coming here? Or would it have happened anyway? She pushed the guilt away. It wasn't going to end like this. She would do exactly as her father said and give them more time together once they were out of danger.

She followed her father's instructions and threw open the second door on the left. Jake waited until she was in before he shut it quietly behind her. The gunshots had stopped and that was usually a bad sign. Was her father all right? She put those feelings aside and concentrated on where they were supposed to go. She didn't want to be a distraction to her father. She couldn't have that on her conscience.

Finding the door to the tunnel, Jake went through first, making sure Mya was right behind him. Footsteps pounded down the hallway and her heart leapt into her throat. Hoping it was her father, but not wanting to stick around to find out if it wasn't, she shut the door and moved to the stairs. "We need to hurry," he whispered, taking her hand.

Mya didn't have to be told twice. They felt their way down the staircase, grabbing a candlestick that was near the entrance and lighting it. When the ground finally leveled off, she moved faster. Jake kept pace, staying just a step away and his presence comforted her. It would have been a lot more intimidating if she were doing this alone.

When the small glow of light from the candle showed the path forked in front of her, she didn't hesitate and kept going to the right.

"Are you sure about this?" Jake asked, stopping in his tracks. "What if we're supposed to go to the left?"

"Yes. He would have chosen the right." It just made sense to her, but was difficult to explain. "Trust me."

"I do." He reached for her hand again and she took it. They'd come a long way from the scene at the U.N. That memory made her smile now, even in the midst of this mess.

Just as her father had said, after they'd gone a few hundred feet in, the path widened into a large shelter to her left. Holding up her candle, she looked around to see the room stocked with supplies, but it was somewhat hidden. If she hadn't known where to look, she would have missed it. "I hope we're not here long enough to need these supplies."

"Me, too. But at least we're safe for now." He stepped closer to her. "Now what? If they find us here, we're sitting ducks. Maybe we should push on and find an exit."

"No." Mya shivered with the adrenaline running through her system. "We should wait for my father." She moved toward the cot at one end of the wall and set the candlestick on the floor. "Let's sit down." She needed to sit down. Her legs were like rubber. Jake didn't even seem like he was out of breath.

He grabbed two bottles of water from a case on the floor and handed one to her as she sat down. He snagged a spot on the other end of the cot and she was sorry he wasn't closer. She was so cold all of the sudden. "How did you know where to go?"

"I didn't. It's just a feeling I can't explain." She opened her bottle of water and took a sip.

"I get those hunches sometimes. I'm always glad when they pay off." He cleared his throat. "I hate to sound like a broken record, but we need to figure out a plan for an escape, even if he comes through. Things are a little chaotic surrounding him and I'm not sure it's safe for you to stay with him."

"He'll come through." She knew it. Secretly, she agreed that it might not be the best idea to stay with her father, but she'd also been shot at while with the task force as well. Was it safe anywhere? "So, do you think he's telling the truth about the CIA?"

"It's possible. Something has seemed off about this mission from the beginning. If it is true, it stings a bit that they chose me for a suicide mission. Especially the Admiral. I looked up to him." He took a long pull of his water.

"Maybe he didn't know. It sounds like this was a CIA op from the beginning. Obviously Ryan was involved, but you don't know the whole story yet." She put her hand on his forearm. He sounded upset and like he was doubting himself.

He turned and gave her a half-smile. "Well, the best thing about this is that your sister is still alive. And if your father can get both of them back, then Edwards and Yasmine can help us figure out this whole mess and who needs to be brought up on charges for it."

"I'm thrilled my sister is still alive. It changes everything." If only they could find somewhere where all three of them could be safe. "I hope my father will let us help him get her back."

She leaned into him, his arms immediately coming around her. She sighed and snuggled deeper, letting his warmth seep into her. "I'm so glad you're here."

"Me, too. When your father said he was going to escort me back to the gate, all I could think of was that I couldn't leave you. Not like that." The candlelight threw shadows over his face, but Mya could only focus on his eyes, dark and captivating.

He touched his finger to her chin and her heart constricted. She wanted him to kiss her, to explore the pull they'd felt between them from the beginning. She swayed toward him, closing the distance and his mouth came down on hers. Her fingers curled in his hair and she was lost in an ocean of feeling. His kiss wasn't demanding, but strong and sure, and it touched something in her soul. She leaned back against the wall behind them and he came with her, his arms trapping her on either side. "Jake," she whispered against his lips when they both came up for air.

His hand cupped her jaw, his thumb running over her cheek. "You're so beautiful." He kissed her again, stealing her breath at the wave of heat he evoked in her, but he broke away when they heard footsteps. It was as if they'd both been thrown in a Siberian snow bank and they straightened, their ears attuned to every sound.

Lightning-fast Jake reached over and quickly doused the candle. They both crouched in the corner with the cot in front of them. He held her against him, trying to be as small as possible, covering her body with his. Her imagination painted pictures of how vulnerable they were without a weapon or an escape and her ribs squeezed, trying to take a breath. Jake didn't have to tell her to be quiet, but even she could hear her gasping as she tried to get air in her lungs. What was she going to do?

This was it.

CHAPTER EIGHTEEN

Jake took the small knife out of the hidden compartment on the side of his boot, glad the guard hadn't found it. At least they had a fighting chance with some sort of weapon. Protectiveness surged in him. He'd do anything to keep Mya safe and not because she was just a mission anymore. He was still reeling emotionally. That kiss had touched him in a way he knew would never happen again. Somewhere between New York and Algeria she'd stolen his heart and he wanted a chance to see where they could go once this was over. All he had to do was keep them both alive.

He could hear Mya's rapid breathing behind him and knew she was in danger of hyperventilating. He turned around and put his hands on her shoulders, forcing her to look at him. "You're okay." He squeezed her shoulders, talking quickly and quietly. "Breathe through your nose while I count to four." She nodded and closed her eyes. "Now hold it for four." The only sound he could hear beyond her breathing was the footsteps getting closer. They needed to hurry. "Now let it out through your lips for four counts."

"Thanks," she said, her voice shaky, but less stressed.

"Just keep doing it. It helps." The tactical breathing had helped him, too. Many times. "Try to relax."

The footsteps slowed down as they approached. Jake kept the knife loose in his hand, not knowing if he'd have to throw it or use it in close combat. Mya was right at his back, still doing the breathing technique. For some reason that calmed him a bit, hearing her breaths and knowing she was relatively safe for now. Jake felt the presence of another person and got ready.

"Mya."

Jake's hand holding the knife relaxed at hearing Amari's voice. He felt her slip around him to step into Amari's flashlight beam. Jake stood up and moved beside her, a little in front just in case her father wasn't alone.

"I'm here," she said as she took another step toward him.

Jake wanted to pull her back, but kept pace with her instead. "What's going on up there?"

"No time for explanations, we have to leave now." He turned back the way he'd come, obviously expecting them to follow.

Jake felt Mya brush by him and he quickened his pace. "What about Elliott? He was waiting in the car while we went in to talk to you. Is he okay?"

"My men escorted him to a side gate and made sure he got away safely the moment we knew there would be trouble."

Amari's flashlight bobbed in front of them, but he didn't hesitate in which way he walked. He knew this tunnel well.

The tunnel narrowed and widened as they walked, but they were able to stand straight at least. Jake had definitely been in worse crawl spaces than this, but the situation was still uncertain. "Before we go any further, I need some answers, sir. Like what's really going on. Who's after you?"

Amari stopped so suddenly, Mya nearly ran into him. "I'll give you some answers when we are safe. Now be quiet."

Jake clenched his jaw, pushing down his irritation. It's not like they were in danger of being overheard down here. "Who breached the factory?"

The flashlight was turned on him, the light in his eyes. "You don't give up, do you?" Amari stepped closer, but Mya was still between them. "We can't tell if it's AQIM or ISIS. Maybe it's someone else on the CIA payroll who is looking for easy ransom money or guns." He turned and started walking again, but Jake didn't let him get away with that.

"So you have no idea. No intel at all. Have you ever thought that maybe there are two factions of AQIM then? One branch working with the CIA to bring down ISIS while the other one is working with al-Qaeda?" He reached out to catch Mya as she stumbled, trying to stay as close to her as possible as the tunnel narrowed again. "Without the whole story we can't accuse the U.S. government of anything."

Amari snorted and took Mya's other arm. "Every terrorist group is out for two things, guns and money and they don't care who provides it, but isn't it ironic the U.S. has their hand in the cookie jar? And as for my intel, there are more factions than two. AQIM, ISIS, Al-Qaeda, and all the other groups combined are like a hydra. You can't cut off a head without growing ten more. There are enough branches to make an entire forest."

"Why are they after you, then? Why come in shooting?" While he had Amari talking, he might as well press for the answers he wanted.

Amari shrugged. "I have many contacts. I know things some don't want known. That's why I'm very careful about security." He glanced back at them. "And they possibly could have been after you two. From what I'm told you were ordered home yesterday. Maybe they were coming to collect their errant Commander."

His step faltered, startled that Amari had that information so quickly. "Do you have a contact in the U.S. government yourself?" Jake wouldn't be surprised.

"No matter." Amari stopped and his light shone on a small metal door. "Where we are going requires extra precautions. I'll need to check you for trackers." He pulled out a small device and Jake stepped forward, his stomach twisted in dread, knowing what Amari would find when he checked Mya. He tried to send her an encouraging look, but it was dark and she wasn't meeting his eyes.

Amari ran the wand over him without any incidents. Mya was next and when it came near her head, it beeped. "I thought as much." His tone was disapproving. He turned, his nose flaring and lips thinned to an almost non-existent line. "I knew you led them to me. Are you working for the CIA as well?"

Jake stepped in front of Mya, wanting to shield her from any of her father's anger. She'd waited so long for this reunion, and it definitely wasn't going to end badly if he could explain. "No, of course not. The tracker was for our own protection. Mya had no idea what you were like or what could happen. We'd had some problems already and wanted to make sure we had her location at all times." He kept as much eye contact with Amari as he could in the semi-darkness. "We took precautions. Surely you understand that when it comes to security."

"What if we did lead them to him somehow?" Mya stepped out from behind his shadow. Her gaze wavered between the two men.

"I don't think we did. We made sure we weren't followed and played your father's cat and mouse game. It would have been nearly impossible for someone to use us to get to him." He reached out for her hand, feeling it tremble in his. "It's not your fault." He resisted the urge to glare at Amari and instead focused on her. "We didn't do anything wrong."

Amari stared at them before he dropped the tracker to the ground and smashed it under his heel. With the force he was using it was as if he wanted to smash Jake the same way. "The point is, no matter how they found us, we are compromised and have to leave immediately."

"Where are we going?" Mya asked, her voice bouncing off the stone walls surrounding the small recess they were in.

"I have a meeting I can't miss." He opened the door and a rush of hot air from the outside greeted them. Jake glimpsed a helicopter waiting on a small dirt area.

"Does it have to do with Yasmine?" Mya asked, drawing closer to her father.

"It's about the terms of her release, yes." He stepped through the door and as soon as the pilot saw them, he turned the rotors on. Amari motioned to Jake and Mya. "I have no choice now but to take you with me." He stared at Mya for a moment. "You won't need an escort. I can keep you safe."

Jake's heart sank. He said he'd escort her to her father and let her go, but that was before he knew Edwards was still alive, before he'd realized how much he wanted Mya in his life. "I'd like to see this through," he said to Mya, hoping she could read what he wasn't saying. "You know I can help." Not to mention that Mya didn't really know what she was walking into. She might need his protection no matter what her father said. And he couldn't leave her. Not now. Maybe not ever. "Partners?" he said loudly over the noise of the helicopter.

She nodded and took his hand. "He can help us," she said to her father. "Please?"

Her father looked like he would say no, then nodded. Jake and Mya ran for the helo, trying to keep low and as invisible as possible. As they got seated and buckled in, though, gunshots rang out behind them. Her father bolted for the co-pilot's seat and scrambled in just as the gunmen came around the corner. "Go, go," he yelled. The gunmen rushed forward, emptying their clips at the aircraft. They took off without incident, however, and no one looked back.

They flew for about an hour, staying low and avoiding radar detection. The longer they were in the air, the more Jake suspected they were heading for the Tizi Ouzou region of Algeria. There were plenty of mountainous areas and places to hide there and it would be the perfect place for a prisoner exchange.

He glanced at Mya. She was looking pensively at the ground below them. Would she see her sister today? It was such a miracle both Yasmine and Edwards were still alive, both personally and professionally. Getting Edwards back would be his first priority. Making sure Edwards testified against whomever in the U.S. government authorized gun-running to terrorists in Algeria would be his second. He rolled his neck, knowing he had to extend a modicum of trust to Amari if he wanted to be in on getting them back. If only they'd been allowed to keep that tracker on, then he could have counted on Elliott, Colt, and Nate for backup. As it was, they would have no idea where he'd been taken.

The pilot began his descent and Jake had to admire his talent as they landed on a small piece of low ground near the summit of a mountain. They all got out and followed Amari down the incline without a word. As soon as they were clear, the pilot took off again. The breeze from his liftoff felt good on

Jake's face as the sun beat down on the rocks all around them. From the looks of things, they were the only sign of life for miles around.

Amari was like a mountain goat, having no problems getting over and around the rocks. Jake reached back for Mya, trying to help her get over the largest ones. When they made it over the first rise the view opened up of them on the side of the mountain and a stark rocky valley beneath.

Amari stopped and turned to Mya. "You'll be safe here." He spread his arms before he turned back to climbing over the rocks.

"Safe where? On the side of a mountain?" Jake muttered under his breath.

"Just follow me," he said over his shoulder.

Those words prickled down Jake's spine. That was the thing that made Jake nervous. They didn't really know this guy and they were blindly following him with no back up and no idea where they really were. He kept pace with Mya. As long as they stayed together, though, they would be okay.

And for the moment, staying together was the only plan he had.

CHAPTER NINETEEN

If she'd known she'd be hiking, she definitely would have worn different shoes. The rocks were sharp and her palms were already raw from the few times Jake hadn't been able to stop her from falling. She'd been trying to gauge their progress by how far they were from the valley floor, but her father seemed to be moving along the face of the mountain now, not down. So she'd given up and just concentrated on getting there in one piece.

She looked at her father's back a few feet in front of her. He'd put his keffiyeh on over his head, mouth and nose to protect himself from the wind and dust. She was grateful for her borrowed hijab, since it kept the wind from whipping her hair. A memory flashed through her mind of her grandmother and her colorful headscarves. Her mother hadn't worn them, but Mya hadn't thought to ask about it until now, when it was too late. Maybe she'd get a chance to ask her father.

Jake came up beside her, bare-headed and windblown. He leaned against a rock jutting out from the rugged path and she joined him to catch her breath a little. “It’s pretty rocky. You okay?”

She pulled the hijab closer around her face for the millionth time. “Yeah. I just can’t figure out where we’re going. I don’t see anything remotely resembling shelter.”

“Me, neither. But your father seems to know exactly where we’re going.” They both looked over at him and simultaneously pushed off to follow before he got too far ahead. Rest time was over. Maybe this little hike is to throw off anyone following us,” Jake suggested.

“Well, this is a pretty elaborate goose chase then.” Mya caught herself before she fell again. “How come you’re not even out of breath?”

“I spend a lot of time outdoors hiking, biking, that sort of thing. You’re not doing too badly, though.” He glanced over at her before stepping behind her when the path narrowed.

“I run. Marathons. It helps keep the stress of my job away most of the time.” She tentatively put her foot down on a section of the path that was eroding away. Small rocks cascaded down and she shuddered. She didn’t want to start rolling down this mountain. Jake’s presence behind her made her feel safer on that account.

Her father went around a corner and Mya followed, but when she got to the last place she’d seen him, he’d disappeared. “Hello?” she called.

Her father appeared at the opening of a small hidden wrinkle in the rock. “Here.”

He led them inside and Mya could hardly keep her mouth from dropping open in surprise. It was more like a sumptuous home than a cave. "Welcome," Amari said, his eyes watching their every reaction.

"This is where you live?" Mya took in the couches, pillows, and tables that she would find in any Algerian home, the silks that covered the stone on the walls, even the bowl of fruit on the side table. A multitude of candles lit the room, completely protected from the wind outside.

"Sometimes, yes. I have several places to call home." He moved to the fruit table near Mya, who was still at the entrance. He looked at the room as if trying to see it as she was seeing it now.

"Has the danger really driven you here?" she asked softly. "To a cave?"

"Do you judge me, daughter?" His voice was just as soft as hers. "My mission to help people gain freedom has required me to sacrifice some of my own."

"Aren't you paid well for your services?" Jake joined their small circle and her father cringed at his words like cold water had been poured on his head.

"You know nothing of what you speak," Amari answered, his expression hardening into an angry stare as he looked at Jake.

"So you don't get a cut of the ransoms?" Jake pushed harder, not letting the subject drop, meeting her father's stare head on.

"Jake," Mya admonished, surprised he was continuing with this. Talking about money while they were here under her father's protection seemed out of place.

His father put his hand on her arm. "Would you pour us some tea, chérie?"

"I've drank more tea in the last five days than I have in the last five years," she said with a smile, hoping to dispel a bit of the tension. Mya walked to the tea service across the room and brought it to the low table in front of the couches. She carefully opened the lid, surprised to see it steaming hot. "Is there someone else here?"

"Of course. My men are all around us, but remain unseen." Her father watched her prepare the drink. "There is soup in the covered dish." He motioned with his hand toward the tray. "You should eat. It is spiced and will warm you."

Mya ladled the soup into small mugs and handed one to her father first, then Jake. "It smells wonderful. Thank you."

Her father acknowledged her and took a sip of his soup before he spoke. "The two of you have complicated things. Nazer doesn't like any change to his plans."

Jake stiffened at the mention of Nazer, the casual, but alert air he'd had around him turned to laser-like focus on her father. "Nazer is here?" He looked around as if he expected Nazer to appear. "I've been chasing him for months and almost had him in Texas, too." Jake put his soup on the table and sat next to her father.

"Yes, I heard about the former vice-president's kidnapping a few months back. Your government was fortunate to get him back." Amari didn't seem that interested in the topic of Nazer, his attention mostly on Mya. "You make an excellent hostess, my dear."

"Mother taught me well," she said, raising her eyes to meet his. "She was all about elegance and refinement." Something Mya had hated as a girl, but appreciated now.

"Yes, your mother was an incredible woman. I've never met another like her." He took a sip of his tea. "I missed you both."

Mya leaned back, feeling content for the first time in days. "I missed you, too." How she'd longed for moments like this with her father.

But the mood didn't last. "As much as I'd like to reminisce with you and discuss what has happened since you left Algeria, we need to discuss the situation at hand." Her father bent forward to pat her knee. "I know you trust Commander Williams, but this negotiation is so delicate." He twisted in his seat to look at Jake. "Perhaps it would be best to leave him behind."

Mya's stomach sank at the thought of leaving Jake behind. He'd want to be a part of it and she wanted him to be a part of her life when this was over. It was easy to see he had some feelings for her with the kisses and confidences they'd shared, but that might not extend further when this was over. Had he thought that far? And what could she say to her father to convince him that Jake could help? "He's a Navy SEAL. Highly decorated. And he's protected me from the very beginning." Even if he didn't think so. The hotel attack had been out of his control.

Jake gave her an appreciative look, but jumped in to give his own list of why he'd be an asset. "You said you knew of the former vice-president's kidnapping case. I was one of the lead investigators and have been chasing Nazer ever since. I know him." Jake shifted to face her father head on. "Nazer has a lot to answer for. I'd like to bring him into custody."

Her father gave Jake a hard stare, as if taking his measure. "You have a lot to recommend you, but I only have one question: If you could save your diplomat or capture Nazer, which would you choose?"

Jake was quiet for the space of a heartbeat. "Save Edwards."

Her father nodded in approval and Mya felt like nodding along with him. He'd passed the test her father had given. Proven that saving Yasmine and Edwards was the first priority. "I'll consider your offer to help," he said. "Especially since you've shown you can take orders today, but it will take more than that to gain my trust."

"It'll take more than that for you to gain my trust as well," Jake said, finally taking a sip of his cooling soup.

Mya's father inclined his head slightly as if accepting a challenge. "My first priority is the safety of my daughters. Just to be clear."

"So how do you plan to get Yasmine back?" Mya cut in, wanting to know more of what the plan was from here on out, now they'd come to some sort of agreement.

Her father didn't even blink and went for her subject change. "There are two meetings. One to talk terms and one to pay the ransom and prisoner exchange." He sat back in his seat, adjusting his position with his arm across the back of the sofa, seemingly relaxed, though Mya could tell from the tightness around his mouth that he was still stressed.

"Will both meetings be here?" Jake said, also trying to keep it casual. "And what prisoners are you exchanging? Surely not Abdul, Adnan, or Fadel." When her father didn't answer, Jake tensed. "Not any of them. Right?"

"The CIA managed to get Fadel. AQIM agreed to exchange both Edwards and Yasmine for him. As well as twenty million." This time, her father looked uncomfortable.

All pretense of casualness disappeared. Jake sat forward, his head shaking back and forth. "You can't do that. Fadel is one of ISIS's leaders. His capture cost the lives of several good men and he needs to stay where he is. The only reason ISIS is even in any disarray was because three of their top men were in custody." Jake's eyes flashed with anger. "There's no way you can exchange him."

"I will do what I have to. They have my daughter." Amari's fist came down on his thigh. "Fadel can be caught again. If we do not comply and hand him over, Yasmine will die and there's no coming back from that."

"We can think of something else," Jake countered. Even Mya knew that wasn't an option with the time constraint, but she could see the worldwide ramifications if Fadel were indeed set free.

"There is no time." Amari finished his soup and drink before he spoke as if trying to decide on how much to tell them. *Trust us*, Mya said silently, hoping her father would feel that he could. He finally spoke. "I will agree to the terms here, yes. The meeting is in the morning."

"Father, let me come to the meeting. I need to do something." Maybe if she were there she could find a way out of this somehow. See an angle her father hadn't thought of. She'd been waiting too long to be part of the solution.

"No," he said, immediately shaking his head. "They do not know Yasmine is my daughter and you might give that away. For now, she is alive and her ransom attainable. If you slip or tell anyone she is related to us, she will be killed or her ransom raised so high we will never get her back."

Mya straightened her back, understanding his reasoning, but wanting to argue. Only the thought of her sister's safety kept her from speaking her mind. "Yes, Father."

"Will I be allowed at the meeting?" Jake asked.

Part of Mya cried out that if Jake were allowed to be there, she should as well, but she held her tongue. He was the next best thing to being there herself.

"You will stay with my daughter." Amari stood. "And keep her safe as you have promised. When my meeting is over, I will come for you."

"Do you think you can get her back?" Mya asked, the fear she'd been holding in for so many days finally leaking out in her question.

Her father reached down and touched her chin. "I know I can. Trust me. I've been looking out for you and your sister your whole lives whether you could see me or not."

"I wish I would have seen you." Mya could feel her throat constricting when she remembered all the times she wished she'd had a father near. "Especially after Mom died."

He looked away. "My job holds me captive here. No family member is safe with me and I won't be the cause of harm to you." He turned his entire body away from them as if he couldn't bear to have the conversation any longer. "I'll show you to your rooms."

They walked a short distance to a small hall off the main room near the entrance. "Mya, you will stay here. Commander, you will be in the room next to hers. My men are everywhere and will not tolerate any disrespect shown to my daughter." His warning was clear.

Jake nodded. "Of course."

"Get some rest. We will have a busy day tomorrow." Mya nodded and went into her room, the curtain coming down behind her. She could still hear them talking, but it was as if they thought if the curtain was down, their conversation was private.

"There are no doors, but she will need her privacy. Hands to yourself. Do not enter without hearing her verbally give her permission." Amari's voice was commanding.

"You have nothing to worry about," Jake said with conviction. "She's safe in my hands."

The part of her that had responded to Jake's kisses protested, wanting him to be tempted to kiss her again, to not listen to her father's rules. But it was probably for the best that he was honorable and did as her father asked. For now.

She could tell that the conversation was over and her father had walked away, but Jake didn't move. His shadow was still under the curtain and she leaned closer, debating whether to pull the curtain back or not.

"Mya, no matter what, don't go anywhere without me, okay?" His words whispered to her through the flimsy barrier.

She pushed the curtains aside. He stood there, his arms folded, looking every inch the warrior he was with a severe look on his face. "As long as you promise the same thing to me."

He hesitated for just a moment then put out his hand. "Deal."

They shook on it and the heat of his hand sent tingles up her arm. Did she dare pull him closer? She looked up at him, the same emotions she was feeling warring in his eyes as well. They were being watched, though, and word would get back to her father. After a moment he reluctantly dropped her hand. "Good night, Mya." His voice was low, mesmerizing.

"Night." She drew back and pulled her arms around herself for warmth as he drew away.

"If you need anything I'm right next door." He backed away toward his room and she shivered. That was one thing he didn't have to remind her. She wouldn't forget that detail. It was a comfort and a curse to her heart that was pounding so loudly she was surprised Jake hadn't heard it. Taking a deep breath she pulled the curtain up and let it fall. This day hadn't gone at all like she'd thought and tomorrow promised more of the same. But with Jake at her side she knew she was up for whatever was ahead.

CHAPTER TWENTY

Jake curled up on the small rug in the cave room and pulled the scratchy wool blanket around him before he closed his eyes. Would Mya stay put? She was so anxious to help, it worried him, but she'd promised and he trusted her. He rolled over. She'd dominated his thoughts all day. What did she think of her father? If only they'd had a moment alone to talk. He'd sort of gotten used to sharing a cup of tea alone with her at night. There wouldn't be a chance of that now.

He flipped onto his back, trying to find a comfortable position. He'd slept on the ground with nothing but rocks for pillows before, but he'd always had someone to watch his back while he slept. In this cave he was exposed, especially when AQIM would be meeting here in the morning. That would be a new experience, sitting down or being close to men who belonged to the organization he'd spent months ferreting out as a SEAL.

His thoughts turned to the team. Would Elliott call the Admiral? He was probably trying to figure out exactly what to do next. Would he reach out to Ryan? Jake hoped not. After his stunt at the Canadian safehouse, he couldn't be trusted. Elliott would keep his head, though, and be methodical about it. Colt would make sure of that.

He pillowed his head on his hands. The cave was brilliant from a defensive standpoint. Hidden, comfortable, and hard to get to. Since Amari was inviting terrorist group leaders here, it must be his showcase as well, letting them know he was a man to be reckoned with. Were they here already? He pulled back the Velcro strap covering the illuminated face of his military-issue watch. Two a.m. This was the longest night in history.

Usually he was able to easily fall asleep, but his mind wouldn't stop asking questions he had no answers for. Would the CIA really supply AQIM with guns, knowing they were being used to arm ISIS? Ryan had mentioned they were tracing them, but obviously hadn't foreseen the circumstances or backlash of ISIS getting hold of the weapons. Someone needed to be held accountable for that. Yet, on the other hand, what if Amari had been lied to? Was it an elaborate ploy to frame the U.S. somehow? There were just too many angles to consider.

He stared up at the ceiling, sleep not anywhere in sight, when he saw a shadow under the curtain moving toward his sleeping area. He jumped into a crouch and quietly moved to the corner.

"Jake, are you asleep?"

Mya. A smile spread across his face. Was she missing their late night chats like he was? Too bad he didn't have any chamomile tea on hand. Maybe she couldn't relax enough to sleep either. He got up and moved the curtain aside. "No. What's wrong?"

The candles from the wall sconces placed strategically in the hallway gave her dark hair a burnished glow. It was strange being in a place with no windows or natural light, but seeing her in candlelight was worth it somehow.

He stepped out beside her and was about to make a suggestion that they find a kitchen area for some food, but she put her finger to her mouth. "I can hear voices. Follow me," she whispered.

He complied, but took her hand. He could see a bead of sweat on her forehead as if she'd been running. Was she nervous? "What's going on?"

She shook her head and silently led him down and around a corner to several hand hewn stone steps that led to another level. He could hear voices, one of them obviously Amari. "Are you going to tell me what this is about?" he whispered in her ear.

She didn't answer, just glanced back at him with one eyebrow quirked. They stopped and she peeked around the corner, inviting him to do the same. Her father was there, in another large room like the one near the entrance and he was standing with a man who looked like he'd just stepped out of a magazine. His suit was impeccable and not a hair was out of place. There was no way he'd hiked here like that. They were speaking in low tones, but the walls echoed a bit so their words carried.

"We've brought them down to twenty million and Fadel. Don't worry, it will all go as we planned." Suit Guy had a British accent and seemed to be trying to reassure Amari of their meeting tomorrow, but who was he? A partner?

"Nazer will try to re-negotiate at the last minute," Amari said, shaking his head. His shoulders were slumped and he was the opposite of the man they'd talked to just hours ago. "You know he will."

"You won't let him do that." Suit Guy put his hand on Amari's shoulder. "Tell me about your younger daughter and the U.S. Navy SEAL you've brought here." Jake tensed at that. They sure seemed to have a line on him and his background.

"She used the old emergency protocols my wife and I put in place. I couldn't turn her away." He sounded defensive. After what happened at the refinery, Jake wasn't surprised. Did they still think Jake had something to do with the attack at the refinery?

"Can we bring them in?" Suit Guy was a little more animated as he floated that idea.

"No. At least, not until the SEAL is properly taken care of. Then I'll bring her in." *What does he mean by properly taken care of?* Jake thought, glancing at Mya. The puzzled look on her face told him she was wondering the same thing.

"He could be useful. Didn't you say he's been after Nazer for a while?" Suit Guy wasn't ready to let him go so easily.

"Let's just concentrate on getting Yasmine back. Sticking to the plan as you said." Amari dismissed Suit Guy's thoughts without a backward glance, straightened and transformed back into the confident Amari he'd shown Mya and Jake so far. Their conversation seemed to be winding down, but so far Amari had been consistent. He'd said his priority was the safety of his daughters and from his conversation with Suit Guy they had a plan in place of some sort. *Too bad they don't trust me*, Jake thought. *I could have helped.*

"Have I ever let you down?" Suit Guy was getting ready to leave. Amari agreed and the men shook hands before they parted.

Mya leaned against the wall as if all the energy had drained from her body. "What do you suppose that was all about?" Mya asked, turning her face toward him.

"I have no idea. How did you even find this place anyway?" Had she broken her promise to not go anywhere without him?

"I heard whispers near my room and when I realized what they were talking about and that they were moving, I immediately came to get you. Promise." She met his eyes, their brown depths sincere.

"What else did you hear when they were near your room?" He was grateful she hadn't gone on her own. His heart stuttered at the thought of her being discovered eavesdropping. If AQIM was here and spotted her, she would have been in danger.

"The other guy's name is Julian and he's helped my father with hostage negotiations before." She furrowed her brow. "Maybe I should have acted like I was looking for a snack or something and had my father introduce us."

He closed his eyes and pulled her into his arms. "You did the right thing coming to get me." Holding her close, knowing the possibilities of what could happen just being in the same vicinity as AQIM, he couldn't hold back any longer. He pressed a kiss to her forehead. "Mya, it scares me to have you here. I care about you and want you safe." He tucked her hair behind her ear, letting his hand caress her face for a minute, giving her a chance to move away.

She stayed right where she was. "I care about you, too." She rose up on her tiptoes and lightly kissed him. "Believe me, I wasn't expecting that."

He gave a low chuckle. "Yeah, I can imagine." Bending to rest his forehead against hers, he inhaled, the spicy scent he'd come to associate with her filling his senses. "I don't want anything to happen to you. Promise me we're in this together."

"We are." She ran her palm over the stubble on his chin, her touch gentle and contemplative.

Warmth curled through him at her exploration and thoughts of kissing her more thoroughly went through his mind no matter who her father might have watching. At the same time he knew they should get back before they were missed. "Are you still hungry?" She looked up at him with those golden brown eyes and his heart melted a little bit. "Mya— ," he started.

Her entire body tensed and she pushed him away. "Look out!" she screamed.

Jake instinctively crouched, bringing her down with him, but it wasn't in time to completely ward off the blow to his head. He hit the ground hard, stars dancing before his eyes. "Get out of here," he ordered Mya.

He pulled himself up, trying to shake it off and get in front of her so she could get away, but the attacker was faster. He roughly took her by the arm. Jake landed a hard right, feeling a rush of satisfaction when he let go of Mya and fell back.

The commotion had drawn Amari's attention and he came into the little alcove with an exasperated look on his face. "What is going on here?"

"I caught them eavesdropping, sir," the man said, rubbing his jaw and shooting a savage look at Jake.

A trim, athletic-looking man joined the group and Jake started in surprise. He'd been chasing him for months all across the U.S., and here he was face-to-face with Nazer al-Raimi in a cave in Algeria. His fist clenched reflexively, wanting nothing more than to pull the guy's hands behind his back, cuff him, and take him into custody. But they weren't in America anymore.

"Who are these people?" Nazer said, imperiously. He gave Mya a once-over and Jake moved to block his view, drawing Nazer's gaze. It was easy to tell the moment he recognized who Jake was. "Agent Jake Williams. How convenient to find you here instead of having to search for you. I've been wanting to meet you since you ruined my plans for Vice-President Chalmers."

"Starks wasn't your best choice to carry out that deal." Jake shrugged one shoulder. "Maybe you should have done it yourself."

Nazer tensed at that. Jake watched his fists clench and unclench before he put his hands behind his back and walked over to Jake. He was a head shorter than Jake and reminded him of a little Napoleon. "You have a reckless bravado considering the circumstances." Nazer turned to Amari as if he'd just come to a conclusion. "I want to re-negotiate the terms of our deal."

Jake flicked his glance to Amari. He was trying to cover his nervousness, but it wasn't working. "To what?" Amari asked carefully.

"I will take Fadel, the twenty million, and this man," he pointed to Jake. "In return, I'll give you the diplomat and his translator. And the German."

Amari's jaw dropped and his face turned as red as the silk on the wall behind him. "You said you'd never negotiate for her. That I didn't have anything you wanted."

Nazer motioned toward Jake with his hand. "Now you do."

This time Mya got in front of her father. Jake widened his eyes, trying to give her a silent message to stay back, but she wasn't looking at him. She was focused on her father. "Don't do this."

"You don't understand." He stared hard at Nazer, setting Mya's words aside. "How do I know Klein is even still alive? You've held her captive for nearly two years."

"She's alive." There was a gleam in Nazer's eye. "And I'll happily add her to our trade."

He must mean Luisa Klein. Jake vaguely remembered the details of her kidnapping. She'd been working for an aid organization and was taken from a market in Yemen. Germany had worked tirelessly for her release, to no avail. How did she end up in Algeria?

"It's a deal." Amari reached out his hand and the two men shook on it. "You may take him now and I will deliver the money and Fadel to our exchange place tomorrow."

Mya clutched her father's sleeve. "No. Not him. Please. Don't let him be taken."

Jake caught her eye this time. "It's going to be okay." The anguished look on her face twisted a knife in his heart. "It's okay. Try not to worry." But he knew she would. She took too much on her own shoulders. That was one thing he'd learned about her up front, but right now she needed to stay calm and as objective as possible if they were both going to live through this.

Nazer laughed, the sound bouncing off the stone walls, echoing through Jake's mind and Jake had to steel his emotions. This guy wasn't going to rattle him.

"Yes, don't worry, my dear. We'll just be getting acquainted. Closely acquainted." Nazer stood in front of Jake. "You must be wondering why I spent extra time in America. I was learning every detail of your life. Where you were born, where you lived, who you love."

Jake went very still at Nazer's words. Where was he going with this?

"I want you to pay for interfering and now I have the means." His eyes met Jake's and his lip curled in disdain. "I know all about your foster sister Chivonn, but never fear, I plan to send you back to her. Piece by piece."

Mya's sharp intake of breath was all he heard as rage blasted through him. He didn't even think, just blindly struck out, connecting with Nazer's jaw. His body hit the wall, but he kept his feet. He drew himself up and touched the blood on his lip. "You'll answer for that, too." Nazer turned to bow to Amari before he walked away.

"Jake," Mya said, fear in her voice.

"It's okay," he said again. The guy who'd attacked them in the hall earlier now grasped Jake's arm in a vise-like grip and marched him after Nazer. Jake glanced back and gave Mya his best smile—the one she thought had women falling at his feet. If that was the last time she was going to see him, he wanted to have a smile on his face.

Facing forward, he followed Nazer. Once again, he was a half-step behind the man. Even in his wildest dreams, though, he never thought he'd be exchanged for Luisa Klein. They stopped in front of another cluster of sleeping areas. Nazer pulled back a curtain and called to someone else inside.

When the man sleepily appeared, Nazer faced them, rubbing a hand over his neatly trimmed beard. "Both of you will take our prisoner to the exit point. Our business is concluded here and we'll be leaving within the hour."

Jake's stomach sank. He had to think. If they got him out of here, there was a really good chance he wouldn't be seen again. Half the world had searched for Luisa and turned up nothing. He could fight, but his odds weren't great at three to one. If only he had a knife or some sort of weapon.

A quick glance around the area didn't give him any ideas that would help him in a fight against three men. He knew Nazer was skilled in hand-to-hand combat and his men probably were experienced killers as well. Jake would have to bide his time and wait for a chance at escape.

And as soon as he was free, he'd come back for Mya.

CHAPTER TWENTY-ONE

The moment she was alone with her father, she whirled on him. "You have to stop this. You know what they'll do to him. He's American!"

"I know." Her father hung his head. "I'm sorry, but Nazer was willing to trade for Luisa Klein. It was a once in a lifetime opportunity."

Mya wanted to shake the dazed look off her father's face, but she got a rein on her emotions. She had to think rationally if she was going to help Jake. "I understand wanting to help her, but Jake is your guest. He's been protecting me." She stopped then added with conviction. "I care about him." It felt good to say it out loud, but would it make a difference?

Her father looked at her and she could see pain in his eyes. "I know you care for this man, that was obvious by looking at you, but what do you really know about him?"

She took his hand in hers, wanting him to really hear her words. "I know enough." Biting her lip, she looked up into her father's face. "Please. Help me get him back."

"Chérie, we'll be able to rescue a woman who has been captive for nearly two years. Her family will be ecstatic. And as a SEAL, your Jake has been trained to resist torture. We will see him again, I promise."

I promise. Nearly the last words she'd spoken to him. If only she hadn't overheard anything and brought him down here. He'd still be sleeping in his room. Her heart burned with self-recrimination. "You know they'll torture him and yet you still won't help me?"

"I have a plan." He squeezed her hand, then let it go. "You can trust me."

She didn't know who to trust anymore. Everything about this felt wrong. "I want to know the plan."

"All right then." Her father took her arm and led her to a small room with only a table and four chairs in it. The walls weren't covered, and it felt more like an interrogation room. The man with the suit was waiting inside and her father nodded to him as they entered. "Mya, I need to introduce you to someone."

The man stood up as they came in, his hand outstretched in greeting. "Mya, it's good to finally meet you. I wish it had been under better circumstances."

She shook his hand, wanting to dispense with the pleasantries and talk about how they were going to get Jake back. "And you are?"

"May I introduce Julian Bennet?" Her father motioned for both of them to sit. "He's been my partner for many years now."

"Partner in what?" Mya appraised Mr. Bennet as she sat across from him. He had a refined air about him, as if he didn't belong here in a cave, but he was also comfortable in it.

"I help your father try to break up as many terrorist cells as he can and rescue hostages that got caught in the crossfire." Julian crossed his legs and picked a bit of lint off his pants. "And we've done a fairly good job of it so far, if I do say so myself."

"What do you mean, you break up terrorist cells?" She turned to her father. "I thought you were a hostage negotiator?"

"My position is unique and allows me access to leaders of different groups that no one else has." He glanced at Julian. "Julian is the head of a very elite team of fighters that, once we have pinpointed information and location, tries to cut off a head of the hydra."

"So, you have a plan for Nazer, then." And a plan to get Jake back, she hoped.

"I know you must have heard us speaking in the hallway." Amari glanced at Julian. "That was a mistake on my part. But I want you to know, we will get your friend back."

"I want to help." She felt like she was echoing all the previous conversations she'd had over the last few days. From the very beginning she'd wanted to help get Yasmine back, but now it was an urgent need to get both Yasmine and Jake back.

"There's nothing you can do. We'll go to the exchange tomorrow with the money and Fadel. Once the exchange has been made and we have our three prisoners, we'll work on getting Jake back. He won't get far without us knowing." Julian sounded so confident, Mya wanted to believe him.

"Nazer is smart. He'll know to check for trackers." She picked at her nail, resisting the urge to bite it. She'd given up that habit as a child and wasn't about to start again.

Her father reached out to put an arm around the back of her chair. "Please. Trust us. Don't panic just yet. Jake is a strong man who will get through this."

The image of Jake being led away was permanently imprinted on her mind. She didn't want that to be the last time she ever saw him. "You gave him up pretty easily." She shifted in her chair away from her father. Her need to reconnect with him was strong, but it had stung that he'd just let Jake go like that.

"I didn't think Nazer would ever negotiate for Luisa. The fact that he has was an unexpected bonus I couldn't pass up." Her father looked her in the eye. "You must understand what that woman has probably been through and we had the power to end it."

"By trading Jake."

"It's only for one night, chérie. You will see."

One night of torture. "Can I see him before he leaves?" she asked quietly.

"I'm afraid not. Nazer is taking him to the helicopter landing right now." Julian looked at her, sympathy in his eyes. "I know you've been through a lot yourself, but it's almost over. If all goes well at the exchange tomorrow, we'll be celebrating."

All Mya heard was Jake was being taken to the helicopter landing. "I've got to tell him one more thing." She didn't want that scene in the alcove to be their last words, their last looks between them. "I've got to see him." She rose and headed for the door.

Julian met her there. "I strongly advise you to stay here."

She calmly met his eyes, pulling herself up to her full height. "Get out of my way. Now."

He moved to the side, his palms up in surrender. "Okay, but let me escort you, then. Just to be safe."

She nodded and didn't look back as she strode to the entrance. Going through the opening, she found her footing on the path, but without a flashlight and in the middle of the night, she wouldn't be able to find her way. It had been hard enough getting here in daylight. With a groan of frustration she turned back.

Julian produced a flashlight and handed it to her. "He's hiking up the hill, just ahead."

"Thanks." She started after him, hopeful she could at least say goodbye, but the wind and the terrain made it slow going. Julian was right behind her, but even as quickly as they were moving now, Jake seemed to get further and further away. His captors were picking up the pace. No matter how fast she was, she would be too late. She gave it all she had, but when she heard the helicopter, her heart sank. She wouldn't make it. They were taking Jake and there was nothing she could do.

Julian put his hand on her arm as she watched the shadow of the helicopter pass over her. “It’s going to be okay,” he said, echoing Jake’s words to her. “We’ll get him back.”

Mya nodded, unable to speak with the lump of emotion in her throat. Everyone she’d ever cared about had been taken away from her. Would Jake just be another one she mourned? Her heart ached at the thought. *Please let him be okay*, she said, raising her face heavenward.

They went back to the cave without a word between them. Julian was kind enough to let her have her space, escorting her back to her sleeping area and leaving her in peace. She curled up on the rug, knowing she wouldn’t sleep tonight. Her thoughts were on the man who was flying away into an unknown. Mya was just going to have to trust Julian and her father, but she was going to be there when Jake was finally freed.

That was non-negotiable.

CHAPTER TWENTY-TWO

Jake was blindfolded and his hands ziptied in front of him. He'd been trying to count and get some sort of idea of how long he'd been in the helicopter so he could calculate distance, but he'd lost count when it got too high. Either they weren't staying in Algeria or they were flying in circles to throw people off. He sank back, trying to get comfortable. So far, it hadn't been too bad, but he knew this situation had the potential to go south fast.

They started to descend and his stomach knotted. This was it. His thoughts turned to Mya and the team waiting for him in Algiers. They would be looking for him and he needed to figure out a way to give them a clue.

The helicopter finally landed and he was taken off and shoved forward. Jake caught himself and was able to keep his balance since the terrain was smooth. It felt more like a road than a mountain. That was good. The guard at his arm pulled him forward, obviously anxious to get where they were going.

He was led along for nearly a hundred feet and he could tell they'd entered a house of some sort. The floors beneath his feet were tiled and he could smell something baking, like bread. He kept up his counting, and was led upstairs. Doors were opening and finally Jake was pushed and sat down hard. "We'll be back for you in the morning," the guard said. Jake could hear the man step out and lock the door as he left.

He worked off his blindfold, but couldn't see much in the pitch dark. He used his teeth to pull the Velcro strap covering his watch face off. The room glowed green. He quickly looked around to get his bearings. There wasn't any furniture to speak of and he was in a small room with no windows. It was not much bigger than his bedroom at home. When he pointed his small beam of light to the far corner, there was a shadow and a soft moan. "Who's there?"

A familiar voice cut through the darkness. "I'm Colin Edwards. Who are you?" His voice was weak and raspy, but Jake could have hugged him.

"It's Jake Williams, sir." He walked over and sat down next to Edwards, unable to keep the smile off his face, even though Edwards wouldn't be able to see it in the dark. "We've been looking for you."

"Jake," Colin said, surprised. "I thought you were with Homeland now? This is pretty far out of your jurisdiction, isn't it?"

Jake chuckled. "They brought me back for a special assignment."

"Let me guess, they lured you back trying to rescue me." Edwards turned serious. "I'm sorry about that. I know what a tough decision it was for you to leave military ops in the first place. How's Chivonn?"

"Better, thanks." He'd confided in Edwards about what Chivonn had been going through and how much he wanted to be there for her during a long night when they both had too much time on their hands. He ran a palm over his forehead, the sweat started to roll down the back of his neck. The heat in the room was suffocating. "We need to get you out of here."

"I guess since you're here with me the rescue operation isn't going well?" Edwards coughed, deep and long. It worried Jake.

"We've had a few unforeseen circumstances." He moved closer when he realized Edwards was trying to sit up. "Have you seen Yasmine Dorval?"

"Not for a while. We were separated, but every now and then I hear screaming. I'm worried it's her."

"Have they questioned you?" Jake was concerned with how weak Edwards sounded. That would make any escape attempt harder.

"Yes. I think my hand is broken actually."

Jake exhaled. He'd expected that, but it still angered him to hear it. "Any other injuries?"

"Cuts, bruises, some cigarette burns, but nothing serious." He shifted as if he was uncomfortable talking about it. "So what's our status?"

"Actually, there's going to be an exchange for you and Ms. Dorval tomorrow." He winced, hoping Edwards wouldn't ask him about his own status.

Of course Edwards picked up on that immediately. "What about you?" Edwards' voice was getting stronger the more he talked. Maybe he'd just been here by himself for too long.

"They already exchanged me for Luisa Klein." Was she here? Or did they keep the hostages in different locations?

"Luisa Klein?" Shock emanated from Edwards. "I didn't think they'd ever find her alive."

"It was a surprise to me, too." He pushed himself over to lean against the wall where Edwards was, going shoulder-to-shoulder. "Are there any other exits out of here?"

"Other than the door you came in, I don't think so." Edwards nudged his shoulder. "What can I do to get you out of here?"

"Nazer seemed to have other plans for me." He tested his zipties, but they were tight. "If the exchange doesn't go well tomorrow, we'll talk about creative escape plans."

"How about we get both of us home no matter how it goes tomorrow?" He tilted his head back and looked toward the ceiling. "I've been sitting here thinking about all the times I took a warm bed and good food for granted." He shivered. "This was going to be my last diplomatic mission for the U.N., you know. I just wanted to finish what I'd started six months ago trying to find solutions for the unrest in Mali and driving AQIM out of Algeria."

"I can't imagine you doing anything else, sir." Jake had never seen anyone able to put others at ease and work toward delicate solutions in war-torn countries like Edwards did. "You have a talent for diplomacy."

"Thanks for saying that." Edwards turned toward him. "The world is so different now, though. One mission always has a shadow mission. I couldn't look the other way anymore. Not when guns were being given to the enemy by my own government."

"How did you find out?" He scratched the whiskers on his chin, wishing he could see Edwards' face with more light than an illuminated watch. It's a good thing Jake wasn't claustrophobic because the darkness was suffocating.

"Yasmine overheard a conversation and alerted me. I looked into it and realized several CIA gun exchanges had happened each time I was in Algeria." His voice lowered. "I tried to discreetly look into it, but didn't get far."

"Coincidence?" Jake's mind was running over possible scenarios of who could have authorized such a thing. The only person that came to mind was the CIA director himself.

"I don't know if they were using me for cover, or what. But when I flew in this last time, Yasmine told me the guns the U.S. was supplying were being re-sold to ISIS. She had evidence, but before I could report it, we were taken." His voice filled with sadness. "We lost some good men."

Jake reached out and found Edwards' shoulder. "I know." They were both silent for a moment before Jake continued. "We had a CIA operative with us when we first came to Algiers. He did a gun exchange at our safehouse, but claimed they were tracing the guns and using them to track AQIM."

"So do you think they already knew AQIM was selling the guns to ISIS and they're tracing them? If that's true, then maybe there's some sort of logical explanation. It's a slippery slope, though, providing weapons to any one of these groups."

"Do you think it stops at the CIA director? Would the White House know anything about this?" Jake knew there had been arms scandals in the past, but this one seemed unprecedented in its scope.

"And with everything at their disposal, this is the only way the CIA could think of to track them?" Edwards was starting to sound tired and weak again and Jake ducked his head, once again helpless to do anything for his friend.

"The moment you were taken, a task force was set up to rescue you. They got a lead that you were in Kabylie and sent in the SEAL team, but the insurgents set off a bomb. We all thought you were dead." Jake turned toward him. "I'm really glad you aren't."

"Me, too." Edwards coughed again. "I've been in this room the entire time. I don't even know how long I've been here. Wherever here is."

"I don't know exactly where we are, either, but you were kidnapped six days ago." He thumped Edwards' back. "Once we get out of here, we can get some answers. If the CIA director is the one running guns, I think he should have to explain himself."

"Agreed." Edwards caught his breath, but didn't raise his head again. "It'll be the second thing on my list, right after getting you home with me."

"You're the priority, sir." Jake felt Edwards lean back again. They were a similar height, so their backs were aligned and it made it easier to talk.

"I couldn't save anyone in my security detail it all happened so fast, but I'm not leaving you behind." His voice was full of as much conviction as he could muster after the last coughing attack.

"Thank you." Jake was touched. He wouldn't turn down any help in getting out of this place. If Edwards was on the outside and could help a rescue team find him, all the better.

"When you get out of here, track down Elliott Burke. He was on the team and he'll know who to contact to help find me." He'd probably go to the Admiral first. Jake didn't believe the Admiral was involved in the gun-running scheme. He'd come for Jake, if nothing else, because of the background they shared.

"If I can't take you with me, I will." He was quiet for a moment and Jake thought he might have dozed off, but he turned his head toward him. "Are your hands and feet tied?"

"My hands are tied, but my feet are free." Jake pulled at his bonds. "Are you tied as well?"

"My feet are shackled to the wall and my hands are tied. It's really uncomfortable." He let out a sigh. "There are a lot of things I won't take for granted anymore."

What he wouldn't give for that small hidden knife in his boot now. "Okay. So tell me the schedule. Do they come in here often for questioning? What's the food and water situation?"

"They pretty much leave me alone. I've been questioned a few times, but not often after they broke my hand. They wanted me to sign something, but since they broke my right hand, the swelling made it so I couldn't hold a pencil to write a legible signature." He chuckled softly. "It was nice to see their plans upended even in a small way."

"Have they made any videos of you or anything?" Jake was listening closely to everything Edwards was saying since his schedule would probably be Jake's shortly.

"No. And if I've been here six days, they've been feeding me once a day with a jug of water every so often."

Foreboding filled him. With the history between him and Nazer, he might not even get that, but there was no use worrying about it. He needed to concentrate on the here and now. "We should probably try to get as much sleep as we can. It's going to be a long day tomorrow."

Edwards nodded and laid back down where he'd been when Jake first arrived. "I'm glad you're here, Jake."

Jake was, too, in a way. At least Edwards wasn't alone anymore. He pulled the Velcro back over his watch and scooted a little further up the wall to lay down himself. The tile floor was cold and hard. Jake missed that scratchy wool blanket he'd had at Amari's cave since he had nothing here. Edwards was right. He wasn't going to take very many things for granted anymore.

He closed his eyes, feeling the exhaustion press down on him. He'd lived a lifetime in these few days and he knew there wasn't going to be much relief in sight unless he got out of here. The look in Nazer's eyes had been pure evil and Jake knew he enjoyed making people suffer and would especially enjoy making an example of Jake. A few escape scenarios ran through his mind, but he discarded them all. He hated having his hands tied literally and figuratively.

He turned his back against the wall, hopefully facing where the door was in case anyone came in. Edwards was right. They needed to be as rested as possible for what was to come. If nothing else good came of this, hopefully the exchange tomorrow went well and Edwards could make sure someone came back for him. The thought of staying here for months on end held no appeal. There had to be a way for him to escape.

And he'd find it or die trying.

CHAPTER TWENTY-THREE

Mya spent nearly an hour arguing with her father, using every strategy she'd ever learned in law school to convince him to let her go to the hostage exchange. He finally gave in, but with some conditions: she had to wear a hijab and be silent. She agreed.

She put on the now familiar hijab and made sure she was the first one ready and at the entrance when it was time to go. There was no way they were going to be given a chance or an excuse to leave her behind. When they hiked to the helicopter landing, Julian brought along a hooded man with them and Mya couldn't stop staring at him. Fadel was suspected of killing dozens of people in horrific ways. He was a man without a conscience and passionate about his leadership in ISIS to establish a new Islamic caliphate throughout the Middle East. It was hard to believe the U.S. was letting him go in a prisoner exchange, but the selfish part of her thought if it got her sister back, she was grateful.

The helicopter ride seemed to take forever. She was crammed in the back with Fadel on one side and her father on the other. Being in such closed quarters with a known terrorist filled her with revulsion. She couldn't stop staring at his hands that had perpetrated so much suffering. What had brought him to this point? She didn't know anything about him, but it was because of men like him that she'd had to be sent away to Canada and lost out on a relationship with her father while she was young. She turned away, preferring to watch the pilot maneuver the aircraft than spend any more time thinking about Fadel.

Her thoughts turned to Jake and what he was doing right now. Had they hurt him? Had he seen Yasmine? Her chest squeezed, remembering Jake's admission of caring about her and the happiness that had bubbled up in her knowing that he felt the same way she did. No, they had to get him back today and do whatever it took to make that happen.

Her father finally picked up her hand to stop it from drumming on her thigh. "Did you sleep well?"

"No, I didn't sleep at all." She met his eyes, the somberness of the moment weighing heavily on her shoulders. "I just want everyone back safely."

He shifted closer to her, leaning in so Mya could hear him over the helicopter noise. "I know we don't know each other well, but whatever happens today, I love you. I always have."

She bit her lip, the moment she'd dreamed of marred by the danger they were flying into. "I love you, too, *bābā*." It was funny how easily her pet name for her father had come back to her right when she needed it.

Her father squeezed her fingers. "When this is over we will talk. I don't want to let you go again."

"I'd like that." She looked over at Fadel who hadn't moved since they'd seated him in the aircraft. "Is there anything about today I should know about?" Had they said too much in front of Fadel? Her father didn't seem particularly concerned so she hadn't thought much about it until right now. Surely he would have said something if she'd talked out of turn.

Julian sat in the co-pilot seat, but turned around at her words. "Just let your father do the talking. That's the main thing."

"Okay." And she would keep her eyes open for any information or opportunity to find Jake. That was her personal mission for today.

The rest of the helicopter ride was quiet. Sitting between the two men, she began to feel crowded, as if she couldn't breathe. Doing the breathing exercise Jake had taught her when they'd been in the tunnel under the refinery helped. When she looked back at all the time they'd spent together, even from the very beginning he'd always been there for her trying to anticipate her needs. Now it was her turn to do the same for him if she could.

She was about to ask how much longer when the helicopter began to descend. When she was finally able to get out, she gulped in a breath of air. The sudden onset of claustrophobia had set her nerves on edge. This was not a good start to trying to find Jake.

She continued the tactical breathing as they approached a sprawling compound in the middle of nowhere. It was rectangular in shape and the dark-colored stone blended into the natural surroundings. There was a steep wall of rock going around the entire complex, with small windows at regular intervals. Usually Algerian homes had a garden or plants around it of some sort, but this one was bare. Sharp rocks and gravel were the only features of the courtyard.

They walked through the gate of the outer wall that surrounded the home and outbuildings and were greeted by armed guards who followed them to the door. Her ribcage squeezed painfully as a strong sense of apprehension washed over her. Pushing it away, she focused on her father. He was well-known for getting hostages out. *He has a plan*, she reminded herself.

They were led through a broad entryway to a large room with a low table in the middle of it. Pillows surrounded it and the men were guided to their seats. Mya was told to stand in the corner, which she did. She pulled the hijab closer around her face, watching as Julian pulled out a laptop and set it on the table. Her father seemed focused on the man at the door who was watching the hallway. Were they waiting for someone?

Finally, Nazer arrived and when he sat down, he clapped his hands twice in a rapid, staccato rhythm. "We will make the exchange." He snapped to the guard who immediately left the room. "One moment."

They waited in silence, but they didn't wait long. The door opened and the three prisoners were led in. The man was hooded like Fadel and wearing a ragged suit. He had to be the ambassador that Yasmine had been with. But the other two women were dressed in heavy burkas and she couldn't tell which one might be her sister. The prisoners were told to stand where they were, practically in the doorway.

"Do you have the money?" Nazer asked, leaning forward on his cushion, his eyes bright with greed. Mya wanted to lash out at him, ask him what he'd done with Jake, but she held her tongue. Now wasn't the time.

Julian opened the laptop. "We just need the account numbers and the money will be transferred."

Nazer nodded to the man standing behind him and he stepped forward with a paper in his hand. "The numbers are there and we will wait for verification."

Julian began tapping the keyboard, his focus completely on the screen in front of him. "Done," he announced, finally.

Nazer's man had his own laptop in the corner and he nodded. "Verified."

The prisoners were pushed forward. "Remove the hoods," Nazer ordered. His man stepped forward to remove the hood from the ambassador while Julian got up to remove Fadel's.

"I want to see the faces of the women," her father said. "For verification."

Nazer nodded and the head coverings were removed from the women. Mya couldn't take her eyes from the scene and it was the biggest lesson in self-control that Mya had ever endured. She couldn't hold back the gasp as she saw her sister for the first time. Her face was bruised on one side and she was squinting as if she hadn't seen daylight in a while. Her face was dirty, but she was alive. It was all Mya could do not to rush forward and hug her.

Her gaze went to the two other prisoners who were in even worse shape. The woman standing next to Yasmine had very short hair, as if it had been haphazardly cut and her cheekbones jutted from her face like she'd been starved. *That must be Luisa.*

Her father raised up from his cushion and stood stiffly in front of Nazer. His jaw was clenched tight and Mya could see how hard he was working to maintain his control. "We have made the exchange," he said as Nazer rose to stand before him. Both men bowed. "We thank you for your hospitality."

"Won't you stay for a drink to celebrate?" Nazer invited. He held up his hand. "Fadel loves a good drink." Nazer smirked in Fadel's direction. "Right, my brother?"

Fadel looked around, dazed, but didn't reply.

"Brother," Nazer said again. He looked back at Julian and her father. "What have you done to him?" He got up and crossed to Fadel, holding his face in both hands. "You're safe now," he murmured. "We will get you home."

Fadel bowed his head, but still didn't speak. Mya watched a look pass between Julian and her father. They were packing up, not hastily, but methodically. Something wasn't right.

Nazer turned to them. "He isn't himself." He took a step away, then whirled around, taking Fadel's arm in his and pushing up his sleeve to reveal the inside of his elbow. "This is not Fadel." He pulled the man forward. "Fadel has a scar here," he jabbed at the man's arm. "It would not have miraculously healed."

They didn't have the real Fadel! It was a fake. Mya's whole body drooped in relief and she nearly missed the pop of the gun as Nazer shot in Julian's direction. Mya let out a scream and immediately crouched low to the ground.

She could see Julian and her father returning fire and she crawled to Yasmine. "Come on," she said, pulling her sister's arm back toward the door.

Yasmine didn't question her and the other two prisoners followed suit as quickly as possible. When they reached the hallway, a bullet whizzed over her head. She turned right, looking for a way out or at least some cover for them. There was no way they were going to come this close to freedom and die in some forsaken compound in the middle of Algeria.

They headed toward the door, but the ambassador stopped her. "We have to go back for Jake Williams."

Mya looked back at him, hope rising in her chest. "You know where he is?" she asked urgently. "Is he here?"

"There's a room above us that they're using for a prison." He turned back the other way. "I know I can find him and I can't leave without him."

The gunfire was spilling out of the room and her father ran out, holding his shoulder. "Let's go."

"Jake is here. We can take him with us." Mya was right behind the ambassador. She wasn't going to let him out of her sight.

Julian came out, shooting back into the room. "We don't have much time," he said to her father. "We've got to leave."

"Jake is here. We're going after him. Take Yasmine and Luisa to the helicopter," Amari ordered.

Julian shook his head. "Let's stay together. Go through the back exit."

More men were coming in from outside now, so they ran for the back. "There's only one other exit," her father said as they ran down the hall. "I will go and get Jake. Go to the room next to the kitchen and let Julian take you and your sister to the helicopter through the back door."

She nodded, her breath coming fast. They were so close to freedom.

"Here, he's here," Edwards pointed to a stairway. "At the top. The only door on the left."

"Go to the back," her father instructed as he started up the stairs. "I'll be right behind you."

Yasmine and Mya supported the other woman between them and they raced for the room at the back of the house. Footsteps pounded behind them and Julian turned and opened fire. Gunshots started whizzing through the air around them and they practically fell through the door to the room at the end of the hall. Julian turned and locked the door.

"This is the kitchen," Mya said, gasping for breath. "We need to be in the room next door."

"I don't think we'll be exiting that way." Julian eyeballed his gun. "We're going to have to make our stand here."

Mya looked around and her heart sank. There wasn't a back door here and barely a window. They were trapped. She slid down next to the cupboard, bringing Yasmine with her. They were both breathing hard and Mya clutched her sister to her. "Yasmine," she said over and over, stroking her hair, not caring that it was stringy and probably hadn't been washed the entire time she'd been in captivity. "I found you."

Her sister returned her hug, her voice breaking as she cried on her shoulder. "Princess."

Julian was near the doorway and when he heard a shout followed by a break in between the volley of gunshots, he unlocked the door, opening it slightly to peek out into the hall. "I'll cover you," he shouted and quickly opened it wider to shoot from his crouch on the floor.

Jake and her father rolled in, low and panting, before Julian slammed it shut. "We're pinned down," Julian said to her father as he reloaded his weapon.

Jake's hands were on his thighs and he leaned over to catch his breath. But as if an invisible cord bound them, his eyes quickly found hers. He didn't waste any time and immediately strode over to her, crushing her to his chest. She clung to him and pulled his head down to hers, kissing him with all she had. She didn't care who saw them anymore. If this was where they were making their stand, her last memory would be of kissing him. He was alive. Real. And standing in front of her. It was almost the best she could have hoped for. She reached up and touched his dimple, relief and happiness at having him in her arms crowding out any other thought. "I think I could fall in love with you," she said. "I hope you don't mind."

"I think I'm already a little in love with you." He gave her a quick kiss before gunshots started pinging the door again. "Let's get you out of here." Pivoting, he turned to Julian. "Do you have an extra weapon?" His t-shirt was torn and he was rubbing his wrists, but other than the raw skin she saw there he looked unhurt. It was a fierce relief after all the worrying she'd done.

"No, we were lucky to smuggle these two in," Julian said as he backed away from the door. "And we're almost out of ammunition."

Jake eyed the small window. "I don't think that's an alternative route."

Mya looked around. There was a table, some chairs, cupboards, dishes, oven and a fridge. It was like any other kitchen. She opened the drawers and found knives, but in the face of the enemy gunfire, they wouldn't do any good. "What do you want to do?"

Before anyone could answer her, a large explosion rocked the entire house, knocking them off their feet. Jake crawled back to her, not caring about the debris all around them. "Are you okay?" He anxiously pushed her hair back to look in her face.

"Fine." She brushed off the dime-sized chunks of ceiling that had fallen on her, the dust covering her clothes. "What was that?"

"I don't know, but maybe it will be a big enough distraction we can get out of here." Jake stood and helped her up. "What do you think? Can we make a break for it?" he asked Julian.

Julian opened the door a crack and they could all hear a voice shouting through the house. "Commander!"

"Is that . . . ?" Mya asked, leaving the question open, knowing Jake would know who she was talking about.

"I'd know that bellow anywhere. It's Ryan. The cavalry is here." He went to the doorway and yelled back. "I'm in here." He kept his arm around Mya, a grin on his face.

Ryan finally burst into the hallway with Elliott, Colt, and Nate right behind him all dressed in tactical gear. They looked as relieved as Mya felt. "Boy, am I glad to see you." Ryan said as he picked his way toward them.

"I never thought I'd hear you say that," Jake said, good-naturedly.

"I had to redeem myself." He looked back at the hallway he'd come from, then turned around with a satisfied grin. "I told you the gun tracers would work."

"That's how you found us?" Jake was giving a side hug to Colt while Elliott fussed over his wrists. "I'm fine. We need to check out Ms. Klein and Yasmine."

"We saw a large concentration of the guns gathering here and knew this was the place to be," Ryan admitted. "As soon as I saw Nazer, I knew you'd be around somewhere."

"You caught Nazer?" Jake's voice was neutral, but Mya could hear just a trace of disappointment. With all the work he'd done chasing Nazer, he had a right to feel down about not bringing him in, but she knew all Jake wanted was to have Nazer in custody.

"No, he got away." Ryan's shoulders slouched. "We were close, but he was a couple of minutes ahead of us."

Jake took a deep breath, as if he'd been half-expecting that. "We'll get him. He can only run for so long." He looked down at Mya and kissed her forehead. "Let's get out of here."

Elliott stood next to Ms. Klein, a hand on her elbow as if she would blow away if he breathed too hard. "Mr. Edwards needs medical attention for his hand, Mr. Amari has a shoulder wound and Ms. Klein should be taken to the hospital as soon as possible." He didn't list her injuries, but it was easy to see she was going to need treatment physically as well as mentally.

"Are you okay?" Mya asked her father, surprised to hear he'd been wounded.

"It's nothing," he reassured her, his arm wrapped around Yasmine.

They all left the kitchen and followed Julian down the hall. Mya's father hadn't let go of Yasmine since the shooting had stopped and Mya stayed right behind them, feeling a sense of security having them right in front of her. It was better to look at them as she tried to avert her eyes from the carnage on the floor. Several men were lying dead, their guns still in their hands. Seeing the sheer number of fighters, she knew if Ryan and the team hadn't come, they wouldn't have lasted behind that door much longer. She turned and reached for Jake's hand, suddenly needing to feel his warmth. He was alive. Yasmine was alive. And they were heading to safety.

They made it to the cars waiting outside and it looked like an army of SUVs were surrounding the compound. Ryan was directing several men in order to secure the scene. Their small team gathered around the lead car. When Ryan was finished, he joined them. "Mr. Edwards, I think I have some explaining to do." He was still limping slightly, but walked forward and shook Edwards' hand. "I'll tell you as much as I can."

Edwards put a hand over his eyes, as if the sunlight were giving him a headache. "After what I've been through, that better be everything."

Ryan looked chagrined. "You know I'm bound to keep some things classified, but I'll do my best."

Jake put his arm around her and Mya smiled. Was he remembering when she'd been so put out that he wouldn't share classified information with her? From the look on Edwards' face, he was feeling the same way she had.

"Mr. Edwards, with AQIM openly rebelling against ISIS policies we took a chance that we could use them against ISIS. All they wanted were guns, so we used new tracer tech that would allow us to trace them to within a small radius. When we saw the tracers all congregating, we had drones and teams ready to do a sweep. We were getting some great intelligence about where AQIM was training and we'd raided some compounds, but then we figured out they were selling to ISIS and the op took on a whole different angle."

"Because you could see where ISIS was and what they were up to." Edwards leaned against the car and he closed his eyes. "So you knew all along they were selling to ISIS and didn't want that to stop."

"We were monitoring the situation closely," Ryan confirmed Edwards' statement without coming right out and saying it. "So, we didn't want you saying anything so they would know we were on to them, but I swear we didn't know AQIM would kidnap you. I don't think one had anything to do with the other actually. Your kidnapping was purely for ransom in my opinion."

"Sir, you should sit down," Jake said, opening the car door. "We can debrief once we're back on American soil."

"Thank you," Edwards said, sitting down heavily in the back seat of the car. Mya's heart went out to him. What a nightmare they'd all been through.

"I need to take my daughter home as well," her father said. He was holding Yasmine in his arms, but was looking at Mya. Was that an invitation for her, too?

Ryan held up a hand and turned to Jake and Colt. "I just wanted you to know I didn't betray anyone. I kept you all as safe as I could. And without that gun exchange we wouldn't have been here when you needed us."

Jake held out his hand. "Thanks for saving my life, man. I owe you."

Ryan shook his hand. "Let's call us even." The handshake turned into a back-slapping hug and Mya put her fingers to her mouth, happy to be a witness to it. It was easy to see making things right with Ryan meant a lot to Jake.

Before they could head toward the helicopter waiting to take them back to Algiers, Julian joined them and the man who'd played Fadel stood next to him. Julian put his hands in his pants pockets. He could feel their stares and nodded toward Fake Fadel. "This is an associate of mine, Kamal."

"Using a Fadel lookalike was a big risk," Edwards said from the car.

"We know, but there was too much red tape and only a slim chance the U.S. would release the real Fadel. Kamal and I go way back when we were MI6 and he agreed to help." Julian looked around at each team member in the circle. "I know we haven't been formally introduced, but my name is Julian Bennet." Mya felt her stomach tighten at the deliberate look in his eyes. He definitely had something on his mind to discuss.

"Thanks for your help back there," Jake said, reaching out a hand.

Julian shook it. "I'd like to help you even more. Or rather, help you help yourself." With a nod at Amari, he continued. "I've discussed it with Ibrahim and we agree that you can help our cause."

"What cause?" Colt spoke up.

"I run a specialized group called the Griffin force. We're mostly former Spec Ops soldiers, dedicated to tracking down terrorist cells and breaking up their operations. I'd like to offer you four a spot on my team. Especially now that Nazer is our top priority."

Mya could feel Jake tense as he always did when Nazer's name was mentioned. "What would it entail?"

"A dedicated effort. My team has no other life when we're going after these guys. No leave, no vacations, nothing until the job is done." He clasped his hands behind his back. "It's not an easy life, but the work is rewarding. I've looked into all of your backgrounds and think you'd be a good addition to the Griffin Force team."

"And Nazer is your first priority?" Jake asked.

"Yes. He's climbing the ranks in AQIM and has had extensive dealings with ISIS groups in Syria. We need to get him in custody." Julian tilted his head. "I know he's a personal cause for you and we have an idea where he is. Not to mention, we're tracking the money we just gave him."

"You don't need to give me any more incentive. I'm in." He tightened his arm around Mya. "But it's only until we catch Nazer. I have plans and other people in my life to consider."

Was she one of those "plans?" Was he asking her to wait for him somehow? "I'd like to help," she said, looking at her father, then back at Jake. They could do this together.

"Me, too," Yasmine spoke up for the first time. "As a translator, you'd be surprised what is said in front of me."

"Count me in." Colt said, turning his attention back to Julian. "Part of our original mission was to help capture Nazer, we might as well finish what we started."

"You'll probably need a m-m-medic. And a mediator," Elliot chimed in. "So I better go along."

Nate was the last one to answer and he looked around their circle, weighing his words. "We were just getting our team chemistry together. Why break up a good thing?"

Julian smiled and clapped Jake on the back. "Brilliant. Welcome to the Griffin Force. As soon as you're all patched up, we'll put you to work."

"Looking forward to it," Jake said, his words intense as they all felt the energy surrounding the team while they processed the new mission they'd just been handed.

They all started moving toward the helicopter together, nearly in step with one another. For Mya, there was a lot to think about with what was ahead of them, but she could look around at what they'd already accomplished standing next to them: The hostages they'd saved, the family they'd reunited and the team they'd become.

Jake stopped and put his hands on Mya's shoulders, his gaze warm. He pulled the hijab from her head, his hands threading through her hair. "Are you going to be okay with us possibly working together?"

"Us saving the world?" she asked with a smile, happiness filling her heart at the opportunity she'd have to get to spend more time with him. "Definitely. But I'm not known for my patient nature."

"And I'm told I can be a little bossy." He grinned, showing off the dimple she loved. "But I think we can work it out, don't you?"

She reached up and put her arms around his neck. "Remember when I said I wasn't patient?" And then she pulled his head down to hers and kissed him in a way that would leave no doubt that they could work it out. They were in this together.

About the Author

Julie Coulter Bellon is an award-winning author of nearly two dozen published books. She loves to travel and her favorite cities she's visited so far are probably Athens, Paris, Ottawa, and London. She would love to visit Hawaii, Australia, Ireland, and Scotland someday. She also loves to read, write, teach, watch Castle, Hawaii Five-O, and eat Canadian chocolate. Not necessarily in that order.

Julie offers writing and publishing tips, as well as her take on life on her blog http://ldswritermom.blogspot.com/ You can also find out about all her upcoming projects at her website www.juliebellon.com or you can follow her on Twitter @juliebellon

10516968R00164

Made in the USA
Monee, IL
29 August 2019